DARKNESS COMES

John Lynch

ISBN: 978-1-910194-28-7

Published by Mandrill Press www.mandrillpress.com

Also by John Lynch:

The Making of Billy McErlane (First published as *Zappa's Mam's a Slapper*)

Sharon Wright: Butterfly

<u>Historical Fiction</u> (by R J Lynch)
A Just and Upright Man

Poor Law

Disclaimer: This is a work of fiction. While some of the characters have the names of real people, none of the people carrying those names did any of the acts described in this book.

When everyone knows something, the only thing you can be certain of is that the something everyone knows is wrong.

<u>*Chapter 1*</u>

It was 1960 and Ted Bailey was fourteen years old, a good-looking boy, already five foot eight and still growing with skin unmarked by acne and curly hair that his father thought he wore a little long though his mother said that was the fashion now. He didn't know he was good-looking because no one had told him. His parents believed modesty befitted a boy on the verge of adulthood and, anyway, there'd be time enough for that. In the Newcastle of 1960 fourteen was still too early for boys and girls to take an interest in each other. Instead, Ted had two passions: cricket and chess. His father wanted to send him to boxing club to toughen him up and get him to make his mark instead of accepting whatever life sent his way but Ted didn't like violence and his mother would prefer not to see cauliflower ears on her only child.

When he came back from the Chess Club with a leaflet about a weekend tournament in York his parents wanted to know the logistics. How would he get there and where would he stay? Ted explained that the leaflet came from one of the older players, there'd be a car with space for him and a local club was providing rooms and breakfast. It was a reciprocal arrangement; been going on since before the war. 'They stay with our members and we stay with theirs.' If he took a sleeping bag, which as a Scout of course he had, they'd find room for him on the floor. 'We'll go at lunchtime on Friday and I'll be home on Monday.' It was holiday time, so what objection could there be?

Ted had expected to see more than one man in the car but Mister Walton, who said Ted should call him Charlie while they were on this trip, explained that the others had gone on. 'We have to pick up Arthur and his pal and then we'll be off. I don't think you've met Arthur.'

No, said Ted, he hadn't met Arthur.

'He doesn't often come to the club. He had a bad war, Arthur. The Germans held him prisoner for four years. I don't suppose he'll ever get over it. But he likes to see a new face sometimes.'

When they reached Arthur's isolated old house south of the Tyne outside Ryton, Charlie said they'd better both go in. 'Arthur's never ready on time. We'll have a coffee while we wait.'

The house looked as though it might once have been a farmhouse and it still sat in the middle of three acres of land. Immediately around it was what had been a garden but was now overgrown with dock leaves two feet long and great arching stems of seeds. Two dogs were chained to the wall by the door. Ted was grateful for this, because the yellow eyes, the drooling saliva and snapping jaws told what they'd like to do to him if they could just tear themselves free.

Arthur must be six feet four inches tall and weigh twenty stone, every ounce of it muscle. Half his face was hidden by an untrimmed black beard but there was no avoiding the eyes that stared at Ted, as crazed as the eyes of the dogs outside. He didn't introduce his friend, a skinny man who seemed unable to stop smiling.

'So this is Teddie,' said Arthur. 'He's as pretty as you said he was.'

Fifty-nine years later, Ted is no longer pretty. Seventy-three isn't so old now, not as old as it was in his father's day, but Ted hasn't aged as well as he might and now it hardly seems to matter because this is the classic out-of-body experience: him up here, calm, lucid, unafraid as he floats in the angle of wall and ceiling; him down there, dying. And the girl, of course. Mustn't forget the girl.

She must have realised by now what's happening but she hasn't the strength to push him off. Whatever the little blue pills were, they clearly don't stop working after a heart attack. She's half his weight, flat on her face because doggy-style is what he wanted and he's wedged tight. He was always too big for comfort in that department.

He's laughing, up here in the corner. And it's a relief. Because, if being dead doesn't really mean being dead, he's not going to like it if he can't laugh. He's always been able to laugh. Maybe if he'd been able to cry, things might have turned out differently, but he hasn't cried since he was fourteen and we are what we are.

He wonders what happens next. No one believes in Heaven any more. Do they? Whatever. He's always had the luck so far. It won't fail him now. It's just a matter of holding your nerve.

The room is becoming less clear. There's a tightness, like being in a tunnel. This is how it must be when you go potholing although he's never been in a pothole in his

life. Never fancied it. And it's getting darker. There's a
darkness coming.

He isn't laughing any more.

Chapter 2

Alex knows she's never been in this place before. Heaven for the most part is what you want it to be and for Alex that means gardens, streams and lonely places. This is a room in a building of grey stone. The building is a house, or was once, and it could be new or thousands of years old. In the room is a table about eight feet long. There is one person on each side of the table and another at the end. It's helpful that the dead wear the clothes of their time and place; Alex places the woman on one side of the table in the twentieth century and somewhere in the West – Britain, America, maybe Germany although her jacket lacks German formality. The man opposite her is harder to date because as far as Alex knows that Arab gear went unchanged for centuries.

The person at the head of the table is simple because that's Peter. The fishermen Alex saw as a child on the North East coast were thin and wiry in ganzies and jeans and Peter is nothing like that. You'd take him for a farmer before you thought he might have made his living in a fishing boat. He has the shoulders of a weightlifter; the legs that jut from beneath his short robe are as thick and muscular as trees on the edge of the Sea of Galilee. Are there trees by the Sea of Galilee? Twisted old olives, possibly, and dates? You'd think you'd know stuff like that when you get Here. Maybe they should run tours for newbies. The Holy Land, guided by people who were there when The Holy Land was holy.

Peter says, 'Sit down, Alex. This is Kay and this is Hani. They're here to help us.' He turns towards the window which a moment ago looked out on nothing but a courtyard and another wall. Now, as close as the room next door but such an unimaginable distance away, is an hotel room There, and a bed, and a girl, and a man.

Alex says, 'Where is this?'

'Lanzarote,' says Peter. 'Ted Bailey lives in the Canaries now.'

'Lives?'

'He's not dead yet,' says Peter. 'Though it doesn't look good.'

They watch in silence. Ted is on the point of departure. Tear tracks have dried on the girl's cheeks. She's stopped trying to push him off. There she will have to lie until a chambermaid arrives to clean the room.

Peter looks from face to face. 'Alex,' he says. 'Kay and Hani arrived before you did and they know why we're here. Ted Bailey has very little time left and there's a decision to be made. It isn't clear-cut; there will have to be a trial.'

'I don't see why,' says Kay. 'He's a murderer. He's used people. Sexually and every other way. He's never controlled his temper. He's destroyed lives with his bribery and his drugs.'

'Kay has summed up the case for the prosecution,' says Peter. 'And I think it's clear this man isn't coming straight through. Is there a case for a second chance? That's what we need to decide.'

Kay is staring at the hotel bedroom. 'It's too late. I think he's gone.'

'Lazarus was in the tomb four days,' says Peter. 'The situation is never irreparable.'

'Isn't that frowned on now?' asks Kay. 'All the attention miracles get from hysterics and self-publicists? We know how the popes feel about that. Is it something we'd want to recommend?'

'The popes have no say Here,' says Peter. 'Even if they think they should. They don't run things any more than the rabbis or the imams do. And I don't know what you think you mean by "now".'

'Who *does* run things?' asks Hani. It's something Alex has wondered, too, but Peter simply glances at Kay and says nothing.

'The popes have a special relationship, though. Don't they?' asks Kay.

'Why?'

'On this rock...?'

'That was never said. Like so much in that book, it's pure invention. I should know. And look how many popes have failed to make it through the darkness.' He looks directly at Alex. 'The prosecutor is already in place. We need a defence counsel.'

'Defence? He has a defence?'

'He thinks so. I agree with him, actually. But he needs a friend down there with him. Acting as his own counsel...how well would he put it across?'

Alex realises with a shock what Peter is suggesting. 'You want me to go back There and defend him? *Me*?'

'You were close to him once.'

'I loved that man and he got me killed. When I was by no means ready to go.' In the face of Peter's silence, she says, 'I thought he loved me, too. Well, I knew he didn't, not yet, but I thought he would come to love me. I was kidding myself.'

Kay says, 'That's what women in love do.'

Peter says, 'We'd like you to go. Please.'

She doesn't want to do this but she knows he's not really asking her. "Please" is for form and the look of it; in fact, she has to do what she's told.

Peter pushes a thick folder across the table. 'This is Ted's file. Your ex-lover's past may surprise you.'

Once, they'd have said, 'Well, he had a good innings.' Today it's more likely to be, 'Seventy-three. It's no age.' Average life expectancy for males of Ted's generation is seventy-four. He's being cheated of a year. But that's average life expectancy. Some people will live to a hundred and some he knew in the sixth form are already gone. Michael, drowned in the Liffey with a stomach full of Guinness when he was twenty-three. If Ted had been there he'd have reminded Michael that he was the one who never learned to swim. Darwin, dead of a heroin overdose in New York at twenty-five. There are others. Quite a lot of others.

The fact is, the Reaper collects when he feels like collecting.

Darkness is everywhere. Ted is moving through it and he can't see an end. So far, it's on the fringes, the way his grandmother said it was when macular degeneration was reducing her eyesight to tunnel vision. He can see what's in front of him but at the edges are threats that are so much worse than they might be because they're invisible.

This is a fairground midway. The Hoppings, probably, the huge fair that comes once a year to Newcastle Town Moor.

But this is not The Hoppings. It's heaving, teeming with life, but it isn't any midway Newcastle Town Moor ever saw. Someone has put a cage on the ground. In the cage is a man. A crowd is gathering. There are shouts, catcalls, laughing. The man looks terrified.

The crowd parts to let someone through. These look like people who stand aside for no one but they shrink back for this newcomer. He's a big man, well over six feet tall with a wrestler's chest and shoulders and a flat stomach. Big thighs that stand out because the green suit he's wearing is a shade too tight. His dark hair is brushed back and pasted down in a nineteen thirties movie star way and you could take him for a villain in the Béla Lugosi mould. His eyes lock with Ted's and Ted can't look away. The man twists a lock on top of the cage. The door falls open.

The man in the cage disappears from sight, smothered by the mob that drags him out and drowns him in a sea of flailing men and women. Still looking at Ted, Béla Lugosi says something and the mob becomes quieter; he holds up a hand and they shrink back to let the man become visible again. He's on his hands and knees and he's sobbing. Lugosi speaks again and four people step out of the crowd. Two men, who hold him up, and two women. The women, without haste and without violence, begin to undress him. The crowd hoots approval.

When the man is naked, the two women push him to the ground, face down. One of the men steps between his outstretched legs and kicks them apart. He kneels and unfastens his belt.

Lugosi looks at Ted. He smiles. And Ted sees that his skin isn't like normal people's. It's thick, and scaly, and it's as much pale green as it is white. This man could be a lizard as easily as he could be a man.

'Take Ted away,' he says. 'He isn't ready for this.'

Two people of restricted growth take Ted by the hands and lead him at something approaching a run until they reach the hotel where, a few moments ago, Ted was in bed with the second Bella, but it's changed. The wall has gone. The space where it used to be is guarded by thickset men and well-built women in camouflage clothing who separate the peace of the hotel from the rising hubbub out here in this place Ted doesn't want to put a name to. The guards are armed. A red-haired woman carries a sword with a blade that must be eighteen inches long. It's oiled, that blade, and it's been used on occasion because the edge is not entirely straight; there are small chips where it's met something hard and dealt with it. The woman looks like someone who could deal with things. Near her is a man with a mace, and another carries a short wooden staff from which hangs a spiked iron ball.

The two midgets try to lead Ted into the hotel, but the guards stop them. The woman with the sword separates their hands from Ted's wrists and waves towards the hotel's interior. 'Get in,' she says. The dwarves are dismissed.

This room is essentially a very large bar. When Ted has been in it before, the chairs were arranged in twos and fours around scattered tables. Now the tables are gone and someone has pulled the chairs into rows. People are sitting in them, staring at a sofa and another chair on the stage the hotel uses for evening entertainment. The chair is a big one and it's been raised by a plinth. Next to that is a huge screen, positioned to hold the whole room's attention.

Maybe he should introduce himself, the way alcoholics do. "I'm Ted Bailey and I'm a dying sinner." But they'll find out soon enough. They can't see him yet, because he's standing in a corner. But one of them can see him, because he's staring, and he is the weirdest person Ted has seen in a long time. All the others here are dressed like twenty-first century tourists out for an evening's entertainment, but this man looks like Tut-en-Khamun after he was embalmed. Where did he get that outfit? A cape of golden cloth. A headdress. And all of it cut for a man twice his size. His eyes are cold, and watchful, and what he's watching is Ted.

The sofa and chairs are empty. At the front of the stage a song and dance man is warming up the audience. He says, 'I should steer clear of the entertainment business. That's what got me expelled from school. In drama club we were doing a play about some guy called Hamlet and I completely misinterpreted the stage direction, "Enter Ophelia from behind." She didn't object but the head teacher was furious.' He looks expectantly and gets a few obliging laughs and Ted wonders what this has to do with the fact that he's dying. 'I was in Australia two weeks ago. I met my wife in Australia. I said, "What are you doing here?"' The laughter is a bit more widespread this time. 'Hands up everyone whose been to Australia.' A few hands go up, not many, and he says, 'Hands up all those who don't like audience participation.' He points at a very overweight man in shorts that reach half way down his calves and a horizontally striped shirt that strains open across a monstrous belly. 'I said, hands, sir, not pairs of fingers. Well, as the tomcat said, these balls won't lick themselves.' Then he throws out his arms and shouts, 'Ladies and Gentleman, **Barry *DOLAN!!!!*'** and the audience stamps and shouts and screams as a man who looks extremely pleased with himself comes through an arch at the back of the stage and makes his way to the big chair and sits in it. He waves his hands at the audience and the stamping and shouting and screaming rise in volume and tempo and then he turns his hands over and they stop. Completely. Just like that. The comedian, his job done, walks towards the bar.

'Ladies and gentlemen,' booms Dolan, 'do we have a line-up for you tonight! We've got Peter Sellers and Henry Blofeld, Kenneth Tynan and John Betjeman and a very special guest from two thousand years ago whose name I don't yet have. But first, let me introduce the star of the show!' He beckons and Ted finds himself walking forward out of the shadows. The audience doesn't stamp and scream for him, or even mutter in a "Who the hell is this?" sort of way as he walks down the stage and takes his seat on the sofa.

And now the point of Dolan's plinth becomes clear, because Dolan is something of a shortarse but Ted is looking up at him. Looking up at a man who can't be a day over thirty with a smooth face, unruly hair and a charcoal grey Mao suit.

'This is a new experience for today's main guest,' Dolan says, and he's looking at and talking to the audience. Then he turns, but the voice is still loud enough to reach the back of this large room. 'Ted Bailey, you usually stay well away from occasions like this.'

'People in my line of business try to avoid publicity. Chat shows aren't really our thing.'

'Your line of business. For the folks at home who don't know, what exactly is that?'

Folks at home? And Ted sees a television camera, which he feels sure wasn't there a moment ago, and a man with a beard operating it. Who is Dolan, that he can generate props out of nothing? He looks at the audience, faces red and mottled by the sun, the hideous colours and shapeless clothes masking the horrible fat bodies. 'This must be a first for you, too, Barry.'

'Yes,' Dolan says. 'We don't usually do the Dolan Show in the bars of resort hotels. But there didn't seem much choice if we were going to get you in at all. Your predicament being what it is.'

'My predicament. You mean, dying on top of a twenty-year-old I've paid to have sex with me? Here in this very hotel? Right now, while we're doing this show?'

The lopsided face creases in a smile that embraces the whole audience. "What a wag!" it seems to say. "What a humourist!" He holds up a finger. 'I think you're trying to draw attention away from my question.'

'You do? What exactly was your question again?'

Another smile hugs the audience. It isn't the nicest smile. It conveys no warmth or friendship. There can't be much doubt that this man is capable of enormous, all-encompassing regard – for himself. There may not be a single person on the entire planet who enthrals Dolan as he captivates himself. And yet, the audience loves him. 'Your line of business, Ted. What is it?'

'Oh,' says Ted. 'This and that. Whatever comes to hand, really.'

'But not much of it legal, Ted?'

'Oh, no, Barry. Not much of what I do is legal.'

Again the complicit smile sweeps the audience. A woman in the second row sets her face like stone. Mostly, though, the reaction amounts to titters and smirks. What a wag, indeed.

'In fact,' Dolan says, 'the story we're going to hear today, ladies and gentlemen, is one of murder, fraud, the bribing of foreign officials and the smuggling and sale of proscribed drugs. And the way the accused treated women was a disgrace.'

There's a stir beyond the wall that yesterday seemed so solid and has now vanished. A woman is weaving her way down the midway towards them. She ignores the freaks on either side and they draw back from her. Her head is lowered but there's something familiar about the way she holds herself. If she'd just look up, Ted is sure he would know who she is. And then she does, and his heart soars. She's carrying a big folder and she marches straight past the guards, into the bar and up to the front, steps on to the stage and stops. Dolan says, 'Do you mind? We're doing a show here.' He looks away, through the arch he walked in by, as though he's looking for help.

'Don't bother calling Security,' she says. 'I have a pass.'

'What?'

'You didn't think you'd get away with this, did you? Stringing the poor guy up with no one to speak for him?'

'Poor guy? Ted Bailey? Who's going to speak for a blackguard like him?'

'I am.'

'Well, good luck. This is a hanging case, open and shut.'

Of course, Ted is listening to this with interest, given that it's him they're talking about, but there's a question that must be asked. 'Alex,' he says. 'You're dead. What are you doing here?'

'Oh,' says Dolan, looking as though things have become clearer. 'So this is Alex. How did you two meet?'

'Can we leave that till later? I want to know what she's doing here.'

'I'm here to take part in this trial. I'm counsel for the defence.'

'My trial? My defence?' She nods. 'That is not fair. That is just not fair.' He points, over her head and through the space where the wall used to be, to the midway. 'And what is that? That wasn't there yesterday.'

'It's always there, Ted,' says Alex. 'The living can't usually see it, but it's always there.'

'We'll push on, shall we?' says Dolan. 'This dreadful life of yours, Ted. How did it start?'

Alex says, 'Not so fast. First, I need somewhere to put my papers.'

Dolan looks annoyed, like this is his show and Alex is horning in on his chance to shine, but she raises her arms and a table appears in front of her. If Ted didn't know it was impossible, he'd swear the stage and the room just grew to accommodate this new furniture. The bearded TV man has been pointing his camera at Alex and Dolan snaps his fingers to get his attention and, when he does, points at himself and the camera veers away from Alex and on to him. Alex places her folder on the table, takes some papers out of it and looks up. 'What's he doing here?'

Ted looks where she's pointing and sees the bizarre old man pressed against the wall and doing his best to be invisible. He says, 'You mean King Tut?' and she says, 'That's no Egyptian god-king. That is Ras Tafar. Haile Selassie, Emperor of Ethiopia. He's barred for ever from where I live now. There are signs all over the place with his picture on them. I'm supposed to report his presence the moment I set eyes on him.'

'I thought Haile Selassie was a goodie.'

'So do lots of people. Ask the Eritrean people he misled, betrayed and slaughtered what kind of saint he is. If you survive this hearing he'll be hoping to enter your body and slip in to Heaven as you. You may allow yourself a moment of pride because that little runt is the Conquering Lion of the Tribe of Judah, the King of Kings, the Elect of God and he has standards. He doesn't pick on just anyone's soul to steal. Ignore him. Right. Carry on.'

'First,' Ted says, 'I need a drink.'

'Is that wise?' asks Dolan. 'In your condition?'

'I'm dying, Barry. I don't think an Armagnac's going to make much difference now.'

Dolan nods at the justice of this and a waiter steps briskly onto the stage. On his tray is a brandy balloon half full of warm water, an empty shot glass and a bottle. He tips the warm water into the shot glass, pours a generous slug of Armagnac into the warm balloon and hands it to Ted.

'Muchas gracias,' says Ted.

The waiter bows slightly and steps back towards the bar. And Ted has already had more surprises than enough today but now something astonishing happens because someone has come through the arch and it's him. Him as a youth. Young Ted fresh out of school with all the hair a young man could want and an engaging manner.

Young Ted sits on the sofa beside Ted, the two Teds five decades apart and Ted is amazed, although to the audience it's just one more marvel of television. It isn't clear they even realise who this is, this young man who is Ted, Ted as he was. Ted envies the years his younger self has to come, though he hopes he'll live them differently. The screen starts to glow.

A dance hall of the early Sixties, all glitter balls and men in suits with jackets that are a little too long and women with bouffant hair and brightly coloured dresses that spread out over massed petticoats.

Beside the screen stands Carol with a microphone. Carol at Young Ted's age; Carol as she was then. Ted hasn't thought of Carol for nearly fifty years. When she speaks, her accent is pure Geordie and Ted wonders how the foreigners in the audience will understand her. Look what happened to Cheryl Tweedy when she tried to make it in the States. She starts to speak.

'This is the Oxford Ballroom. In my day this was where the young people of Newcastle came to meet each other. Ted Bailey was one of them and I was another.'

The Ladies' Powder Room. Carol sits on a stool in front of a mirror, make-up bag open beside her.

The girl at the next mirror pauses, lipstick in hand. 'Rita's engaged.'

'Rita? Who to?' says Carol-on-the-screen.

'That fitter she was gannin' oot with. What's his name? Bobby.'

'A fitter!'

'She's eighteen, man. Like you. Time's passin'. There's only you left from our class.'

'Ah'm not marryin' any bliddy fitter.'

'You'll be an old maid, man.'

'Ah want someone gans to work in a suit an' a white shirt. Nee bliddy fitter.'

Carol-on-the-screen stands, raises her skirt, turns her head to peer down her back and straightens her stockings.

Carol-by-the-screen speaks. 'Pretty Polly Holdups are four years away and tights a year farther off than that. Like every other girl there, I still hooked my stockings to my suspenders. For a while, the thing Ted wanted most in the world would be to get his hand past the tops of those stockings. That was the window of opportunity. That was when you had to hook your fish and land him. He'd think he was the one doing the catching. Boys. What are they like?'

Dolan gestures to Carol-by-the-screen and she comes down and takes the sofa between the two Teds. Young Ted grins at her; her look might be cutting him dead and might be inviting him to make his move. On the screen, the camera has left the powder room and we're looking down from some point on the ceiling.

> *The young Ted enters the glittering ballroom on one side; Carol emerges through the grey door on the other. The camera zooms in as each reaches the edge of the dance floor. Closer still as Carol becomes aware that the young Ted is looking at her from the other side of the floor.*

The screen shows something Ted didn't see at the time as Young Ted picks his way round the edge of the sprung and polished wooden circle. 'You were tracking me every inch of the way.'

Carol-by-the-screen who is now Carol-on-the-sofa says, 'Of course. My granddaughter can walk up to any man she chooses and ask for a date. We couldn't do that in my day. All we could do was wait. Like a spider in a web. It wasn't a nice way to be. I'm glad things have changed.'

'You have a granddaughter?'

'One that I know of. Thanks to you I may have ten grandchildren I've never heard about.'

Ted looks at the floor. 'I'm sorry, Carol.'

'Are you, Ted? Are you? I think about my little girl so often. Especially on her birthday. How is she? What's she doing? Were her new family good to her? Is she happy?' Her lip is wobbling. 'Do you ever think about the damage you've done?'

Ted shakes his head as if trying to expel a thought he finds unwelcome.

Carol says, 'Oh, what's the point? Get on with your show.'

Alex hasn't been paying much attention to any of this. She's going through the papers in her folder, skipping over some and reading others two or more times, and making notes. Ted has been aware once or twice that she looked at him in a thoughtful way. He'd love to know what's in those papers.

<u>Chapter 4</u>

A young man in a powder blue jacket with black velvet lapels and a shoestring tie asks Carol for a dance. She takes in the oil under his fingernails and shakes her head. Close on Carol and the young Ted as they come together. The young Ted speaks.

'Would you like to dance?'

Convention in Jane Austen's day said that, once you had refused to dance with one gentleman at a ball, you could not dance with anyone for the rest of the evening. Those times are far in the past. Carol and Ted move smoothly out onto the floor. Carol's dinky blue handbag hangs from the arm she raises to place round Young Ted's back. The rejected suitor turns to someone else.

As they dance, the girl from the powder room catches Carol's eye. She looks at Young Ted and gives Carol an approving nod. Carol smiles demurely. Young Ted spots a youth he knew in sixth form who leers at Carol and gives a lecherous grin and an obscene gesture.

Later that same evening. Carol at a table, handbag on her primly closed knees, hands crossed on the bag. The young Ted approaches with a half pint of beer and a sweet vermouth. He sits.

'Thank you. I haven't seen you here before.'

'I come most Saturdays.'

Young Ted sniggers and his older self asks what he's laughing at and he says, '"I come most Saturdays." How's that for a *double entendre*?' Ted laughs and says, 'Well, I did,' and Young Ted says, 'Yeah. In your hand,' and Dolan tells them to shut up and watch the screen, which they do in time to see Young Ted asking Carol where she lives.

Ted's old school friend is already at the bar.

'She looks all right.'

'She lives in Walker.'

'Bloody hell. You'd better get rid of her.'

'Maybe. She's quite nice, isn't she? Lovely arse.'

'Look around, man. No shortage of nice arses in here.'

'Yes, I know. Even so.'

'And most of them are on girls who don't have perms. Some of whom don't live miles away from yours.'

'Has she got a perm?'

'Stands out a mile. It's up to you, man. I know what I'd do.'

Even later. A place unobserved enough for the rites of courtship close to a respectable girl's

The screen goes blank. Dolan speaks to Carol-on-the-sofa. 'By the time I was old enough, that sort of courting was out of date. Tell us what was going on.'

'It was a game like any other. It had rules and we both knew what they were. Well, actually he didn't know what they were because I found out later I was his very first date. But I knew enough for both of us. He'd kiss me, I'd kiss him. He'd press himself against me, I'd moan. If I felt something sticking into me that shouldn't, I'd moan a bit louder and lean away. That's as far as I went. Sex was for the man. Still is, if you ask me. It came in return for marriage. The night I got that gold band on my finger he could have all the sex he wanted. Well. Mebbes not all he wanted.'

'How long did it go on?'

'As long as it took. Boys who gan to work in a suit and a white shirt don't marry as early as bliddy fitters. After I'd dangled the hook in front of him for a few weeks, I put more bait on it.' She pauses, as though she's done, and then she adds something, speaking directly to the audience. 'If we're going to watch what I think we're going to watch, there'll be a bit of trembling and moaning. A bit of gasping. Don't let it worry you. He wasn't hurting me.' She smooths her permed hair with her hand (yes, it was permed, Ted can see that now). 'Actually, I quite enjoyed that side of things.'

Carol and Young Ted, kissing on the sofa. Instead of removing his hand from her breast, she moans. She moans and trembles as he unbuttons her blouse, unhooks her brassiere, slips both from her shoulders. She turns her head, lowers her eyes and gasps. His hand moves across her belly; she moans some more. She strokes the back of his neck and moans again, but when he reaches for the hem of her skirt she catches his hand.

'Pet, I can't. Please.'

Young Ted goes on trying to get the skirt up. 'Please, darling. Please let me. I do love you, so much. Please let me touch you.'

'No!' She drags herself upright. 'Ted, I can't. It's all right for you. You're a man. Do you think I don't want you as much as you want me? I do. I love you. If you love me, you won't ask me to give myself to you.' She covers her little goose-bumped breasts. 'I've gone too far already.'

The young Ted removes her hands and stares at her. 'Oh, you haven't my darling, you haven't.'

The midway flares into sudden noise. It's the man who was in the cage. Ted says, 'Why doesn't someone help him?'

'Like who?' asks Dolan.

'Well. Us?'

Alex raises her head. 'We can't go out there, Ted. Only the dead can walk the Midway. I was spared it and you aren't ready. Judgement on you has not been passed.'

'What about the guards?'

'The guards are there to keep the dead from the living. The darkness came for that man and he did not come through it. The guards don't care what happens to him now. Nobody does.'

'He's being buggered.'

'Yes, I do believe he is.'

'How can he be dead? Can a dead man scream like that?'

'The evidence is before you.'

Lugosi the lizard man leans back against the wall, his face a picture of contentment. King Tut rustles his robes. What's happening on the midway brings back the memory Ted believed he had buried so deep it could never return.

The room Arthur and his smiling friend took Ted to was a bedroom, at least inasmuch as there was a bed in it. The mattress was covered by a single sheet that looked as though it had not been washed in a long time. A mahogany wardrobe, battered and scratched with a cracked mirror on the front. No other furniture. Paint had been spilt on the floor but the shabby dirtiness it shared with the rest of the room suggested it had happened some time ago. There were no curtains on the unwashed window whose grime turned the sunshine grey.

They put Ted face down on the bed. Arthur's friend sat on his neck and held his wrists while Arthur went to work with a bottle of oil. Ted was crying, but not because of what they were making him ready for with the oil. Or not only because of that. He cried out of helplessness.

Dolan says, 'Shall we get on? You decided you'd waited long enough. What the other person wanted took second place.' For a moment, Ted thinks he's talking to Arthur but then he realises that Arthur isn't here and Dolan can't see him.

Another Saturday night. Young Ted removes Carol's blouse and brassiere as before, presses her back onto the sofa and moves his hand across her belly. As usual, when he reaches for the hem of her skirt she stops him. This time, he wraps his arms round her and rolls her onto the floor.

'What are you doing?'

With the weight of his body on her right arm, his knee between her thighs and his left hand holding hers above her head, his right hand is free to do what it chooses. It chooses to unhook her skirt. She babbles in breathless protest but she is looking up at the face of a man who is not about to stop. 'Ted. You do love me. Don't you?'

Her skirt is round her ankles and her waist slip is following it. 'Darling, of course I love you.'

'I mean really love me. For ever.'

His hand makes short work of her suspenders. He kisses her. 'Oh, darling, you know I do. I love you, I love you, I love you.'

'Ted, I'm frightened.'

He tugs her knickers past her knees. 'Darling, don't be frightened. You know I love you. If I didn't love you, I wouldn't want to do this.'

He has to let go of her to get his trousers off. She lies on the floor, her fate out of her hands. 'Ted, I'm only letting you because I love you so much. You know that, don't you? I'd never do this with anyone else. Never. You do know that, don't you?'

He unzips. 'Of course I do. I told you, my darling, I love you for ever. I'll never leave you.'

'You won't, will you? You won't leave me? Oh! Oh, darling, be gentle. OH!'

'Well,' says Dolan. 'My word. That was a bit steamy.'

'Not the kind of thing you usually get on your show, Barry?'

'Indeed not. So, how did you follow that?'

'We cleaned the carpet.'

'That's not quite what I meant.'

'Learned to hold on a bit longer, for a start.'

Dolan smiles at the audience, waves his finger at Ted. 'So it went on? The sex?'

'We were at it like rabbits. Every Saturday night.'

'But not rape anymore?' says Dolan. 'Not after that first time?'

Ted finishes his Armagnac and holds up the empty glass. The waiter arrives, goes through the same business with the warm water, the shot glass, the balloon. Ted is looking at the darkness. On the floor, in the corners, still distant but slowly getting closer. Is he the only one who sees it? He shakes himself. The darkness does not retreat. And nor does King Tut, still lurking in a corner and still staring at him.

'The first time wasn't rape, Barry.'

'That's what they'd call it today.'

'We're not talking about today.'

'She didn't want to have sex. You did. Because you were bigger and stronger, you got your way. By force.'

'It wasn't rape. Not the way rape was defined then. Today, yes, you'd call it rape. Then, no. I'm no rapist.'

Dolan says, 'Why don't we see what Carol thinks? Carol?'

Carol coughs, clears her throat; even after all this time the subject still embarrasses her. 'Well,' she says. 'If you really want to know, I was feeling better than I'd expected.'

'But it was rape,' says Dolan. 'He did rape you.'

'And, you know, maybe it was okay because it was true love. If I felt let down at all, it was by the brevity of the thing.'

'Carol, did you feel...'

'No. All right? I don't know why this is so important to you, but, no, I did not feel as though I'd been raped. This is nineteen sixty-two we're talking about. It's a world that's gone, swept away and quite right too because it had very little to do with the way people really are. It was more the end of the Fifties than the beginning of the Sixties and the Fifties in Britain was a very dishonest decade. But it was real then and we all knew what the rules were. The man...what am I saying, the *boy,* they weren't men in those days, not at nineteen, they were boys, the boy would push as hard as he could without hurting you, and if you were a decent girl you had to resist him. If you actually got him to the altar without giving in you got extra points for that but if you'd kept him at bay as long as you could and then passion got the better of the pair of you, or of just him if you couldn't fight him off, then it was a matter for shame, you couldn't avoid that, but it wasn't the end of the world so long as he married you. He had to marry you.'

Dolan looks satisfied. 'So Ted broke the rules? He welshed on the bargain?'

'He didn't marry me, if that's what you mean.'

'And these rules. Did all girls think the same way?'

'A real filthy little trollop wouldn't. And the kind of posh girl who went to Larsser Jess thought it didn't apply to them. Like the stuck-up bitch he went with after me. They could do what they wanted and if they got themselves in trouble their parents would send them away for a while and the baby would be adopted and nobody would say a word and they could still have their pick of boys to marry. But nice girls kept themselves decent.'

Dolan looks satisfied. 'I think a jury would see that as rape. Anyway, you carried on. And always the long walk home afterwards, Ted? Was it worth it?'

Ted jerks his head in Young Ted's direction. 'Is this him you're asking? Or me?'

'I'm looking at you.'

'I bought a car. In those days most people of my age went everywhere on the bus, or they cycled, or they walked, but I paid three hundred and fifty pounds for a one-year old Hillman Minx. My father lent me the money and I paid him back at ten pounds a month. I could afford it. I was living at home and I wasn't expected to give my mother anything for my keep. But even without the car, I'd have thought so. Young men of nineteen didn't expect unlimited access to a willing female body, Barry. Not in those days. You had to fight for every inch above the knee. Be grateful for a bit of tongue. You're too young to remember how it used to be.'

'And she *was* willing?'

'Couldn't get enough. I think she surprised herself. But we did it in her bed. It's nicer in a bed. More yielding. You get more bounce.'

Carol's face has turned bright red. She says, and she's standing up and walking towards the arch as she says it, 'I didn't come here to be called a slut in front of people I've never met.'

Young Ted scrambles to his feet. 'I'll just have a word before she disappears out of my life for another fifty years,' he says, and he goes too. Dolan doesn't seem to notice. 'You took precautions? As they say?'

'Usually. You don't think he's hoping to get his leg over again, do you? After everything that's happened?'

'You should know. He's you, not me. In matters of contraception, usually is often not enough.'

'As we found out later.'

'When you were beginning to cool towards Carol. When you'd already found someone else.'

Ted nods. A hiss passes round the audience. As before, the meaning of the hiss divides according to the sex of the hisser.

'Tell us about the someone else.'

Chapter 5

1966. Summer. Saturday afternoon in the drawing room of a well-appointed Jesmond home. A small drinks party. The furniture is chintz and polished rosewood, the velvet curtains are swagged, the window panes leaded, the carpets deep and fitted. In a cabinet, glassware and porcelain figurines. On the wall a large seascape; opposite it, a reproduction of The Hay Wain. Almost everyone is smoking.

Beside the screen once again is a girl with a microphone. Ted's face softens. After all these years, Annabel can still do that to him. He'd thought at the time that everyone must go through that feeling before they married or marriage would never happen. It's love and he had it for the first time with Annabel because what he had with Carol wasn't love, it was sex, and if he didn't know that before Annabel came into his life he did once he had her. When he was with Annabel he didn't want revenge, didn't want to hurt anyone (and certainly not her), didn't want to prove he was a man and not some other man's pretend girl.

Annabel isn't speaking, standing there by the screen, but on the screen she is. Standing by the French windows, she's talking to the twenty-year old Ted.

'Durham's the best of both worlds. It's only twenty miles away, so getting home's no problem, but you have to live in college.'

The young Ted stares at her face in silence.

'You could still go there. My father says your father wishes you had.'

Oh, those full red lips. Her frank blue eyes, and straw-coloured hair pulled back in a ponytail.

'I can hardly wait. I mean, I love the parents but I feel stifled here. You know what I mean?'

She has a tiny scar just to the right of her beautiful nose.

'Ted, if you don't talk a bit more and listen a bit less I'll start thinking you fancy me.'

Was ever eye as blue or gaze as clear as Annabel's? Ted didn't think so.

'I see.' In a louder voice, 'Mother, I'm going to show Ted the garden.'

They walk slowly, close together without touching. Annabel says, 'Tell me about your plans, Ted. What do you want to do with your life?'

'Well. Get away, I suppose.'

'You do have a voice, then. Get away from where? Home? Newcastle? Carol?'

'What do you know about Carol?'

'Your parents tell mine. They think you're going to throw yourself away.'

'No chance of that.'

The camera leaves them in the garden and trundles into the drawing room. Ted watches closely because he wasn't part of this conversation and he knows nothing of it. Before he can hear it, though, the Annabel who isn't on the screen, the Annabel who is standing beside it, places her microphone neatly on the table and walks across to the sofa. She sits down beside Ted and takes his hand in hers, hugging it to her. Her face turns to his. She's smiling. And Ted is in love again, transported to a place of happiness he hadn't known before Annabel came into his life and has experienced only once or twice since she left it. And he's wishing that she could have grown old, and done it with him. Annabel pats his hand, sees that he can't stop staring into her eyes and says, 'Let's watch the screen.'

> *Ted's father and Annabel's mother watch Annabel and Ted through the open French windows.*
>
> *'You worry too much, Charles. A young man needs experience. God knows I'd have hated Henderson to come to the marriage bed a virgin. One of us was quite enough.'*
>
> *'I wish he'd hook up with someone more suitable.'*
>
> *'Young men like Ted don't marry shop assistants. It'll blow over. He'll forget her before the year is out.'*

'He's too passive. He lets things happen. I sent him to Boys' Club to learn to box. Toughen him up.'

'It didn't work?'

'He was a good fighter.'

'He's a big boy.'

'He had a streak of aggression I never suspected. Beat a couple of lads no one expected him to beat. Bigger and more experienced boys. Just went crazy and battered them. The coach thought he could turn professional. I wouldn't have wanted that, of course. But he's still too ready to sit back and take what comes. I wish I'd let him go to university.'

'Why didn't you?'

But Ted doesn't hear the answer, because the screen has switched. In any case, he doesn't need to hear it because he knows it. His father had left school when he was fourteen and he thought enough education was enough. That time, late Fifties, early Sixties, it wasn't like it would be later. University was still for a minority. Ted's father played snooker at the Conservative Club. He got an estate agent friend there to give Ted a job.

Annabel says, 'You haven't asked what I'm looking forward to most.'

'Tell me?'

'Losing my virginity.'

As she says it on the screen, the Annabel sitting beside Ted squeezes his hand tight.

'Don't look so shocked. My mother thinks I'll enter the married state unsullied. As she did. She's welcome to think that. You don't think I'll lose my commodity value as a bride, do you? If I've had a penis inside me?'

'Er...no. No.'

Ted had never had a conversation like this. Not with a girl. And especially not with a girl as beautiful as Annabel. Or as intelligent. Carol could never have used an expression like commodity value, wouldn't even know what it meant. He wasn't completely certain he knew himself. He saw in an instant how inadequate the sex life he'd been so proud of actually was.

'I don't want a botched job, though. And I don't want any unplanned after effects. I want it done with a contraceptive. And I want it done by someone who's done it before. My, Ted, you are looking interested all of a sudden.'

'I...'

'Someone not much older than me, ideally. And as intelligent. Does that sound boastful? An intelligent, clean, good-looking young man who's been perfecting his technique with a shopgirl would be perfect. Especially if he'd had a bath before he got here.' Tall herself, she has to look upwards to hold Ted's eyes. *'The*

parents play a round of golf every Sunday. Then they have lunch at the club. I'll be at home tomorrow, finishing an essay. If a qualified candidate turned up about ten he'd have plenty of time to teach me everything he knows.'

In the car on the way home. Ted's mother said, 'You seemed to get on with Annabel.'

'Yeah. Yes, she's okay. She's grown up a bit since last time I saw her.'

'So have you. You seeing Carol this evening?'

'No. Yes.'

'No, yes?'

'I'm supposed to. I've got a bit of a headache.'

His parents exchanged glances. 'Probably the sun,' said his mother. 'You were a long time in the garden. What were you talking about?'

'Oh, this and that.'

Annabel opens the door wearing a dressing gown. Her skin is pink, as after a bath. No make-up. Her ponytail has been shaken loose; straw-coloured hair frames the sweet oval of her face. She steps back to allow the young Ted to enter.

'Hiya.'

'Hiya.'

'Well.'

'Yes.'

'Shall we go up?'

Annabel's bedroom. Narrow bed. Frilled and flowery counterpane.

She lays a towel on the bottom sheet. Then she lays another on top of it. 'No point leaving unnecessary traces, is there? Do you think you might kiss me?'

He does.

'You'll do this nicely, won't you? Not just some quickie conquest?'

The screen fades and then comes back to life. Annabel is again in her dressing gown, folding the towels. Young Ted is getting dressed.

'I can make you a sandwich, if you like? Then you should probably go.'

'A sandwich would be lovely.'

'Was it...you know.'

'It was wonderful.'

'For me too. I'm so lucky it was you. You won't tell people, will you?'

'Who? Who am I going to tell?'

'Friends. People you want to show off to. Her.'

'Carol? You think I'd tell Carol about you?'

'What are you going to do about her?'

'I'm going to end it.'

'You don't have to. I mean, I'd like you to but you don't…'

'I couldn't keep seeing her after we've… After… This has been the most wonderful day of my life.'

'Thank you.'

Dolan freezes the screen with his remote control. He stares at Ted, adult Ted, eyeing him without a word. Then he says, 'You were lying.'

'Yes.'

'You knew you were going to have Carol again but you said you weren't.'

'Yes.'

He goes on staring. Then he looks at the audience. 'He was lying,' he says. 'When he tells you how much he loved Annabel, how she made him feel, remember that. She'd just given herself to him and he lied to her.'

On the sofa, Annabel squeezes Ted's hand again and looks as though she's going to speak but Dolan says, 'Not now' and presses his remote. The screen unfreezes.

Annabel peeps round the front door. 'I won't come further than this. You know what neighbours are like.'

'Can I meet you from school tomorrow?'

'That would be nice.'

'Your parents won't mind?'

'My parents will be delighted. When are you going to tell her?'

'This afternoon.'

'Will you go there?'

'I don't want to finish it on the phone. I owe her that.'

'Good luck. Be gentle with her. She's going to be very upset. I don't think you know what a desirable hunk you are. Ted...'

'Yes?'

'I love you.'

'I love you, too.'

The screen goes blank, and Annabel gently removes her hand from Ted's and stands up. She faces the audience full on. In a voice that sounds as though she's learned a little speech and she's going to say it, whatever happens, she says, 'Ted Bailey was the best thing that ever happened to me. He was the best thing that could ever have happened to anyone. If we'd stayed together, his life would have gone differently and he wouldn't be here now. And he's a good man, whatever people might say. He deserves another chance.' Then she leans over and kisses him on the forehead and says, 'God bless you, Ted.' And she's gone. Vanished. Out of his life.

When Mr Walton came back, Ted refused to call him Charlie. 'Everything going to be all right?' the man asked.

'We've had a great time,' said Arthur. 'Right, Teddie?'

'That isn't what I asked. Is he going to be sensible?'

Arthur said, 'What Charlie is asking, Teddie, is whether you're going to blab when you get home.'

Ted shook his head.

'That's what I thought. This is just going to be between us. Right?'

The movement of Ted's head could mean anything.

'Yes or no, Teddie. You're not going to tell anyone what happened here. Say it out loud.'

'I won't tell anyone.'

'Good boy. Give him back his clothes.'

In the car, Ted didn't speak. Mr Walton dropped him in town with his rucksack and Ted took the bus home.

'Good weekend?' asked his mother.

'It was okay.'

His father said, 'A whole weekend playing chess. A bit too much, was it?'

Ted nodded. 'I think I've lost interest in chess. Can you get me into that boxing club you talked about?'

'So,' says Dolan. 'You told Annabel you were going to finish your relationship with Carol. You didn't, though. Did you? Not that afternoon.'

'No,' says Ted. 'I didn't finish it.'

'In fact, having tupped Annabel in the morning, you drove Carol to the Town Moor and shagged her in the afternoon.'

'I suppose I did. Yes.'

'Deceit had entered Ted Bailey's life.'

'Yes it had.'

'Twice over. You were lying to Annabel and you had to start lying to your parents. They couldn't know you were still seeing Carol.'

'Dad might have said something to Annabel's father.'

'And we couldn't have that, could we? Not if you hoped to find yourself between Annabel's thighs again. Which you did.'

'Oh, Barry, how I did.'

'It couldn't have lasted.'

'I didn't know that then.'

'But something else started that day.'

Newcastle in the early Sixties was still one of the most attractive cities in England. Wide streets, handsome buildings, parks, trees. A sense (whatever happened to that?) that the future was here and it was going to be better for most people than the past had been. And there was the Town Moor. Nearly a thousand acres of common land, bigger than Hyde Park and Hampstead Heath put together and all of it close to the city centre. This was not the first time Young Ted had taken Carol there.

She lies on the blanket. Her skirt is raised high on her stomach, her legs widely spread, her knees bent. Her knickers hang from one ankle. She reaches for Young Ted's belt and starts unbuckling him. 'Please,' she murmurs. 'Please.'

He sits back. Carol grabs his arm. 'Darling. What is it?'

'I haven't got a blob.'

'Oh, is that all.'

'Carol, we can't. Not without protection.'

She has him out of his trousers now. 'We've done it before. Pull out like you did last time.'

'But it's a hell of a risk.'

'You're not leaving me like this, Ted Bailey. You started it, you're going to finish it. And look at this big boy. Don't tell me he doesn't want his oats.'

'But what if you have a baby?'

'I finished my period on Thursday. I can't get pregnant now. We're safe as houses.' She pulls him towards her. But when he is ready to climax and tries to withdraw, her legs are locked around his back in a grip he cannot break.

Later. Young Ted is driving Carol home. A memory comes to him. 'You had your period two weeks ago.'

'No.' Her voice is drowsy and slow with pleasure.

'You did. You told me.'

'You're imagining it, Teddie. Everything's fine. Are you staying for tea?'

Next day, Young Ted leaves the office early. He parks a little way from La Sagesse, the girl's school everyone in Newcastle called Larsser Jess. When Annabel emerges she ignores her friends' giggles as she walks towards him. He takes her schoolbag and entwines the little finger of his free hand with hers.

'Did you tell her?'

'Yes.'

'How did she take it?'

'I think she was expecting it, quite honestly.'

'She must have known it couldn't work.'

'I suppose.'

'Her and you. The differences are too great. Does she know about me?'

'No. She suspects there's someone.'

'Why? What did she say?'

'She asked if I'd found someone else. I said not exactly.'

'Thanks a bunch.'

'Well, you didn't want me to tell her about you. Did you?'

'When did she ask?'

'When I refused to go to bed with her.'

'You refused?'

'Well, I should think so. It'd be a bit disloyal, don't you think?'

'To me?'

'Who else?'

'Oh, Ted. If we weren't so close to school I'd kiss you.'

'I wouldn't mind.'

'The Head would have a fit. You'll have to be patient. Daddy's coming home early. He wants to talk to you.'

'How did you feel, lying to her like that?' asks Dolan.

'I felt like a shit. I remember wishing I hadn't put myself in a position where I had to do it.'

'Regrets like that are cheap. It's what you do that counts, not what you think or what you say.'

'Just a minute,' says Alex. 'You're very hard on Ted, but you let those girls off a bit easily.'

'They aren't on trial here,' says Dolan.

'Maybe they should be. Ted, did you ever think you were being played for a mug?'

A mug? Him? 'What do you mean?'

'Annabel knew you and Carol were an item but she wanted you. She was better educated and nicer to look at and she simply took you away from Carol. Using her body to do it. And Carol decided she'd waited long enough for you to declare yourself so she tried to trap you. She told you she wasn't fertile when she knew she was, and when you tried to pull out she made sure you couldn't.'

'I don't like to think of them like that.'

'By "like that" you mean cunning, devious and manipulative. That's not how you like to think of women.'

Ted shakes his head.

'That's one reason you got into so much trouble, Ted. Because there are manipulative women, and you seem to have been drawn to them.'

'Oh, far out!' says Dolan, and he's laughing. 'You're going to try to get one of the biggest bastards of the last fifty years off his charges by saying he was led astray by women. Good luck with that.'

Alex says, 'I didn't know anyone still said, "Far out".'

'Annabel's father wanted to talk to you, Ted,' says Dolan. 'That must have made you sit up.'

'It did, a bit.'

'She didn't explain what he wanted?'

'Annabel liked to tease. In a nice way.'

'But as it turned out, he wasn't asking about your intentions towards his daughter. That meeting was to be the start of your criminal career.'

'What I did with Henderson Wilde wasn't criminal.'

'It was fraud.'

'That's a very strong word.'

'It was fraud. Not as bad in the public mind as some of the other stuff you've done, but still something the courts send people to jail for. I'm beginning to wonder why it was me you sent for. You don't need a chat show, you need This Is Your Life.'

'No. With Eamonn Andrews, maybe. We could talk about boxing. But he's dead. And they bring in all these people from your past. I'm not sure I'd like that.'

'So. Henderson Wilde had a proposition for you?' He turns back towards the screen. The audience is silent, intent on the unfolding story. Ted feels like ripping off a loud fart, just to break their concentration, but he doesn't. Breaking wind may not be the wisest thing for a man in his condition.

'Property, Ted,' says Wilde. 'That's where the money is.'

'Yes?'

'When my parents got married, they bought a house for five hundred pounds. And they expected it to go down in value. Property was a wasting asset. But now look. Even here in Newcastle, a three-bedroom semi will set you back three thousand. And they're going up. Buy that semi today for three thousand, you'll

probably be able to sell it in a couple of years for another four or five hundred.'

'Yes?'

'That's a return of eight per cent a year, Ted. You won't get that by sticking your money in a building society.'

'Interesting.'

'Very,' said Wilde.

He looks amused and though Ted didn't realise it at the time he sees now that Henderson thought he'd made a pun.

'And if the house is rented, you've got the rental income, too. But you can do better than that, Ted.'

'Yes?'

'Most people haven't realised yet what's happening. Especially older people.'

'Mister Coomes says that. When older people want to sell their houses, they're amazed by what they're worth. They think the house might go for a thousand or so, and he tells them it could be three times that.'

'He tells them, does he?'

'Well, yes. Of course.'

'Not much of a businessman, your Mister Coomes. Is he?'

'How do you mean, Mister Wilde?'

'Henderson, please. Suppose he didn't tell them, Ted?'

'Well...they'd know, wouldn't they? When they sold the house?'

'Not necessarily. Let's take an example. Suppose an old lady rings up, says she wants to sell her house. Husband's dead, children gone, it's too big for her. Maybe she's buying a flat. Moving in with her daughter and her daughter's family. Going into a home. Whatever.'

'Yes?'

'She thinks the house is worth a thousand. So somebody buys it from her for a thousand. Or even eleven hundred. Give her a bit of a bonus. She's happy. Isn't she?'

'Well, yes. I suppose so.'

'Course she is. She's like my parents, Ted. Thought the house she bought thirty years ago would go down in value. Instead of which, she's getting two, three times what she paid for it. She's happy. Bound to be.'

'I suppose so.'

'Then the somebody who bought it from her for eleven hundred sells it for three thousand. Which is its market value. So they're happy, too. Yes?'

'I suppose so.'

'Everyone's happy. It's what they call a win-win situation. Ted, I want to spread happiness around like that. I want to be that somebody who buys the house for eleven hundred and sells it for three thousand. I want to set up a company to do that.'

'Oh.'

'See, Ted, what you need to do that, you need two things. You need the money to buy the house. Me and a friend of mine, we have that money. And if we don't have it, we have the credit to raise it. But the second thing you need is the information on where the house is. And my friend and I, we don't have that. But you do.'

'Me?'

'You, Ted. When someone wants to sell their house, what do they do?'

'Well, sometimes they come to the office. But usually they phone.'

'And who takes the call?'

'Me. I do.'

'You do. So you're the person who has the information. Right?'

Ted didn't say anything. The conversation was moving into an area he'd never been in. He hadn't thought about it a lot but he'd always assumed he'd lead a blameless sort of life. Okay, the shagging, but shagging is what young men do. Young men are in thrall to their dicks. The young man says: "Please marry me; I love you and I want to cherish you and be with you for ever." What the young man means is: "I need to be inside you. I'm so certain I'll always want to be inside you I want to marry you, to make sure your furry little mott is there for me any time I want it." But he was never going to get involved in anything illegal. And that was where Henderson was taking him, he knew that. He hadn't spelt it out yet but it was coming. And Ted was going to say "No" because he was not a crook, wasn't born or raised to be a crook and didn't intend to become one. He'd let Henderson make his pitch but he knew he wasn't buying.

'What do you do when the call comes in?'

'I log it. Write it down in the book. Then I assign it to one of the sales people.'

'And they go and see the seller?'

'The vendor. Yes.'

'Do you think you can tell when the caller is an old person, Ted?'

'Usually, Yes.'

'So. Suppose, Ted, instead of logging the call and assigning it to a sales person, you call me. Give me the details. I go and see the vendor.'

'Saying you're us?'

'You'll have said someone will call. I just say, "I've come about the house." I let a week go by, and then I tell them I've got an offer for the house, and my company...our company,

Ted…buys it. And then sells it. And everyone's happy.'

'Our company, Henderson?'

At this distance in time, Ted sees things he didn't see then. Henderson's eyes were fixed on him with what, as Young Ted, he probably saw as friendly interest. What he sees more clearly now is that Young Ted had something Henderson wanted and Henderson intended to have it. In a way, Henderson was no different from Arthur except that Henderson saw a way to make a lot of money and what Arthur wanted was sodomy. He looks across the room at Haile Selassie and sees there the same desire for something Ted has.

'I don't expect you to do this for nothing, Ted. There's me, my friend, and you. You probably shouldn't be a shareholder, just in case anyone checks. But you'll get a one third share of the profits, Ted. A completely even three-way split. So now you're happy, too. What do you think?'

'But I work for Mister Coomes. He pays my salary.'

Henderson puts his hand on Young Ted's arm. 'Ted. I've seen the way you look at Annabel. I've seen the way she looks at you. You're going to get married one day, Ted, and if it isn't to Annabel it's going to be to someone like her. Or so you hope. Right?'

'Yes. Right.'

'Girls like Annabel, they have certain expectations. How much does Coomes pay you?'

Ted is no longer the young buck who shagged two girls in one day. He looks at his feet. 'Six hundred pounds a year, Henderson.'

Henderson takes his hand away. 'Six hundred a year. That won't go far with a girl like Annabel. And even when they make you a salesman, what will you start on? A thousand?'

'Less, probably.'

'Under a thousand. Do you have any idea what my wife spends on clothes, Ted? Annabel won't be any different. Girls like Annabel, they know their worth to a man. They take it in with their mother's milk. They learn it at schools like La Sagesse. Which, by the way, costs me more every year than you earn. Do you think Annabel will want her children to go to Chillingham Road? Will you? Where did Carol go to school, Ted?'

'North Heaton Secondary Modern.' He whispers it.

'That's the girl's equivalent of Chillingham Road, right?'

'Yes. I suppose so.'

'Well, that's the choice you're looking at, Ted. Young men reach a crossroads, they have to decide which way to go. La Sagesse or Chilly

Given the year in which they were eating it, dinner was quite adventurous. During the meal, Annabel was at her most captivating. The difference between her and Carol could not have been clearer. Little currents passed between her and Ted which Ted hoped were invisible to the adults. Which is the word he used because, right then, he wasn't feeling very adult. He felt like someone who'd been put very firmly in his place.

The roses were fragrant in the evening sunlight, and so was Annabel. That doesn't come across on the screen but everything about that evening is vivid in Ted's memory.

Annabel says, 'What are you thinking about?'

'Cricket.'

'Oh, that's very flattering.'

In fact, of course, he wasn't thinking about cricket. He was thinking about being a criminal, and how it simply wasn't possible, and how was he going to tell Henderson that without cutting himself off from his daughter? But he couldn't say so to her, so he talked about cricket.

'I always wanted to be a cricketer. Barnes, our headmaster before Leaping Arthur, was President of Northumberland Cricket Club. He encouraged me. But they have better coaching at the Royal Grammar. I'm wondering whether I would have made it if I'd gone there.'

'You don't seem to play now.'

'Cricket's a cliquey game. I couldn't get into the kind of club I wanted, so I gave up.'

'I didn't think you were a giver-up.'

Ted shrugs. He isn't happy, she knows he isn't happy and she ignores it. 'End of term next week. I've got the whole of the summer. Then Durham.'

'I'll lose you then.'

'That'll be up to us, Ted.' She turns to face him. 'I suppose that's when I'll find out. Whether you're a giver-up.'

The conversation seems to be over, but then she turns back. 'Why did you call your headmaster Leaping Arthur?'

'Olympics. He was in the Long Jump.'

'Oh.' She smiles. 'Aren't boys funny?'

<u>*Chapter 6*</u>

The screen doesn't bother to go blank; it merely switches to the next day. Watching it, Ted is sunk into deep gloom. He'd been invited to enter into an arrangement that was certainly immoral and probably criminal. He'd known it was coming and he'd known he was going to turn it down. And he hadn't. Pretty soon now he was going to have to take out Henderson Wilde's card, phone him, tell him he couldn't help. Wilde wasn't going to like it.

And what would his unhappiness with Ted do to Ted's relationship with Annabel?

Ted jerks his attention to the screen. There he is, Young Ted, and there with him is the first personal visitor he's had at the office. Young Ted has seen the man on the back pages of the *Chronicle,* and he isn't the only one because people are looking at him. He has an easy, friendly smile.

'Ted Bailey?'

Ted nods.

'I hear good things about you, Ted. Henderson Wilde tells me you were an opening bat at HGS?'

Ted nods again.

'I wondered if you'd like to turn out for our seconds on Saturday? No promises, but if you do well, who knows?'

It's clear the young man on the screen can't believe this is happening. You don't get to be twenty without learning to handle disappointment; having a dream come true can be harder to deal with.

'I'd love to.'

'It's an away game. You know where our ground is?'

'Yes.' It's a croak, so quiet the man almost fails to hear.

'Be there at nine thirty with your kit.'

Ted sits at his desk, staring at Wilde's card. He'd been so sure that Wilde's proposal was not for him, and now he isn't. One thing is inescapable—he wouldn't have been invited to join such a prestigious club without Henderson's intervention, and Henderson couldn't have made it without being briefed by Annabel because on his own he would never have identified cricket as a way to get to Ted. Which meant that Annabel wants Ted to join her father in his plans. His criminal, fraudulent plans. She's talked about finding out whether Ted was a giver up and now she is testing him. Almost as though she's asking: How much does he really want her?

Ted picks up the phone.

After the screen goes blank, Dolan gets up and walks off the stage, through the audience in their seats and out of the bar. He's gone.

No one else seems ready to panic, so Ted doesn't. Someone must know what's going on, and Dolan is a professional. He'll be back. Presumably. And in the meantime Ted can stare at the darkness spreading, slowly but inexorably, in his direction. Is he the only one who sees it? Apart from King Tut? He seems to be.

He's here on this sofa in this plushly over-decorated bar. But he's also somewhere else – in what looks like a tunnel, arms trapped by his sides, not knowing how to get from where he is to where he might want to be if he even knew where that was. It's a strange feeling, being in two places, two modes, at once.

And, actually, it's three places and not two because he's also lying like a dead weight on top of that poor girl with the sweet-smelling arse.

That darkness is moving. Slowly, but it's moving.

Towards Ted.

Then Dolan bursts back into the room and the smell he carries with him tells what he's been doing. 'You can't smoke anywhere now, you know that? You have to go and stand outside, like a delinquent. It's all about the rights of non-smokers but what about smokers? Eh? Don't we have rights?'

'It doesn't bother me. I gave up.'

He's brought someone back with him, and this man smiles at Ted in a distant sort of way and takes his place on the sofa. He's wearing a bow tie, which is something you don't see so often, and large glasses and his face is a sort of triangle in that it goes from a broad dome a little light on hair to an almost pointed chin. It's a familiar face and Ted should know who he is but he doesn't, and the man doesn't introduce himself and Dolan doesn't do it for him. Ted is about to take the ice-breaking task on himself when Dolan launches off in another direction.

'"I want to spread happiness around like that." What he meant was, "I'm going to rob people blind, old people, people who don't have much and can't really afford to lose what they do have, and I need you to help me." And you agreed. Why? So that you could play cricket and screw his daughter.'

Ted stares at his feet. 'I was young. There was so much time to make amends.'

'And you think you've done that, do you? Made amends? You, with the life you've led?'

'You don't think, when you're barely twenty, that someday you'll have to defend yourself. You know in your head you're going to die, but you don't know it in your heart. That comes later. I read once that Hindus, I think it was, split their lives into two halves. In the first, they do everything and anything they have to to make their pile. Then, in the second half, they retire from the world and make their peace with God. But I haven't had time to do that. And, if I had it, I didn't take it. I don't suppose Hindus do, either, if I think about it. What I've learned…'

Dolan shakes his head. 'Never mind what you've learned. Whatever it is, you learned it too late. Hard to be a twice a day man when you're playing cricket.'

'Impossible.'

'But you'd made up your mind anyway. If the cricket hadn't worked out, you'd still had enough of Carol. Now that you'd seen what else life could offer.'

'The cricket did work out. I played five games with the seconds and then they gave me a run with the first team. I wasn't a fixture, but I was there.'

'Scored a few runs.'

'More than a few.'

'And you enjoyed it.'

'Duck to water.'

'Got on with the other guys.'

'House on fire.'

'Learned to hold your drink. Learned to make small talk with the committee wives. In your element.'

'Loved it.'

'You couldn't have taken Carol there, even if Annabel hadn't been around.'

'I wouldn't have been there myself if Annabel hadn't been around.'

'So how did she take it? Carol?' He turns to the screen, where Young Ted is speaking into one of those big black Bakelite phones the GPO provided in those days. 'Let's watch, shall we?'

'It's an away game, Carol. I won't be back till nine. Later, maybe. And I'll be tired.'

'What you're saying is cricket is more important than me.'

Young Ted doesn't answer.

The Geordie is coming into her voice. 'You're finishing with us on the phone. You couldn't even do this to me face. After everything Ah've given you, do you not think you owe us that? Or am ah not worth the bother?'

Ted keeps his mouth shut. Let her end the thing herself.

'What about Monday night?'

'I can't. I have things to do.'

'Who with? Ah said, who with, Ted?'

'Why does there have to be anyone?'

'Because there is. Isn't there? You've taken everything Ah had to give you and now you're dumping us. Aren't you?'

His silence says as much as any words could have done.

'Ah'll never believe anyone when he says he loves us. Not ever again.'

She waits in vain.

'You're a shite, Ted Bailey. A nasty selfish little shite.'

'You'll be glad to be shot of us, then. Pet.' And he puts down the phone. He stays beside it for a while, waiting for her to call back. But she doesn't.

Chapter 7

There's a stir of interest as a new guest comes through the arch, shakes hands with Dolan and the other man who still hasn't been identified and grasps Ted in a bear hug. That's something Henderson Wilde would never have done at the time. When Ted was young, British men did not hug. They'd have seen it as impossibly Italian, as unthinkable as speaking to another man in the Gents or an earring on a professional footballer. Henderson goes to stand beside the screen. Poor Henderson. He was so big, so powerful, so full of beans. He got his suits made in London and this one does an excellent job of hiding what is becoming a substantial stomach. Ted is beginning to wonder why he'd said he didn't want people from his past on the show. They were all coming anyway.

Wilde says, 'We sold the first house three weeks later. At my suggestion, Ted didn't leave the call unlogged after all.'

1968. The sitting room of the Wildes' Jesmond home. Henderson Wilde and Young Ted.

Wilde says, 'Suppose there's ever a check, and every house they check on failed to be recorded. Who are they going to blame?'

'Me.'

'Is there someone in that office you don't like?'

'Marcus Thomas. Supercilious little rat. He did my job before me and now he treats me like dirt.'

'Book them all to him. Just in case.'

The words "Eight Weeks Later" flash on and off the screen and there is Henderson Wilde giving Young Ted a passbook and asking him to sign some bank mandates. 'The bank's in Jersey,' he says. 'They'll pay you interest, you can get money out any time you like but it might be wise not to put the cash straight into your own account here. In case anyone checks.'

Dolan picks up the remote and stops the action. 'These references to people checking. Do you still maintain that you weren't doing anything you shouldn't?'

There's no answer Ted can think of. At the time, he hid from the knowledge that what he was doing was wrong, but Dolan isn't leaving him room to do that. But the sum in that passbook was more than Ted earned in a year, after tax, and they'd sold two more houses since that first transaction. Dolan looks at the audience and raises his eyebrows. Then he presses the button on the remote and the screen comes back to life.

'Don't start any mad spending,' Wilde says. 'You don't want to draw attention to yourself.'

'I'd thought of buying a flat.'

'No harm in that, I suppose. Good investment; it can only go up in value. But tell people

you're renting. And don't buy it in your own name. Form a company.'

'In case anyone checks.'

'You're learning, Ted. I'll get my accountant to call you. He can help you set the company up. You'll be inviting Annabel to this flat, I suppose?'

'I imagine so.'

'Treat my daughter with respect, Ted. She's young and impressionable. I don't want to see her hurt.'

'I wouldn't hurt her for the world.'

'No, I don't think you would.' He pats Ted on the arm. 'I have great hopes for you.'

Henderson gives Ted a little wave and walks off, not through the arch but into the audience where he keeps on walking, out of the room and, as far as Ted can tell, out of the hotel. The screen does its scene-changing thing and the man who came back with Dolan after his smoke break and has been sitting since then on the sofa gets up and takes the microphone in his hand. And when he speaks Ted recognises him, and when he does he realises why he failed to identify someone so well known. It's because he's famous for his voice and not his face. Ted has listened to him for so many years on *Test Match Special* through his long wave radio and then on the Web, but only occasionally seen his photograph. Henry Calthorpe Blofeld. Blowers. Son of the man who gave the James Bond villain his name. Brother of a High Court Judge. Nephew of an England captain. Might have led England himself, had a bus not removed him from his bike on his way to captain Eton and left him in a coma for a month.

The screen is showing film of Ted's early matches when Blowers begins his commentary. Oh, that impeccable Eton diction. In his day, they didn't see the need to pretend to be ordinary people. The British used to admire people like Blowers, and Ted still does. A class act.

'It was a good cricketing summer for Ted Bailey. He only scored twenty in his first match, but they'd put him in at number six and he was still there when the last wicket fell. In his next two matches he moved up the order and did better, scoring an unbeaten fifty in one of them. Then, on a terrible wicket, he was out for nine, but no one else stayed long at the crease. The following Saturday, he was dropped in the slips on eighteen and went on to hit his first century. When one of the first team openers sprained his wrist, the number three was promoted and Ted took his place. He was back with the seconds three weeks later, but with decent scores and fine fielding to his name. People at the club were starting to talk about him.'

The images on the screen switch from the cricket field to the inside of Young Ted's flat. The Blofeld lip curls as he starts on the next bit of his commentary.

'He hadn't heard from Carol for several weeks and didn't expect to. That side of his life was over. Or so he thought. Her call came out of the blue, just after breakfast as he was putting his kit into his cricket bag.'

'How did you get my number?'

'What do you think? Your parents gave it to me. You must be doing well, Ted. A flat of your own. That's good. I wouldn't like to start married life living with my parents.'

The young Ted laughed. Married life? With Carol? Dream on. Ted remembers that laugh at that moment. It didn't last.

'It's no laughing matter, Ted. I've missed two periods. It must have been that day on the Moor.'

'That day you said you couldn't get pregnant. That day you wrapped your legs round me and wouldn't let me pull out.'

'You'll have to do your duty, Ted.'

'You scheming little bitch.'

'You had nothing to do with it, I suppose. My father wants to see you. This afternoon.'

'He'll have to want. I'm playing cricket today. In Yorkshire.'

'Tomorrow, then. You can come for tea. There's a lot to talk about. We have plans to make. I don't want to look like the side of a house when I go up the aisle.'

This is going to be Young Ted's last match—he doesn't think there's much doubt about that. You get a girl in trouble; you marry her. Simple as that. No one expects the marriage to be happy but the rules are the rules. Everything he's begun to hope for is turning to rat shit.

Blowers is still there, still speaking. On the screen, a small cricket ground, chairs along part of the boundary, old brick walls covered in ivy. The sun is shining but Young Ted's face looks like thunder.

'It's a game they shouldn't really be playing,' says Blowers. 'The opposition isn't their standard. But it's a school a past president of the club went to, and a tradition has grown up, and where would cricket be without tradition? Every summer, towards the end of the season, the club seconds play the school's first eleven. The school never wins, but it's understood that their noses won't be rubbed in it, that they'll be allowed to lose by not very many. And afterwards there's a nice tea, and for the adults sherry in the Headmaster's study.

'On the way to the ground, and in the dressing room, Ted was silent. He responded to none of the banter around him. Fury burned in his eyes.'

Ted is opening the batting with Tony Webb, the second team captain.

Tony was a lawyer, about thirty, a good egg who looked after the younger players as an older brother might if he were a nice older brother and not the kind most people have.

Blowers says, 'The first ball is a loosener, fast and short and wayward. Ted watches it every inch of the way as it rises steeply outside leg stump and hooks it high over square leg for six.'

Ripple of applause. The bowler looks hurt as he walks back to his mark.

'The second ball is pitched up more, and straighter. Ted steps forward and drives it hard back past the bowler for four.' Blowers can't feel it from inside but, oh, the pent-up rage in that shot.

'The third ball is better; an attempted yorker that Ted does well to get his bat down on.'

The bowler glares and Ted grins back, but there is no humour and no kindness in his smile. When the next ball moves away outside off stump he waits, then cuts late and hard.

'If you're going to cut, cut hard,' says Blowers. 'That's a lesson taught by every coach to every batsman anywhere in the world, and this is why. The ball rises steeply and safely over the head and upstretched arm of second slip and races away for four.'

The applause is louder. As the ball is retrieved, Tony walks down the wicket. 'You all right?'

'Never better. Why?'

'You're being a bit hard on that poor lad.'

'Am I?'

Blowers says, 'This boy is too erratic to be an opening bowler. Every ball so far has been pitched in a different place and so is the fifth—straight and just a touch short. Once again, Young Ted comes down the wicket and unleashes all the fury that threatens to send him up in flames. Straight back over the demoralised bowler's head for the second six of the over.

The school captain speaks to the bowler, and Young Ted watches as a fielder takes up position on the boundary behind the square leg umpire.

Blowers again: 'The sixth ball is like the first: short and climbing down the leg side, an invitation to try the hook shot again but this time dropping the ball down the boundary fielder's throat. Instead, Ted steps down the wicket, takes the ball early and pulls, rolling his wrists so that it bounces where leg slip might have been and speeds towards the boundary, where it is cut off. They run three.'

Twenty-three runs off the first over, and Young Ted still had the strike.

Tony comes down the wicket again. 'Take it easy, Ted. This isn't a competitive game. They're only kids.'

'Okay.' But the second over goes for eighteen.

Tony gives the bowler a maiden in the third, rebuilding his confidence, ignoring easy runs. Young Ted takes five fours off the fourth. It's the fastest fifty ever seen in this fixture and the applause is genuine. Tony walks towards him and they meet in the middle. Tony is smiling, but his tone is stern. 'That's enough, Ted. I don't know what's eating you, but you can't carry on like this. Next ball you face, give them a catch. If you don't, I'll run you out.'

'What if they drop it?'

'Give them another.'

'Okay.'

Blowers takes up the commentary again. 'Tony runs a single on the second ball, and Young Ted takes strike. He looks round the field, taking in the position of every fielder. It's a slower delivery, very straight, and he pretends to be fooled, deliberately taking the ball early and lofting it over the bowler's end. The bowler can't reach it, but Mid On takes a fine catch running backwards and Young Ted's out for sixty-one. Whatever may have been going on inside his head, this is cricket and there are conventions to be observed. He raises his bat towards the bowler who is receiving the well-mannered congratulations of his side. "Good ball," he says. Tony pats him on the shoulder as he walks off. The bowler smiles. "Well played, sir."

Tony Webb is out for fifty-four, playing no stroke at a straight ball that raps him high on the pad and walking before the umpire has time to give him not out. He drops down beside Young Ted.

'Now,' he says. 'Do you want to tell me what's eating you?'

'Oh. I'm okay.'

'You are not okay. And I want to know why.'

Young Ted shrugs. Here on this beautiful cricket ground bathed in sunlight, he's aware of what he is going to lose. There are tears in his eyes. 'I've got a girl in trouble.'

'Annabel Wilde?'

'No! Annabel's as pure as they come.'

'Who, then?'

'A tart in a shop. I went with her before I met Bella. I wish I'd never set eyes on her.'

'Tell me the story. Leave nothing out. I'm not your captain for this, I'm your lawyer.'

So he does. Tony asks questions from time to time, and Young Ted answers them. When team mates stroll up to chat Tony waves them away.

'Do you want to marry this girl?'

'Of course I don't.'

'Right. Here's what we do. When you get home tonight, pack a bag. You won't be home tomorrow, and you won't be at your parents' place. Do you have enough money to rent a room in a hotel?'

'Yes.'

'So do that. I want you completely out of touch.'

'What about my meeting with Carol's father?'

'You won't be there. I'm going in your place. If you had to raise a few hundred quid, could you do it? Would your parents help?'

'I could raise some money.'

'Okay. Money always makes things easier.'

'What are you going to do?'

'Lawyers terrify people like this. I'll ask how they can prove the baby's yours and I'll scare them shitless with what we'll do to their daughter's reputation if we ever get into court.'

'But it is mine.'

'You don't know that, Ted. If we have to, we'll show the court five men she's been with, the filthy little baggage. That'd cost, mind. Now I want you to put your heart and soul into this match, and forget all about this little tart and her baby. Because, after tomorrow, you'll never hear from her again. Deal?'

'Deal, Tony. And thank you.'

Webb smiles. 'That's what lawyers are for, Ted. To get their clients and their friends out of trouble. But do me a favour?'

'Anything.'

'Be more careful who you go to bed with in future.'

Blowers gives Ted a look of disgust, you really couldn't call it anything less than that, and puts down the microphone. He walks out of the room without a backward glance. The upper classes have standards and Ted has failed them. He looks at Alex and sees her lips pursed. She'd thought she knew him and she's realising that she really didn't.

'So Tony Webb extricated you from the mess,' says Dolan. 'And what might happen to Carol and the child she was carrying never crossed your mind,'

'Not then. All I could think of was that I'd been rescued. Got out of jail.'

'In any case, Webb was as good as his word.'

'He did the business. I paid three hundred quid for Carol's trouble and the baby was adopted.'

'Do you ever wonder what happened to it?'

'Her. It was a girl. And we've just heard that Carol doesn't know what happened, so how would I?'

He is on his third Armagnac now, and it's helping to dull his sense of the clouds of darkness creeping relentlessly towards him. How that poor girl upstairs is getting on, he doesn't want to think.

'Did you hear any more from Carol?'

'She sent Annabel a photo of the baby. From before it was taken away. Said she was doing it for Annabel's own good. To let her know what kind of man she was associating with.'

'How did Annabel react to that?'

'She laughed.'

'There's female solidarity for you.'

Alex says, 'I think it's time to put something on the plus side of this ledger of a man's life.'

This is the kind of situation boxing club prepared Ted for. It's nothing like as bad as it will become; louts like these are usually satisfied by a show of submission, like gorillas pissing on trees or whatever it is gorillas do; but you can't be certain.

And, anyway, Arthur had had all the submission Ted was ever going to give.

'Like a bit of pain, do you?'

'Why are you doing this?' asks Charlotte in a thin, nervous voice.

Young Ted says, 'Stay out of it, Charlie.'

'Stay out of it, Charlie,' mimics the youth. 'What kind of a lah-de-dah name's Charlie for a tart?' He leers. 'Does she go?'

People talk about a red mist coming down, but that isn't how Ted experiences it. What happens to him is that rage takes hold, and rage while it lasts makes him impervious to pain. But the rage is tempered by technique and underpinned by strength, size and the knowledge that losing isn't thinkable.

Young Ted drives his fist into the youth's stomach, a deliberately low blow he'd never have tried in the ring, bringing him to his knees. Before the others can intervene, his fist slams into the kneeling boy's face, aiming through it at the back of the head behind as he's been taught to do, smashing the nose. Blood sprays everywhere. The youth isn't unconscious, but neither is he thinking about getting up. He curls into a foetal position.

Young Ted turns to Youth Two. 'You next, is it?' But this one is running for the shelter of the trees, horrified and frightened, and so is Youth Three. They turn and scream abuse, but not till they are far enough away not to be caught.

'Step round him, Charlie,' says Young Ted. 'He'll only try to look up your skirt.'

Charlotte goes to find her doubles partner and Annabel and Young Ted sit by the court with a Kia-Ora. Annabel takes his right hand in hers. 'You've hurt your hand.'

'He had a hard head.'

'You were wonderful.'

'I was defending what's important to me.'

'Oh, Ted. I wish we weren't here. I wish we were in your bedroom. I wish you were on top of me, riding me, right now.' She pauses. 'Do I repel you?'

'Repel? Are you mad?'

She is bright pink. 'It's so hard being a girl. Boys are expected to want girls, aren't they? But girls are supposed to be so demure. But I can't be. Not with you. Girls want boys, too, Ted. I love you with every bit of me. When I'm not with you, I think about you all the time. I think about you on top of me. Inside me.' She looks away. There are tears in her eyes. 'And I worry that you'll think I'm a slut for wanting you.'

'You're crazy, Bella. Don't you know how I feel about you?'

'I think I do, but...'

'Well, I do.'

Ted's first signal of female insecurity. He should have recognised it, but he didn't. It had always seemed to be girls who felt at home in the world. That it was often a front did not become clear for several years.

Charlotte walks onto court with three other girls. She's looking at Young Ted. Annabel says. 'I'll be gone in two weeks, Ted. And Charlie will still be here.'

Charlotte? There had never been anything between him and Charlotte.

'See how she looks at you. You're not just my hero, Ted. Not now. Not after what you did.'

And it was true. He wasn't. Word got around. Charlotte's father was on the *Chronicle,* and the paper carried a story about the young cricket star who saw off three louts while defending the young ladies under his protection. They got a picture of Ted in his whites from the cricket club. They had pictures of Annabel and Charlotte, too, the one of Charlotte larger and better touched up than Annabel's. They interviewed Ted's proud father, Annabel's father, Charlotte's mother, Nigel Coomes. They tried to interview Ted but he refused. The paper noted this modesty with approval. An editorial asked what the police were doing when three innocent young people couldn't walk across a public park in broad daylight without being set on.

'Is that it?' Dolan asks. 'That's the good thing you wanted us to know?'

'It's one of them,' Alex says. 'There are others and I'll get to them.'

Dolan turns to Ted. 'You were still working for Nigel Coomes when that happened, but you also had your own thing going with Henderson Wilde and his partner. Your own fraudulent thing. How did that continue?'

'We sold seventy-two houses in twelve months.'

'That's an incredible number. Didn't Coomes realise his sales were falling off?'

Ted is about to say that they weren't, but Alex holds up her hand. 'I'm defence counsel,' she says. 'Let me do my job.' To Dolan, she says, 'Your evidence for that?'

'Excuse me?' says Dolan.

'Ted says he and Wilde sold seventy-two houses in twelve months and you want to know if Coomes realised his sales were falling off. Who said they were?'

'Well, if six went missing every month...'

'Mister Dolan, if you're going to seek to rub out my client, have the grace to present your evidence in a rational way.' She turns to Ted. 'Nigel's was a big and well known firm, right?'

'One of the biggest and best known in the North East.'

'And the number of house sales was rising?'

'Oh, yes. The economy was booming. People were moving to take new jobs. Or just to spend their improved incomes on a better house. Newlyweds were coming to us whose parents would never have dreamed of owning property.'

Dolan has a book in front of him and he's thumbing through it. 'Look at this sad specimen,' says Alex. 'He calls himself a prosecutor and he's going through law books trying to discover what to do next. Did you take all your sales from Nigel Coomes?'

'Not at all. In fact, given the way the market was expanding, I think Nigel's sales actually increased while we were at work. We branched out. We had leaflets printed, saying "We've just sold a house like yours and we have customers wanting more. If you're interested in selling, call this number." Everyone does that now, but at the time it was a marketing breakthrough. Professional firms in those days didn't advertise.

'We read the deaths columns in all the papers across the region. Ten days after the death of anyone over seventy, we slipped a leaflet through the door of any house that looked owned and not rented. Think of it in those terms, seventy-two wasn't a huge number.'

Dolan slams his book shut. 'So,' he says. 'You swindled seventy-two old people, still grieving for their beloved lifetime partner, out of anything from two thousand pounds each.'

'If you have to put it that way.'

'It's the way it was. How big was your take from that?'

'I suppose I got about forty-five thousand.'

He looks disbelieving. 'That's an amazing amount of money.'

'It certainly was in those days. A thousand was still the marker. In sixty-one, people would say you had to be on a thousand a year by thirty if you wanted to make it onto the board.'

'And you were making forty-five times that.'

'I learned two things from that time. One was that making money is easy, although society keeps that secret from most people. And the other was that making money is not just easy, it's also not wrong. There's enough energy expended telling the British people that being rich is immoral to power the entire British Airways fleet. And it's bullshit.'

'Did you spend it all?'

'Course not. I bought my flat, but that didn't cost much. Couple of Mister Fish suits, kipper ties. It was just starting to be all right for men to wear pink shirts without being shouted at in the street. I wanted a Healey Three Thousand, but Henderson said that would draw attention to me.'

'Shame.'

'Later, when that didn't matter, I bought an E Type.'

'So what did you do with the money?'

'Invested it. Henderson was very well connected. He put me into Rolls Razor shares just before they took off. Then he got me out again just before they collapsed. Must have trebled my money in that one.'

'That was kind of him.'

'Not really. He expected me to become his son-in-law. Which would you rather have? A rich son-in-law or a poor one? Especially if your daughter was someone like Annabel.'

'She was greedy?'

'She was spoiled. Maybe. A little bit. She was an angel. Who wouldn't spoil an angel?'

'So. You were stealing all this money and your well-connected father-in-law-to-be was helping you to multiply it. How much did you have?'

'After a year? About two hundred thousand.'

Dolan whistles. In spite of himself, he's impressed. 'That was a huge amount of money for those days.'

'If I'd done nothing except put it in a building society, the interest would have supported Bella in the style she expected. Of course, we didn't know then what inflation could do to savings.'

'But that wasn't what you planned.'

'No, it wasn't. Nigel was about to move me into sales. What we worked out was that I'd do that for two years, learn the business and then set up on my own. As a property developer, not an estate agent.'

'We?'

'Me, Henderson and Annabel. We'd spend ten thousand or so on buying and furnishing a really nice house for me and Bella. You're too young to remember what ten thousand would buy in those days.'

'An estate, I should think. A park. A palace.'

'Especially in the North East. And then I'd use more of my money to start my new firm. The balance we'd invest for Bella. And our children. I was an only child and so was she and we wanted more than that.'

'So Annabel knew she was going to marry you.'

'Oh, yes. She'd finish her degree and we'd have a big graduation party for her. Then, a week later, a big wedding.'

'She loved you and you loved her.'

'Match made in Heaven.'

'But it wasn't to be.'

'I don't want to talk about this.'

'The audience wants to know what happened to Annabel. You invited them. I think they're entitled. Don't you?'

Ted looks at his feet. 'She died,' he whispers. 'In a car crash.'

'How did it happen?'

'I wasn't there. The car crashed. That's all I know.'

Alex says, 'I think I can help.'

'But you weren't there, either.'

'I didn't know this, any more than you did, but now... Now I've been given access to everything I need. Personally, I think some things are best left alone, but you want me to tell you how Bella died.' She takes a paper out of her file. 'In fact, I can do better than that. If you watch that screen, I'll show you.'

Dolan says, 'Let's hold that for a moment.'

'But you're the one who's been pushing for it.'

'We'll see your film. First, I want some context. Before everyone starts feeling sorry for this piece of filth, let's show them the effect his thieving was having on other people.'

Ted doesn't remember ever seeing the woman who walks through the arch and onto the stage, but it's clear she knows who he is. She and Dolan air-kiss and the audience, assuming from this performance that they are looking at a celebrity, stamps and cheers.

'Maggie Leghorn,' says Dolan. 'Why don't you...'

'Jones,' she says. 'It's Maggie Jones now. I was Maggie Leghorn when this man came into my life.' She points at Ted as she says that.

'Maggie Jones,' says Dolan. 'Why don't you tell us about your dealings with Ted Bailey?'

She takes her seat on the sofa beside Ted. 'Actually,' she says, 'In between being Maggie Leghorn and Maggie Jones I was Maggie Sabal. I married a Jordanian. But that turned out to be a mistake.'

Dolan's eyes have glazed over. 'We all make those,' he says, more pointedly than chat show hosts usually think is necessary. 'Ted Bailey?'

And now Alex is on her feet. 'Who is this?' she wants to know.

'We've just been through that,' says Dolan. 'She is Maggie Jones who was previously Maggie Leghorn before, for a brief while, being Maggie Sabal.'

'What I mean,' says Alex, 'is what is she doing here? My files contain the names of every single person Ted has ever known. There's no Maggie Leghorn there. No Sabal. No Jones.'

'She is here,' Dolan says, 'because she is a witness for the prosecution. Why don't you stand by your table, shut up and listen? Then you'll know why she's here. Maggie. You were about to tell us how your path and Ted Bailey's crossed.'

'When my grandfather died,' says Maggie, 'my grandmother decided she needed a smaller house. These people,' and again she points at Ted, 'sold the one she'd raised her family in. For peanuts. Or they said they did; what actually happened was they bought it for a fraction of what it was worth and then sold it for three times what they'd paid.'

'You objected to that?'

'Well, of course. That money should have been mine.'

Ted has been doing sums in his head. This woman can't be more than thirty now. 'Just a minute,' he says. 'How old were you when your grandfather died?'

'What's that got to do with anything?' asks Dolan.

And then Alex leaves her table to sit on the sofa. 'Move over,' she says, and takes the central place between Ted and Maggie. 'It's a good question,' she says, 'and I think, Barry, you need to be a little less one-sided in the way you decide what's relevant and what isn't.'

'This man is on trial,' says Dolan. 'Defending him is your job, not mine.'

'Then let me do it. Maggie, how old were you when your grandfather died?'

'I wasn't born yet.'

'You weren't born yet. So this story you're telling us – you knew nothing about it at the time. Is that right?'

'My mother told me about it.'

'How many times?'

'What kind of question is that?' splutters Dolan.

'How many times did your mother tell you about her parents' house, Maggie?'

Very quietly, Maggie says, 'Lots of times.'

Alex has looked angry, but now she's calmer. Maybe it's the tears that have started to trickle down the young woman's cheeks, or maybe Alex has become a kinder, gentler person since Ted saw her last. Or, of course, this could all be put on as a way to win the jurors' hearts. He's assuming that there is a jury. Alex says, 'It's all right, Maggie. It's all right to cry.' She reaches out her arms and Maggie slips into them, resting her head on Alex's shoulder. She's crying in earnest now. She says, 'Mum's had a hard life. She's always said, if she'd had the money from the house, things would have been different.'

'If it hadn't been that it would have been something else,' says Alex.

Maggie says, 'Have you got a hanky?' and Alex says, 'Sorry, love. The dead don't need them,' and Maggie looks at her in something like horror, as though she hadn't realised who she was dealing with, what arms she was taking comfort from, and then wrenches herself out of Alex's grasp. She stands up.

'I'd better go.' She says to Dolan, who is looking very depressed, 'Aren't you going to say anything?'

'Like what?'

'I always thought, if I ever got on one of these things, at the end the host would shout, "Ladies and gentlemen, *MAGGIE LEGHORN!*" And everyone would stamp and cheer.'

'We only do that for professionals,' says Dolan. 'Why should anyone stamp and cheer for you?'

Maggie wipes her nose with the back of her hand. 'Well, it was only a thought.'

Ted says, 'Stick around, Maggie. If I survive this, I'll find you and give you some money.' Then he stands up and takes her hand, turns her towards the audience and raises her arm like a boxer's and he shouts, "Ladies and gentlemen, *MAGGIE LEGHORN!*" and the people in the audience stamp and cheer. Though they do look a little embarrassed to be doing it.

Maggie kisses Ted on the cheek. 'I always thought I'd hate you,' she says. 'But you're nice, really. I hope you do survive. And not just for the money.' Then she goes and sits in the audience.

Alex turns to Dolan. 'Well,' she says, 'that was a real triumph, wasn't it? Got any more prosecution witnesses like that? If you have, I may as well leave and let you do my job for me.'

But Dolan is livid. He ignores Alex. To Ted he says, 'That's exactly what you think, isn't it? Give the woman some money, you'll make everything all right. You can't buy your way into Heaven, you know.'

Alex says, 'Who says you can't?' Dolan stares at her in astonishment. Alex goes on, 'What do you think you know about Heaven? Have you ever been there?'

'We've had people telling us for two thousand years what Heaven is like. The Church...'

'Don't be ridiculous.'

'What?'

'The people who tell us who God is and what God wants know no more than you do. What they know is what they want. The State says, Thou shalt not kill, but it also says that doesn't mean you can't kill someone to protect your country if your country tells you to. And, in fact, if you don't we're acting in God's holy name when we call you a deserter and kill you ourselves. The rich say control your feelings of vengeance and envy because that isn't how God wants you to be, but that doesn't apply if you happen to be rich yourself. It's all right then and you can go out and grab anything you want. And let's not even think about adultery.'

Dolan points a finger at Ted. 'That man there is a common criminal. None of this changes what he did.'

'What we've got now is an idea of who God is and what God wants that has nothing to do with reality. People say, "How can there be a God if he lets bad things happen?" The answer is very simple. God is a God who lets bad things happen. You don't like that when it's you the bad things happen to? Tough. God doesn't care very much what you like. What kind of God would allow wars, and earthquakes? The kind of God we have, that's what kind of God. And as for you...who says you can't buy your way into Heaven? You can buy anything you want here on earth, can't you? Is it so hard to believe that when God created a world he made it just the way he wanted it to be? If God created Man in his own image, and if Man is not the nicest person you ever met, excuse me if that sounds Irish, doesn't that say a little bit about God?'

'But everybody knows...'

'Barry. When everyone knows something, the only thing you can be certain of is that the something everyone knows is wrong. God has favourites. Some people get away with murder, and I do mean that literally, and some people live like angels for seventy years and end up discarded. It isn't just. It isn't fair. So what? The atheists, which I used to be, are right when they say that Man has created a model of God that suits them. They abandon logic when they go on from there to say that there is therefore no God. One does not follow from the other. There is a God. He just isn't the God people think he is.'

'God is a He, then?'

'I use the word for convenience. Where I am now, He and She don't exist as separate ways of being. God is not He and God is not She. God is not even a person in any way you'd recognise. But when all the invisible friends have been eliminated, God is still there. Enough. Where were we up to?'

'Hold on. You're the only person who knows anything about what happens after death. You can't just leave us there.'

'I can do anything I choose. And now we'll see how Annabel died.'

'But...'

'Just press the button, Barry, and let's see what's on telly.'

1969. The kitchen of Young Ted's flat. He is putting food and a bottle of champagne into the fridge.

Alex reads from her paper. 'It's the end of Annabel's second year. She and Ted have seen each other most weekends, but now she'll be home for weeks. There's never been any doubt in Ted's mind that she was the one for him, any more than he has ever failed to realise how lucky he is to possess the love of this young woman. It isn't lust that fires him, though there's no doubt he aches to enter that sweet body once again. What he longs for most is just to hold her in his arms. To talk to her, listen to the melodies of that wonderful voice, hear her laughter as she tells him stories of the people she shares her Durham life with. People he has met on his frequent visits.'

Annabel is handing a car key to a man in blue overalls.

Alex says, 'When she went to Durham, her doting father bought her a car. A nice, reliable Volkswagen Beetle, suitable transport for a well-off young student, which hasn't actually been as reliable as expected. Last time she was in Newcastle she left it to be fixed. Ted would have collected her, but she called this morning to say her friend Ferdie was passing through on his way to Edinburgh and would bring her.'

Annabel and a handsome young man who looks a little spoiled are getting into a red Healey 3000. It's a nasty day in Durham, a day of low cloud and intermittent rain. It's midday, but Ferdie has his headlights on as he turns onto the A1 and heads for Newcastle. He accelerates hard.

'Ferdie. Slow down.'

'I'm safe enough,' says Ferdie, shouting to be heard in the open sportster. 'I want to be in Edinburgh tonight.'

'Stay with us. Go on in the morning.'

Ferdie shakes his head. 'I want to be in the Canny Man before closing time.'

'You won't make it like this.'

'Nonsense.'

Alex says, 'Many people are installing seat belts in cars, but they aren't compulsory and Ferdie hasn't bothered. The law doesn't yet require minimum tread depth on tyres, either, and one of Ferdie's is bald. His father sent him the price of a new set, but the money has gone on beer and whisky.'

The car sprints past slower traffic, slipping back into lane just before a bend. Annabel says, 'Whoosh,' and laughs. To any watcher, it looks a nervous laugh.

It happens just outside Gateshead. The A1 here has not yet been dualled. Traffic going in opposite directions shares the same carriageway. Ferdie misjudges the distance to a bend, is still overtaking on the wrong side of the road when he sees an oncoming truck and has to get in.

The audience is silent. Some of them are weeping. So is Ted.

Dolan lets him sit quietly sobbing for a while. Then he says, 'A terrible thing.'

'Yes.'

'A young life tragically ended.'

'Two.' There's a sympathetic stir around Ted. Even through his grief, he is starting to see the audience as a sort of Greek chorus. Boo. Cheer. Hiss. Hooray. 'To say nothing of her parents. It destroyed them.'

'And Ferdie?'

'Didn't even come to the funeral.'

The screen switches to the funeral. St George's is not the most beautiful church in the north of England. Charles Mitchell, a wealthy shipbuilder, gave the land free and paid for the building on condition he had his own way in the design. You get what you pay for, and for its church the parish of North Jesmond paid nothing.

You can't fault it for size, however. The chancel is long, the nave is longer and the roof is a long way from the floor. One thing you have to give it credit for is light; it pours in through big windows, especially when the day outside is as bright as it was that Tuesday. It was as though the heavens were mocking their grief.

La Sagesse sent their choir. Annabel's last form mistress spoke a eulogy, and the Head Girl from Bella's final year gave another. Ted was shocked to find that, for all the misery that possessed him, in his mind he was undressing her. Sliding his fingers between cotton and warm flesh. Spreading her legs. He knows now that the burial of the dead awakens in the living thoughts of sex and the creation of life, but that early experience of conflicting emotions made him feel a rat.

Henderson broke down in the middle of *How Great Thou Art*. Ted tried to maintain his stiff upper lip, but the tears streamed down regardless.

One hour later. The Wilde's house. Present: most of those who were at the funeral. Many have spilled out into the garden.

Mary has wrapped mirrors in black crepe and all photographs have been removed. The only things on show are cards of condolence. There are scores of them. Annabel's school friends look sombre and speak quietly. The university crowd start out noisier but catch the mood and fall silent.

Charlotte is nursing a glass of white Burgundy. 'I'm so sorry, Ted. So very sorry.'

'Thank you.'

'I know how much you loved her. And she loved you.'

'Yes.'

'If there's ever anything I can do…'

'I know. Thanks, Charlie.'

She puts down the glass. 'Well. I must make my goodbyes and go.' She touches his cheek. 'I'll be thinking of you, Ted.'

He watches her go. He makes small talk, helps Mary offer plates and drinks. It all becomes too much and he, too, says goodbye. Henderson

Ted slowed down, but then drove on. Whatever Charlotte wanted to give him was not something he could accept. When he looked in the rear-view mirror she was standing in the road, watching him go. Crying.

'And the next day,' says Dolan, 'you locked your flat and left. Without knowing where you were going.'

'It wasn't quite that cavalier. I had a passport, I sold the car for cash and I had a lot more I could get my hands on when I needed to.'

'What about exchange control?'

'Did we still have exchange control then? I don't know. Anyway, my money was in Jersey so it didn't apply to me.'

'Where did you go?'

'I flew to St Helier from Newcastle on a little BKS Elizabethan. I wonder what happened to them? Booked into a hotel. Stayed three days. Went to see my bank. Drew out five hundred pounds in francs and traveller's cheques. And they gave me a circular letter of credit for another thousand quid. There's another thing I wonder what happened to. Then I took a ferry to France. Bought a car. Citroen. French, left hand drive.'

'Did you cut yourself off completely?'

'Of course not. I rang my parents every Sunday afternoon.

'So there you are, twenty years old, in France, no ties, money in your pocket. You can't have known what to do with yourself?'

Chapter 9

It's 1969. Ted is twenty-three years old and the biggest shock is not having to do anything. For nearly two years he's been getting up five days a week to go to the office. In the summer, Saturdays and sometimes Sundays have been for cricket. He's driven up and down to Durham to see Bella. On top of which he's been involved in a criminal activity—a second employment—that has been, to put it mildly, labour intensive.

And now he has no reason to get out of bed.

It comes as a surprise to learn how deeply the work ethic is embedded. In practice, the only times he isn't up at dawn are when he didn't go to bed alone the night before.

Tourism becomes his work. He buys guide books and goes from city to city, town to town, village to village, looking at things. He stays six weeks in Toulouse and takes conversational French lessons five days a week, seven hours a day. One of his A levels is in French, but that doesn't mean he can speak the language. A level French is about literature. Ted has read Racine and Balzac but he can't carry on a normal conversation with a Frog. He knows Moliere was baptised Jean-Baptiste Poquelin, he can discourse knowledgeably on the *Comedie Humaine*, but he can't discuss a menu with a waiter.

After six weeks, he can. He is completely fluent, albeit with a pronounced regional accent he doesn't realise he has.

He ends up in Marseille.

It's a racy city, on the south coast but not of it. Nice it isn't—whichever way you pronounce that word. There are shops and restaurants as smart as anything at the other end of the Côte d'Azur, if that's what you're looking for, but Marseille has a persona crafted out of crime and travel and a disregard for anything not Marseillais. Walk the Canebière from the old port to the Réformés with your eyes open and you'll see all the things that go with being a busy port—the violence, the drinking, the smuggling. All thriving in Marseille.

One evening, Ted is walking through the twisting alleys behind the harbour when he sees three men dragging a girl into the shadows. He follows with a sinking heart, not wanting to get involved but knowing that he must.

One of the men holds both of the girl's wrists. The other two have her by the legs. They are lifting her onto a skip. She's shouting "Non," and a few other things besides, but no one is taking any notice. When she's horizontal, one of them steps between her wildly thrashing legs.

These aren't the cowardly louts Ted saw off in Paddy Freeman's. They're small but wiry and strong. He steps forward into the light. Surprise will be all. He slams a fist into the back of the one holding the girl's wrists, right where he judges the kidneys to be. There's an oath Ted hasn't heard in his lessons. The man staggers. The girl's hands are free now and she sets about the man between her legs, seizing him by the long hair and twisting his head this way and that.

All three men let go of their prey, more intent now on Ted. One of them draws a knife. Ted shouts at the girl to run, kicks the knifeman in the balls and closes on the third with the same combination of low punch and jab that did the job in the Newcastle park.

It doesn't work here.

Ted's nose breaks, the blood running down onto his lips. He comes close to dodging a second head shot, but not close enough. Someone grabs his ankle. If he falls, he knows he may not get up again. He turns and lashes out with his free foot. The ankle-grabber takes the kick between the eyes and goes down moaning.

The knife is on the ground. Ted picks it up. He's never held a knife before, not this kind of knife in this kind of situation, but he's seen it done in films. He wields it in a wide circle. The two men still standing back off. One of them holds up a hand, palm outward. In French, he tells Ted to stop. Ted is breathing like a steam train, the knife held out in front of him. The man with the outstretched hand points at the man on the floor. Ted nods.

Through all of this, Ted has felt burning rage but no
fear. It comes now as he watches the girl's attackers
hobble backwards. When they have put enough space
between them and him, they turn their backs. They go as
fast as the injured man's weight allows. Fifty feet away,
one of them turns. 'You need to control yourself. You
are a crazy man.' Ted feels an irrational glee that he
understands – his French is not just classroom French.

The girl has not run. She stares at Ted with what looks
on the screen a lot like fear, though he didn't see it at the
time. He smiles, but even from inside his face, he knows
it isn't very warming. When he tries to steer the girl
towards the brighter lights, she shrinks against the wall.
Does she think he wants her for himself? He asks her
that out loud, and laughs when he realises he is speaking
English. She does not look reassured.

Ted was living above an *alimentaire générale*. It helped his French, and anyway hotels had started to bore him. You can't go into an hotel kitchen when you feel like it to make a cup of tea and a sandwich. Entrance was through a door to the side of the *alimentaire*. The girl was only ten yards behind him now. He held the door open, the girl moved forward, slipped past him and up the stairs. She was short, with nice legs under a skirt that showed her hips to advantage. Above that, a denim blouson.

She pauses on the first landing. Ted is making heavy weather of the stairs, limping and holding on hard to the rail. When he gets there, he enters his apartment and leaves the door open.

In the bathroom, he swills water around his mouth. The girl's anxious face appears in the mirror behind his. The knife is still in his hand. He places it carefully on the side of the basin.

She leads him into the bedroom, takes his shoes off and levers his legs up onto the bed.

Ted finds himself hoping she doesn't want sex because he really doesn't think he has it in him right then.

She puts a towel under Ted's head and starts to wash his face.

Ted sinks into a state that doesn't feel like sleep but isn't waking. Annabel kisses him gently on the bruised lips. He hasn't thought of her in weeks, but now she is there. Her hair brushes his face. Then she goes away. Ted hears his keys rattle. The door closes. He struggles to pull her back but she won't come. Sweet, loving Annabel, who never held back when she lived.

Ted comes awake with a jolt. He stands, shakes his jacket, rifles his trouser pockets, searches with increasing panic every flat surface in the room. His money is there but his keys are gone.

What's the French for locksmith? He never learned that, and anyway it's late. There's a catch on the door to stop people outside from unlocking it. He puts the catch in place. Sleep calls once more. He drops face down on the bed and shrieks in agony as his nose moves against the pillow. He rolls onto his back.

Annabel is banging on the door. She's shouting in French. Of course, she would have learned French at La Sagesse, but Ted has never heard her use it. He drags himself out of bed and staggers to the door to let her in.

Only it isn't Annabel. It's the girl, and behind her is a man carrying a bag. Ted tries to swing the door shut on them, but the only result is that he nearly falls to the floor. The girl pushes past him. 'Why did you lock the door? Are you an idiot?'

He slept more comfortably. There were stitches in his cheek, inside and out, and his nose was protected by a sort of guard strapped to his face. Most of all, though, he slept because of the injection the doctor, if that was really what he was, gave him after dressing his wounds and after the girl had stripped off his clothes.

Annabel had not seemed this real to Ted since her death. He felt her close by, sensed her circling, felt her concern. He knew when she knelt by the bed. Her hand crept under the bed clothes. In all the time they were together she never did this, and Ted knew the humiliation he would feel if he failed to take the lead, but she pushed his hands away. With all the sweetness he knew so well, she brought him to his climax.

He felt no shame at all.

He slept.

When he woke, he was alone. He slept again.

'You really hadn't realised?' says Dolan.

Ted says, 'I never got a clear look at her before they hit me. And after they hit me, I wasn't seeing straight anyway.'

'She must have seemed quite exotic to you?'

'I'll say. Here I was, living life to the existentialist full. In France. Speaking French. Arab girlfriend. Even bought myself some black polo necks. Black trousers. Long black coat. Started enjoying the breakfast of champions. Standing at the zinc with the meat porters and the taxi drivers. *Gauloise,* black coffee, a glass of marc, and don't pronounce the "c". It's rough stuff, marc. Cognac was for poofters.'

'Nothing to eat?'

'I cheated. I'd go round the corner to the *boulangerie*, buy a couple of croissants straight from the oven so I wouldn't get hungry while I was posing.'

'Having an Arab girl wouldn't have hurt the image.'

'*Bien sur*. And, of course, she worked nights. I'd come back from zinc duty. Bring some more croissants. She'd have the coffee made. We'd have breakfast. She'd give me free what the customers had been paying for. Then she'd sleep and I'd be free to wander the town.'

'Didn't you mind her working?'

'It got a bit sloppy sometimes. She tried to make the customers wear condoms, but it didn't always work. She liked me to muff dive. There were times I had to decline.'

'I think you know,' says Dolan, 'that that wasn't the question I was asking.'

'Yes, I minded her working. I was brought up to believe that a man's job is to look after his woman. It was Abdul who ended it, though.'

'Her pimp.'

'If I'd had more sense, I'd have known he was going to be trouble.'

'Abdul saw her in the morning before you did.'

'He used to go through her purse.'

'She didn't like that.'

'It was all right before I turned up. But I was her man now. I should have been the one taking her money.'

She keeps her back towards Ted, making coffee. When he comes up behind her, she steps away. He follows, takes hold, spins her round.

'Who did that to you?'

She hangs her head.

'Was it a customer?'

She sits down, tears a vicious chunk off her croissant, dunks it in her coffee.

'Abdul?'

She nods. One eye is closed. Her upper lip is swollen and split. Black and yellow are spreading across the beautiful olive skin. 'He says he will kill you.'

'Why?'

The question is too stupid to ask, never mind answer. She returns to her croissant. 'You will have to deal with him.'

'Talk to him?'

'Kill him.'

'That's crazy.'

'Then he will kill you. And I will be his woman again, and not yours.'

'I will talk to him.'

She shakes her head. How stupid can a man be?

'Where will I find him?'

'He takes lunch every day at the Andalucia. But he will kill you.'

After breakfast, she does not take off her clothes. Instead, she pulls on the denim blouson. 'You must stay here till I return. You must not go out. Promise?'

Ted nods.

She was gone for perhaps an hour. When she returned, she had a gun in her handbag. 'You know how to use one of these?'

'No. Of course not.' Ted couldn't take his eyes off it. Guns were Bonnie and Clyde, Wells Fargo, Shane. Three-Ten to Yuma. He wasn't entirely sure it was real. And why was she showing it to him? Surely if someone was to kill her pimp it should be one of her brothers?

'I will show you. This, here, is the most important part, the safety catch. Like this, the gun will never fire. And Abdul will shoot you. Like this,' and she flicked the catch backwards, 'you will shoot him. Try it.'

'I'm going to talk to him, Ramina.'

'Try it.'

So he did. He practised again and again, until he flicked the catch without having to think about. John Wayne, eat your heart out.

Ramina undressed. 'This may be our last time, Teddie. Make it good. Let them hear me in the Grand Harbour.'

At 1 o'clock, Ted pushes open the door of the Andalucia. He is the only man there whose parents are not from Algeria, Niger, Tunisia, Chad. An absolute silence falls.

He has only seen Abdul from the apartment window, but that is enough. He approaches the table. 'I need to talk to you.'

Abdul says something in Arabic to the blank-faced man as wide as he is tall who sits opposite him. He spits on the floor. The face returns to Ted is openly contemptuous.

Ramina's battered face comes briefly onto the screen. Ted reaches into his pocket. The gun

*comes out as if with practised ease, the safety
sliding backwards as the muzzle rises to point
straight at Abdul's unbelieving brow. The
explosion is deafening.*

*Ted looks round, the gun still in his hand. No
one speaks. No one even looks at him. He puts
the gun back in his pocket and turns towards
the door.*

The screen fades.

Dolan says, 'How did you feel?'

'Elated.'

'You'd just killed a man.'

Ted shrugs. 'What do you want me to say? I'm
dying. If there was ever a time to tell the truth, this is it.
The police aren't going to arrest me now, are they?'

'Weren't you worried about that then?'

'Not worried. Fatalistic. What would be would be.'

'You'd killed a man. A pimp. The police must have
known him. They must have known Ramina.'

'Of course. They took a share of her earnings.'

'You'd killed him in front of a room full of
witnesses. What if they'd talked?'

'These people weren't the kind to talk to the police.'

'You didn't know that then. Why weren't you
terrified? Why didn't you run?'

Ted shrugs once more.

'You put the gun back in your pocket? If they'd
tested your coat they'd have known you'd fired it.
They'd have found the gun itself.'

'Barry. An Arab pimp had been killed. Do you seriously imagine the Marseille Police Department went looking for his killer? They had better things to do.'

'When your father said you let things happen to you, he was right, wasn't he? You got rid of the coat?'

'No. Ramina wanted me to. I had it cleaned, which she said was useless. But the police never asked for it.'

'And the gun?'

'The opposite of the coat. I wanted Ramina to take it away. She wouldn't.'

Dolan turns to Alex. 'Does defence counsel want to say anything?'

'You've watched too much television.'

'He's just *killed* a man.'

'Self-defence. He killed a pimp who had threatened his life and beaten up Ted's woman.'

'*Jesus Christ,*' shouts Dolan. 'She was *used* to being beaten up. She was an Arab whore.'

Alex's face has become very tense. 'If I were you,' she says, 'and knowing what I know now and you don't, I'd be very careful about whose name you use as an oath. Very careful.'

Ted is looking closely at Alex. Is she serious or is this a way to get the prosecution off balance? He can't tell. She looks as though she means it, he'll say that, but does she? Whatever the answer, it's worked because now Dolan isn't so sure of himself. 'It's just an expression,' he says. 'It doesn't mean anything.'

Alex is speaking very quietly. 'Just an expression,' she says. 'The name of Jesus Christ doesn't mean anything. You think that, do you?'

The room has gone very cold. Ted can still see the darkness and it's still advancing, but there's a coldness now. Even though he isn't wearing a tie, Dolan reaches to adjust his collar. And the Lizard – the Lizard is looking round as though he expects something to happen. The noise on the midway rises to a level that means Ted can hardly hear himself think and irritation appears on the Lizard's previously impassive face. He points a finger at the gap in the wall. The empty space fills with something, an opaque gauze that yet looks as though it could stop a tank, and the noise dies away.

Alex says, 'I suggest you remember where we are, what we're doing and *who is listening to us.*'

'Okay,' says Dolan, his voice a croak. 'I didn't mean any harm.'

Alex is staring at him. After a while she says, slowly and quietly, 'What does the name Barabbas mean to you?'

'He was the thief Pontius Pilate let out of jail instead of Christ.'

'He was a thief, was he?'

'Everyone knows that,' says Dolan. 'It's in the Bible.'

'Well, it must be true, then,' says Alex. 'I just wish you could hear what They say about some of what's in the Bible.'

'Wasn't he a thief?'

'If you met an Arab, today, and he referred to someone as Bar Abbas, what do you think he'd mean?'

'I've no idea. I don't speak Arabic. You're the linguist, not me.'

'Bar means son of and Abbas means God.'

'Oh. But...'

'The words were much the same in Aramaic two thousand years ago.'

'But Barabbas wasn't...'

'How do you know what Barabbas was and wasn't?'

'I learned about Barabbas when I was five years old.'

'Yes. And you never asked yourself a single question in all the years that followed. There were two men known as the son of God. One of them taught love and forgiveness. You shall love the Lord your God with all your heart and with all your soul, and you shall love your neighbour as yourself. The other taught that the Kingdom of God would arrive on earth as a result of a violent uprising against the power occupying the land of the People of God. That power being the Roman Empire and the People of God being the Jews. Pilate asked the people of Israel to decide which one he should release and which he should kill. They made the wrong choice. I don't suppose they meant any harm, either. We think of the third century as a time of ignorance but people knew what Barabbas stood for. The Church obscured the knowledge because they wanted to say that the Jews had chosen a thief over the man sent to save them. As rank a piece of anti-Semitism as we have ever had. Where were we? Oh, yes.' She turns to Ted. 'You wanted to get rid of the gun and Ramina wanted you to keep it. Shall we take it from there?'

Ted says, 'How long have you known all this stuff? You never talked about it when we were an item.'

'I didn't know it then. After you go through the Darkness you learn things you didn't know while you were Here. Ramina? The gun? And then we'll ask you to explain why you're choosing to mislead us.'

Dolan is about to speak, but Alex waves him away. 'Later.'

'I knew he was lying,' says Dolan. 'I don't believe a word he says.'

<u>*Chapter 10*</u>

'You are my man. My man must have a gun.'

'I am not your man in that sense, Ramina.'

She unbuttons Ted's trousers. 'You killed Abdul. For me.'

As she takes him in her mouth, he relives the exaltation he felt as Abdul went backwards over his chair, dead.

When she is done, she says, 'I cannot work tonight. Not looking like this.'

'Good. I would rather you never worked again.'

'But how would I live, chéri?'

'With me. I am not poor, Ramina.'

'We will speak of this later. If you are not poor, you can take me to lunch. It will be nice, to walk in the street with my man. To eat lunch. Even looking like this.'

That night, in bed, Ramina holds Ted close. 'It is good to be here. With you. Not out there, with those others.'

He kisses her throat.

'They could be pigs, some of those men. And the ones that weren't pigs were like babies. Poor Maman's boys.'

'Do we have to talk about this?'

'No, we do not have to talk about other men. Not if it makes you feel bad.' She snuggles closer. *'How much are you not poor?'*

'Pardon?'

'How much money do you have?'

'Enough.'

'A lot?'

'You'd probably think so.'

Her leg slides over his. *'I would like you to meet my father. And my brothers.'*

'Why?'

'Why not?'

Ted could think of no reason. The doctor's words came back to him. You must be careful of the girl. Not because she isn't clean. Because she's an Arab.

'My brothers will be glad I do not have to work the streets. They will be grateful to you.'

'What will they want me to do?'

She laughs as she moves down his body. 'Do not worry, my lovely Teddie. They will not expect you to marry me. They would not permit it, even.' She holds him tenderly between two fingers. She licks him gently. Her laugh is a low throaty giggle. 'See? I have the evidence in my hand. Infidel.'

That morning, Ted does not go to the tabac. Over breakfast, he asks, 'What do your brothers do?'

'What they can. Whatever brings them money. They fetch and carry things. They make deliveries.' The livid black and yellow bruises are fading. Her broken lip is losing its puffiness.

'Drugs?'

'Perhaps. Sometimes. Whatever people want to be fetched and carried. They cannot pick and choose.'

'Have they ever been arrested?'

'Of course. They keep a little money in reserve to pay the police.'

'Drugs do a lot of damage to people.'

'How do you know that? What drugs have you ever taken? Apart from your smelly cigarettes?'

'How old are you, Ramina?'

'I am twenty-one. I am sixteen. I am thirty-three. How old do you think I am? Why do you care how old I am? I am old enough to bring you pleasure. Am I not?'

'Where do your brothers get the drugs from?'

'From the people who have them. Where else?' She dips a piece of croissant in her coffee and

holds it to Ted's lips. 'They would like to have their own drugs. Then they could be rich.'

He swallows the offering. 'And how would they get their own drugs?'

'With money.' She holds his gaze. 'The person who lent the money. He would be rich, too.'

'It would be dangerous.'

'Not for people who know what they are doing. Not for people who know who to pay to look the other way.'

'You want me to lend your brothers money to buy drugs?'

'They would make you rich.'

'I am rich.'

'They would make you richer.'

'Dealing in drugs is against the law.'

'Yes? And so? You will think about it?'

'Perhaps.'

'And you will meet them? And my father?'

'Let's take them to dinner.'

'No. They will not wish to meet you in public. We will go to my home.'

'This is your home, Ramina.'

'Then we will go to ex-my home. Yes?'

'Yes. I suppose so.'

'And you will listen to what they say.'

'I will listen.'

'Good. And now, because you are my man, you will fuck me, please.'

There is a swagger about her as they walk through the streets near her parents' home – walking because the taxi refused to go there. Streets where almost everyone is dark skinned and the smells are the smells of the souk and not of France. Ted knows without being told that the swagger is because her man is with her and he is European, white and rich. She was poor here, and now she is somebody.

At the outset, she attempts to walk four paces behind him. He turns and looks at her. She stands still. 'This is our way,' she says.

'It is not my way. Get up here and walk beside me.'

'It shows respect. For the man.'

'Beside me, Ramina. And hold my hand.'

'The people in this quarter will not like it.'

'The people in this quarter can learn tolerance. It is a European virtue, and they are in Europe now.'

He senses her nervousness as she steps forward, but she is smiling as he takes her hand. She says, 'You will not kiss me here?'

'Kissing in the street is vulgar.'

A small apartment so crowded with garish bric-a-brac that it looks even smaller. Ramina's father and mother, two brothers and two sisters. The men offer respectful but wary greetings. The women hurry giggling into another room, taking Ramina with them.

The men sit in the claustrophobic sitting room and drink whisky and smoke cigarettes. Bakhr, Ramina's father, says, 'You are a brave man.'

'Me?'

'You came to my daughter's rescue. And you killed Abdul.'

One of the brothers glowers at the pimp's name. Bakhr says, 'Pierre feels shame, that it was a stranger and not one of us who ended this man's life.'

'Pierre?'

'Both of my sons have their real names. But they have also French names, which I think you will find easier. This is Pierre. And that is Jean.'

'And Ramina? Does she have a French name?'

He shakes his head. 'For a daughter is not necessary.'

Pierre says, 'Our sister says you will lend us money to buy drugs.'

'I said I would listen to what you have to tell me.'

'What must we tell? The drugs come here from Morocco. We take small amounts from the importers. We sell them, pay the people here in cash, and buy more. We make a little money. The importers make a lot. If we can pay the people in Morocco, they will supply us. And we will make a lot, too.'

'Which we will share with you,' says Jean.

'And the importers who supply you now? How will they feel when you cut them out and go direct?'

'They will not like it,' says Jean. 'Of course. They may wish to fight us.'

'With what?'

'With guns. With knives. With what they have. What do you think?'

Ted should leave. He should start running and not stop till he reaches the airport. He knows that.

Ted says, 'We may all die.'

'Yes, we may all die. The police may take us for questioning and tell our family we had a heart attack. We may be shot as we carry our little cargo from one place to another. We may be knifed as we take money to the importers so that we can buy more drugs. We may be forced to defend the honour of our family against someone we cannot defend it against. Life is precarious. Will you lend us the money?'

'I like your philosophy.'

'I do not have a philosophy. I have only a life. Which I can lose. But I would like to be rich. If I have to die, I would like to die rich. Will you lend us the money?'

He must be crazy even to be thinking about it. 'How much do you need?'

'They must be paid in American dollars. For twenty thousand dollars, we can buy drugs we will sell here for eighty thousand dollars. To buy the same amount of drugs from the people here would cost us seventy thousand dollars.'

Jean says, 'Sixty thousand dollars profit instead of ten thousand dollars. That is worth a little risk, no? Will you lend us the money?'

Ramina has come into the room. 'Will you lend them the money?' she asks.

'For you?'

'For them, for me, for whatever you like. You are my man. Will you lend my brothers the money they need to buy drugs?'

Twenty thousand dollars is seven thousand pounds, give or take. And what is seven thousand pounds, to a man who has so much? 'Yes,' he says. 'Yes. I will lend you the money.'

Bakhr and his sons are formal as they shake hands. 'And now,' says Bakhr, 'there is someone waiting to meet you.'

It is the man, as broad as he is tall, who sat opposite Abdul when Ted killed him.

'He wishes you no harm,' says Bakhr.

'No?'

'No,' says the man. 'What I want is justice for the family of Abdul.'

'Justice?'

'It is our way,' says Pierre.

'Blood money,' says Jean.

'They have nothing,' says the man. 'You killed the breadwinner, and now they will starve. They ask you to pay. Money for a life.'

'How much?'

'They are not rich people. Most of what his girls earned, Abdul spent on clothes and drink for himself.'

'How much?'

'Two thousand American dollars.'

'We are in France. Why is everything in dollars?'

'Dollars buy what people need. These people will go home to Algeria. With two thousand American dollars they will be secure forever. They will raise goats and grow vegetables to sell in the market.'

'I can have it for you tomorrow.'

'Bring it to the Andalucia.'

Dolan raises the remote and freezes the action on the screen. He looks a lot less shaky than he did a few minutes ago, which is probably the difference between knowing you're dying, as Ted has accepted that he is, and still having years ahead of you as Dolan must believe he has.

'Let's unpick this, shall we?' he says. 'A few moments ago we heard you telling Ramina that drugs do a lot of damage and now we see you agreeing to finance two brothers who want to smuggle them into France to sell there. Are you going to fall back on the existentialist defence again?'

Alex says, 'I think you've both misunderstood what existentialism actually means. Ted's problem, as his father told Annabel's mother, was that he went along with things too easily, and that is not existentialism. You'd do better to ask him if he regrets it than why he did it.'

'Oh, sure,' says Dolan, clicking the screen back into life. 'Of course he regrets it. Now that it's too late for regret.'

'When will you have our money?' asks Pierre.

'Tomorrow. I will give it to Ramina. She will bring it.'

'You must come too. Ramina must not walk in the street with twenty thousand dollars.'

'Very well. In the morning. Ramina and I will go from here to the Andalucia.'

'She is a woman. They will not let her in.'

'I will need only a moment inside.' He looks at Ramina, who is offering a plate of grilled lamb. 'And then we will take lunch on the train to Nice and dine at the Negresco.'

Going home, Ramina says, 'We will not dine at the Negresco.'

'You don't like the Negresco?'

'I have never been there. I have never been to Nice. I would like to go there. Another time. But not tomorrow.'

'Then what will we do after the Andalucia? Since it seems they will not serve you there?'

'We will go home. We will spend the afternoon in bed. In the evening, you will take me to dinner. But here in Marseille. Not in Nice.'

The screen fades once more.

'This must have seemed a wonderful time to you,' says Alex.

'Well, yes. And no.'

'No? You were barely into your twenties and you were with a woman who wanted to spend all her time in bed with you.'

'Oh, it was very nice on one level. But I think that was the day I came to see that sex isn't everything. You can have too much sex. I'd never have believed that when I was at school, but it's true. And Ramina didn't have anything else to offer.'

'You were beginning to tire of her.'

'I wasn't mature enough to realise that. It takes a while to admit to yourself that you might want something else. Somebody else. As far as I was concerned, Ramina was the woman I loved. I hadn't met you then. Didn't know how fulfilling life with a certain kind of woman could be. I think I need another drink.'

Alex comes over to where Ted is sitting, puts her arms round him and kisses him gently on the forehead. He can see that Dolan doesn't like that. 'In any case,' Dolan says, turning to the screen as the waiter starts to go through his business with the glasses, 'you had some stuff you had to deal with first.'

<u>*Chapter 11*</u>

Ramina goes into the kitchen with her sisters. Her mother, veiled because Ted is there and he is not her husband, her father, her brother or her son, serves coffee to the men. Ted takes the thicker envelope from his pocket and lays it on the low brass disk that serves as a table. They study it. There is a reverence in the eyes of Ramina's menfolk that Ted has seen before only in church.

Pierre picks up the envelope and hands it to Bakhr. Bakhr takes out the notes and counts them, slowly and methodically, wetting his fingers and laying the hundred dollar bills on the table one at a time. There are two hundred of them, and the counting takes some time, but neither Pierre nor Jean removes his eyes from the money for a moment. Ted drinks his coffee, which is instantly replenished by Ramina's mother.

Jean is the first to speak. 'Thank you,' he says. His eyes glow. 'We will repay you completely. With every cent of your profit.'

'Inshallah,' says Bakhr.

'Unless we are all killed,' says Ted, smiling.

Jean bows his head. 'Unless we are all killed.'

Bakhr takes the money from the room. Pierre stands. 'Jean and I will walk with you to the Andalucia.'

When they reach the café, Jean and Ramina wait by the door while Pierre and Ted enter. It is just noon, and there are few patrons. The man who is as broad as he is tall sits alone at a table. Pierre motions to Ted to sit down; he himself remains standing.

Ted takes the remaining envelope from his pocket and places it on the table. The man picks it up and puts it unopened into his pocket. 'Thank you. This matter is closed. You will hear no more of it.'

Ted inclines his head. When Pierre touches him on the shoulder, he stands. They walk out together. When they reach the door, Ted turns to look back. The man has not moved. He nods, raises his hand to his forehead in what might be a benediction. Ted smiles. The man smiles back. It is a thoughtful smile. A serene smile. There is no hostility in it.

When they can, they pick up a taxi. In the apartment, Ramina tells Ted to undress and sit on the bed.

'All right,' says Alex. 'Whatever happened next, we don't need to see it.'

'Ramina gave me a little reward.'

'Yes, I'm sure she did.'

'It took all afternoon. I was exhausted. And then we went out for dinner.'

They eat Bouillabaisse du Ravi and drink champagne. With coffee, Ramina takes a cigarette from Ted's packet and holds his hand as he lights it for her. 'You don't smoke,' says Ted.

'Do I smoke like someone who does not smoke? I smoke when I am content. And never in front of my father or my brothers. You will not mention my smoking to them.' She looks at Ted through her eyelashes. 'You are content also?'

'You know I am.'

Her smile is different. Relaxed. Wider. Ted had never realised how wide her mouth was. She says, 'It is a pity you are an infidel.'

'I could convert.'

'We would have to cut off the little piece of skin at the end of your magnificent baguette.' Ted grimaces and she laughs. 'I could perform the operation myself. I would keep it in a jar, to remember when you were a Christian.'

His legs are squeezed close together.

'No,' she says. 'No, my big man, you will not convert. And we will never marry. But I will be your woman and you will be my man. I am

content.' She leans across the table. 'And if you ever want to take another woman, I will cut off more than just the little piece of skin at the end of your baguette.'

Ramina likes being a kept woman. She visits her family every day, returning with stories of their new status as entrepreneurs instead of lowly employees.

'And everyone knows about the new English gangster who bankrolls them.'

'Everyone?'

'You must carry your gun everywhere, Teddie. And you must meet the police.'

'How? How do I do that?'

'How did you do it in England?'

'In England I stayed well clear of the police.'

'Pfftt. How do the English arrange things, if both sides do not talk to each other? In any case, here it is easy. You already know Mahmoud.'

'Who the hell is Mahmoud?'

'Tch. You do know Mahmoud. You gave him money for Abdul's family.'

'Him? He works with the police?'

'Not with, Teddie. For. He is a policeman.'

Ted sits back in his chair, momentarily stunned. 'I shot a man in front of him. He could have arrested me.'

'Teddie, you are sometimes so silly. Why would he arrest you? How would he get money like that?'

'Yes. I see.'

And Ted begins to think that perhaps he really does. 'So what is it that he will arrange?'

'Protection.'

'Protection.'

'Yes, Teddie. Protection. You are English. They will not arrest you without good reason. For us it is different. Would you like to see my brothers arrested? Or me, or one of my sisters, taken in for questioning? Do you have any idea what our police mean when they say they are questioning an Arab woman? My sisters are good girls. They are virgins. My father will find them good husbands. But no Moslem man will marry a girl who has been questioned by the police, because he would know that they have taken her most precious jewel.'

A little later, when the import of this has sunk in, Ted says, 'Ramina, that means no Moslem man would marry you.'

'Of course not, silly. I am not a virgin. Why would a man want to marry me? But in any case, you would shoot any man who suggested marrying me. So the question cannot arise.'

'Oh,' Ted says. 'Of course.'

Ted goes to meet Mahmoud at the Andalucia. His gun with the silencer Ramina obtained from the same unknown place as she got the gun is in his pocket. It is never, these days, anywhere else.

Mahmoud's face is still as blank as when Ted first saw him, but there is no menace there. What the Arab does radiate is power, confidence and calm.

They sit at a corner table and drink tea. Mahmoud says, 'The girl is satisfactory?'

'In every way.'

'It is a good family. They will not let you down. It is tonight they will bring in the first drugs?'

'I have no idea. I've been careful not to ask.'

'It is tonight. Inshallah.'

'I wonder if Ramina knows.'

'She will know. There may be danger. The boat they have used is not the best boat.'

'It is unsafe?'

'No, no. It is the owner who gives me concern. He has worked for the others.'

'The competition? You think he will tell them?'

'I think they should have chosen another boat. My job is to keep peace.'

Ted holds up his hand, and Dolan stops the on-screen action. Ted says, 'You will think it odd, but it was only at this point that I realised the danger I had put myself in.'

Dolan says, 'I've told you before, that defence is not going to get you anywhere,' but Alex says, 'I don't think you're the person best qualified to judge that.' To Ted, she says, 'Can you explain why you hadn't realised it?' and Ted says, 'No,' and she laughs, but Dolan looks irritated. He presses a different button on the remote and the scene restarts from a couple of lines earlier.

'The competition? You think he will tell them?'

'I think they should have chosen another boat. My job is to keep peace.'

'What do you want me to do?'

'You showed what you can do when you dealt with Abdul. But that should not be necessary. I shall be on the quay when the cargo arrives. If there is trouble, I will try to settle it. There will be costs.'

'You want money?'

'Yes, monsieur, I want money. But not today and not from you. If all goes well, I will be paid when the goods are sold, inshallah. And I will

distribute the money among my colleagues in the way that is needed.'

'And if all does not go well?'

'Then I will need one thousand dollars, to make sure there are no repercussions.'

'What repercussions might there be?'

'There will be none. Because you will give me the money if Bakhr and his sons cannot.'

'But what…'

'Monsieur. If I have to ask you for the one thousand dollars, I will tell you at the time what will happen to Ramina and her family if you do not pay. You have no plans to leave Marseille?'

'I've promised to take Ramina to Nice this afternoon.'

'So she does know it is tonight. You will travel by train?'

'We will.'

'Go. I have colleagues in Nice. I will alert them to your arrival and send them a picture of you and the girl.'

'You want me to give you a photograph?'

Mahmoud smiles. It is the first sign of any emotion he has shown in Ted's presence. 'There is no need, monsieur. The one I have is perfectly satisfactory.' He pauses to let this sink in. 'You will not travel anywhere else, monsieur? I should not like to have to intercept your journey.' He pauses again.

'I think I have the message, Mahmoud.'

'That is good, monsieur. It is always best to understand each other.'

'Did you know it was to be tonight?'

Ramina nods. 'I did not think you would wish to know.'

'What do you think these repercussions are that Mahmoud spoke of?'

'You are English. They will not wish to arrest you. So, if things go wrong, they would say you were shot by drug dealers.'

'Nice. And what about you?'

'We, too, would be shot by drug dealers. But first Mahmoud's friends in the police would try to beat the money out of my father and my brothers. With me and my sisters they would wish to enjoy other pleasures. They have a house they keep for such things. Perhaps my mother would escape the worst.'

'And we can avoid this if I pay Mahmoud one thousand dollars.'

'Of course. Our police are not unreasonable. All they want is to be paid. But you will not have to pay, because my brothers will do so. As they promised.'

'If they are alive.'

'That is why Mahmoud will be on the quay. To make sure there is no trouble. But he is right about the boat. They should have used another. I told them so, but of course they do not listen when a woman speaks.'

'Perhaps we should defer our trip to Nice.'

'Why? It was because I knew it would be tonight that I wanted us to go there today. What would you do if we stayed here? What is going to happen is going to happen. I want to go to Nice. I want to walk along the Promenade des Anglais with my man. I want to stay at the Negresco, and dine there. I want to pleasure you in a large bed in a room overlooking the Bay of Angels.'

'I thought you'd never been to Nice.'

'That does not mean I know nothing of it. My friend Marguerite went there several times with her man. She described it to me. He would do filthy things to her as she leaned on the parapet of their balcony.'

'She didn't like it?'

'She thought it was wonderful. She always wanted to go back.'

'I have never heard of your friend Marguerite.'

'No. He killed her.'

'Deliberately?'

'Of course. He tied her up and hung her from a doorway while he…well. It does not matter now. They sent him to the guillotine.'

'What had she done?'

'How can we know? She had displeased him. He never said in what way.'

'Was he mad?'

'The judge did not think so. Can we speak of something else, please? And I think we should go soon to the station.'

The Negresco was the place to stay and eat in Nice. Ted and Ramina ate Brittany oysters with champagne, followed by John Dory. Then rack of lamb with a St Emilion.

During the pause that follows, while they are contemplating the idea of pudding, a well-dressed man enters the dining room and approaches their table.

'Monsieur El-Diouf telephoned and asked me to call on you, Monsieur Bailey. He wishes you to know that all passed off as intended. There were no difficulties.'

'Thank you, monsieur…'

'Monsieur L'Inspecteur. Names do not matter.'

'Thank you, Monsieur L'Inspecteur. Will you join us in a pudding? They do wonderful things here with chocolate and prunes in Armagnac.'

The Inspector smiles. 'Thank you, Monsieur Bailey, but that will not be possible. There are things I must do. I am pleased only to have been able to bring you this good news. Enjoy the rest of your stay in Nice. Monsieur El-Diouf wishes me to say that you should consider yourselves free to pursue any other journeys you may wish to contemplate.'

'That is kind. If you speak again to Monsieur El-Diouf, please tell him that we shall return to Marseille as planned on Friday.'

With a smiling bow and an almost Prussian click of the heels, the visitor leaves the table and the dining room. Ramina and Ted look at each other. She is radiant. 'I think, chéri, there are more important things now than chocolate and prunes in Armagnac.'

'Like doing filthy things on our balcony?'

It is the first time Ted has ever seen her blush. He raises a hand to attract the waiter's attention. 'We would like to complete the meal in our room. Coffee, please, and petits fours. And a bottle of Krug.'

'I shall have them delivered at once, monsieur.'

Dolan's expression reeks of unbelief.

'What?'

'Enjoy the rest of your stay in Nice!'

'You don't believe it happened like that?' asks Ted.

'Did it?'

'The events were real. I may have tarted up the dialogue. That must happen a lot on your show?'

'All the time. What we don't usually get is the opportunity to re-shoot the scene.'

'You want to do that?'

'In the interests of veracity? Why not?'

In the Negresco that evening, Ramina and Ted eat Brittany oysters. Neither has ever eaten oysters, and Ted would just as soon have a prawn cocktail, but Marguerite and her man used to eat oysters here.

Ted says, 'Marguerite's man murdered her.'

'That is a horrible word. Please don't use it. She said the oysters were wonderful.' Her eyes glitter. 'And they are an aphrodisiac. They will make you feel horny.'

'I always feel horny.'

'They will make you feel more horny.'

Of course, with oysters they must have champagne. Without drawing attention to himself or them, the waiter gently shows Ramina how to deal with the oysters. Ted watches and follows suit. He learns quickly, and wonders why Ramina seems to need so much help from the waiter: why he needs to guide her hands; why she gives him that particular look, head back, eyes raised, that Ted had thought she reserved only for her man. When the dishes have been removed, he asks her.

'To make you jealous, of course. Why do you think?'

'Why do you want to make me jealous?'

She rolls her eyes and sighs theatrically. 'So that you will take it out on me later. So that you will give me an extra pounding in bed. Do you know nothing?'

The waiter suggests they follow the oysters with John Dory, but they have already ordered rack of lamb. How many courses does this penguin suit think they can eat? The sommelier arrives at their table. Under the guise of seeking Ted's opinion, he steers him towards a St Emilion to drink with the lamb – not the oldest Bordeaux on the list and certainly not the most expensive, but when it arrives it fits the bill precisely. The sommelier exchanges an indulgent smile with the waiter as he walks away from the table.

Ted is still smouldering. 'Are you allowed to eat oysters? Are they not haram?'

She lays down her fork and stares into his eyes. 'Teddie. I am Moslem and you are not. Leave questions of haram and halal to me, please. Do you imagine this lamb has been lawfully killed? I assure you, it has not. Perhaps you would have liked me to leave the champagne, too? And the red wine?' She picks up the fork again, but Ted can see she is thinking about something. Then she says, 'But you will not mention the wine to my father or my brothers, please.'

They haven't quite finished the lamb when a youth in the uniform of the hotel comes to our table. 'A policeman is asking for you, monsieur.'

Ramina's face has turned white. Ted knows that his is the same. She stays in her seat, her hand to her mouth, as he walks across the floor behind the boy. He sees none of the diners, hears none of the enjoying bustle. The boy escorts him to the lobby, points out a tidily dressed man and walks away.

'Monsieur Edward Bailey?'

Ted nods.

The man's stare is cold. 'I am an inspector of police. I understand that an officer in Marseille instructed you not to leave Nice without permission.'

'I...yes. What's happened? Jean? Pierre? Are they dead?'

The policeman shrugs. 'I know nothing of any Jean or Pierre. I am to tell you that you are free to go where you wish.'

'But…I don't understand. How are…how are my fiancée's brothers?'

'What do I know of your fiancée or her brothers? I am to tell you that all passed off as intended.' He leans closer. 'As for this woman you call your fiancée, monsieur, do not imagine we do not see her for what she is. We have enough home-grown tarts in Nice without importing blackies from the shit-hole to the west.' He prods his finger into Ted's chest. 'If she so much as blinks at a trick before you're on the train home, I'll have her in the slammer.'

He turns on his heel and walks off. Two smartly dressed receptionists make great show of attending to paperwork. They have heard every word. Ted's face and ears glow red as he walks back to Ramina.

'What is it? What's happened?'

Ted sits down. The waiter approaches. 'It's fine,' Ted says. 'It's all fine.'

'But tell me.'

'They're…they're all right. Everything passed off as intended.'

The colour is coming back into her cheeks. The waiter pours wine into their glasses. 'No one...no one was hurt? Everything arrived safely?'

'Yes.' Exhilaration takes hold of Ted. 'Everything happened exactly as it was supposed to.' He starts to laugh. Diners at the nearer tables are looking at him. He turns to the waiter. 'I'm sorry. I can't eat any more.'

'There was a problem, monsieur?'

'No. No, there was no problem. It was lovely. I just can't eat any more. I think we'd better go to our room.'

Ramina pouts. 'But, chéri, I want the chocolate and prunes in Armagnac. Marguerite spoke of them. And now we have something to celebrate.'

Ted is on the verge of tears. The effort of holding himself together is proving too much. The waiter comes to the rescue. 'Madame, the chocolate and prunes in Armagnac is indeed wonderful. But why not complete the meal in your room? With coffee and petits fours. And, if you are celebrating, may I suggest a bottle of Krug?'

Ramina is radiant again. Ted stumbles to his feet. The waiter says, 'I shall have them delivered at once, monsieur.'

Dolan says, 'Why do you think you did that?'

'Did what?'

'The suave bit. The reality was you'd just had the figurative shit kicked out of you. You'd been humiliated. Made to feel like the child you still were and not the streetwise man you pretended to be. Instead of which, we get a polite copper coming to your table. We get, "That is kind." We get, "We would like to complete the meal in our room." "Will you join us in a pudding?" "A bottle of Krug, please." Did you even know what Krug was?'

'I certainly found out that night. It took its place as my favourite champagne and nothing has ever replaced it. In fact…' He looks towards the waiter, who raises a finger in acknowledgement and hurries off to the bar.

'Nice bottle,' says Dolan. 'Nice label. Bit pricey for what it is, if you ask me. But it's your money. Virtually speaking. If we can come back to the question?'

'As you said, Barry, I was little more than a child.'

'You were a killer. You were financing drug smugglers. You were living with a prostitute. You had defrauded little old ladies out of thousands of pounds. You'd indulged in pretty well every sexual act a heterosexual man can participate in. It has only been the hetero stuff with you?'

'Yes, Barry. I've nothing against shirt-lifters, but only the female body does it for me. I've often said I'm a lesbian trapped in a man's body.'

'You're by no means the first man who's often said that.'

'Doesn't make it less true.'

'You'll forgive me if I've begun to wonder how much of anything you tell me is true. In fact,' and he is looking at Alex as he says this, 'weren't we going to discuss exactly that?'

'Yeeesss.' She says it slowly, thinking, tapping a pencil on her table. 'I think we need a time out.'

Dolan looks amazed. 'You can't just stop like that! Who the hell do you think you are? Television takes priority. It's a law of nature. This is a chat show. It starts at the beginning and goes through to the end.' He waves his arm at the audience. 'These people are here to be entertained.'

'So entertain them,' says Alex. 'Get another guest here. Some celeb nonentity, like you usually have. We'll be back.' She looks at Ted. 'Ted. This is your show.'

'This is *my* show,' says Dolan.

'Your show courtesy of Ted,' says Alex. 'Ted, who would you like on here while we're talking strategy?'

Ted thinks about that. A parade of people he's admired runs through his mind. Or would someone he doesn't think much of be better? 'Does it have to be someone living?'

'Within reason it can be anyone you like. Alive or dead. Some people would be able to pull rank on you. You won't get Jesus here, or Mohamed, or the Buddha.'

'That's a pity. I could have done the one about the Buddhist who goes into a pizzeria and says, "Make me one with everything".'

'Very funny, Ted,' says Alex. 'You were a cricketer. How about Don Bradman?'

'The audience wouldn't enjoy that. Bradman never used two words where one would do. Or just silence. The only miserable Aussie who ever lived.' Ted thinks a bit more. 'How about Barabbas, since you've talked about him?'

'Okay,' says Alex.

'What do you mean, "Okay"?' asks Dolan. 'This is my show. I'll decide who the guests are.'

'Barabbas it is,' says Alex. 'And why not get John Betjeman with him, for a somewhat different perspective?'

And here they are, coming in through the arch as Alex and Ted go out. Two old men, one in goat skins with a beard halfway down his chest who looks as though he doesn't know where the hell he is and one, eager as only someone who knows the chat show circuit and misses it can be eager, in a worn and shiny blue suit with a crumpled white shirt and an old school tie. When they're safely past, Ted says, 'That is the craziest old loon I ever set eyes on,' and Alex says, 'Barabbas? Or Betjeman?'

On the other side of the arch is a big open space with TV production people sitting at desks. Two flunkies in blue hotel uniforms, one carrying Alex's files, lead them past this area to a door in the wall which opens to reveal a meeting room. There's a long table with water jugs, glasses and bottles of squash. In one corner is a coffee maker. There are biscuits in cellophane wrappers and slices of fruit cake.

Ted pours himself a coffee and puts a piece of cake on a plate. 'Can I get you something?'

'The dead don't eat, Ted.'

'I don't fancy that.'

'Do you remember that place in Goodramgate?'

Ted hasn't thought of it in years, but the moment she mentions it, it comes back to him. 'You always ate the chicken stuffed with ham and cheese.'

'I didn't always eat anything. They had a good menu and I worked my way through it.'

'Drank all the wine, too.'

'Chance would be a fine thing, with you at the table. It was over a bottle of Barolo that I realised I'd fallen in love with you.' Then she says, 'Causation,' and it takes Ted a moment to realise she's talking about something else. He raises an eyebrow.

'If you have your way,' she says, 'a big part of your defence is going to be that things simply happened to you. You were a wall, on which other people wrote graffiti.'

'I'm not sure I'd have…'

'But it isn't true,' she says. 'Oh, sure, you stumbled onto Ramina. She was attacked, you went to her aid, that's in your favour. And she happened to be on the game, and her brothers happened to sell drugs. But getting involved with the drugs was your choice. Living with a prossy and accepting what she earned was your choice. Killing her pimp was your choice. And you let Dolan think you simply got away with that, that no one came after you, and that simply is not true.

'So what are you going to do?'

'Tell him. He's got all sorts of stuff about you in Africa, you in Lebanon, you in South East Asia and he's going to present it as just more bad things Ted Bailey did. What we have to show is that one thing led to another.'

'You think he'll take any notice?'

'Ted. Dolan is not the judge. Your case will be decided far from here.'

'I wonder how he's getting on with his guests.'

'Why don't we go and watch?'

Ted finishes his coffee and now he needs a piss. While Alex is walking back to stand by the arch, he finds one of the flunkies and ask him the way to the *mingitorio*. The man gives him a strange look and says, 'You want the men's room, sir?' and takes him to it. When he's done, he joins Alex in the archway and they watch the proceedings from there.

Dolan is looking more than a little brassed off and it seems that Betjeman has taken control in that effortless Marlborough College way. To the aristocracy of his day he may have been a parvenu, and foreign with it, but to most people he was what an upper-class English gent should be. 'When we talk about the Church,' he is saying, 'we normally mean the people in it. Starting with the Archbishop of Canterbury and embracing all of the clergy and the laity. But when the man on the Clapham omnibus says "the church," chances are he means his local parish building. Church architecture has influenced the development of the English character every bit as much as the language of the King James Bible, and certainly more than any Jesuitical philosophising.'

Barabbas has been listening to this with an expression of undisguised contempt. He turns sideways and spits on the floor. Not an Italian "pah" type spatter; this is a full blown, greasy hockle, the type of expectoration a miner coming off shift might have used to clear the coal dust out of his mouth and nose before the days of the pit-head bath. Dolan looks at him in silent horror; Betjeman merely wrinkles his nose.

'What we have to remember,' Betjeman says, 'is that the great monotheistic religions – Judaism, Christianity, Islam – took root in lands as harsh and inimical to human life as it is possible to be, where every day was a struggle for survival. Imagine if God had spoken to us through an Eskimo. The teaching we received from the Son of God as mediated through Gospels written...'

'I was the Son of God,' says Barabbas.

'Yes, of course, dear boy, in a sense you were...'

'In a sense?' Rage simmers behind the goatskin wearer's purple face.

'As Bar Abbas, the Son of God, of course you were. But I was referring to the Son of God who we know as Jesus of Nazareth.'

Barabbas spits again, as full throated as before, and Dolan half rises from his seat. 'Will you please stop *doing* that.'

'The Son of God who we know as Jesus of Nazareth,' Betjeman repeats. 'His teachings came to us first from men for whom every day was a battle simply to stay alive. They are black and white. There is no room for shades of opinion, only what is right and what is wrong. It is the same today in Saudi Arabia. People regard Wahhabism as some form of extremist creed, but what Wahhabis want is adherence to what they see as the pure, original teaching of Mohamed. No shrines, no priests, no mysticism of any kind. They may be seen as simply the Particular Baptists of Islam. There is a difference, of course. If he knows you recognise the authority of a bishop, a Particular Baptist will walk past you in the street without speaking. A Wahhabi meeting a Dervish or a Sufi will feel entitled to kill him for the greater glory of Allah.

'And this is how Christianity came to us, at least before the humanising influence of Rome with its wine and its beautiful food and its art and its adultery. But God is an Englishman, and what He wants are English things. Compromise. Tolerance of difference. Politeness. Look at the cathedrals of Ely and Gloucester, the minsters of York and Southwell and you will see God's will made manifest.'

Barabbas is on his feet, his short hairy skirt swaying. 'Jesus of Nazareth was a Jew!' he screams. 'Like me. The People of God are the Jewish people! You want to know what God wants? He wants this!' And his clenched fist slams into Betjeman's face, splatting the nose and shaking loose a tooth. Then Alex says, 'Oh, my God,' and Haile Selassie emerges from the shadows and strides onto the stage, if a man with such short legs can be said to stride. He is quivering with anger. Barabbas turns to face him, his chin thrust out, looking for a fight.

'The Jews *were* the People of God,' says Haile Selassie. 'You gave that away when King Solomon violated the Empress Makeda, whom the ignorant call the Queen of Sheba. She was searching for his wisdom, but he was what he was and he jumped her. His own people were so disgusted by the way he treated her, the way he broke faith and his promise, that they escorted her back to Abyssinia and they took the Ark of the Covenant with them. It sits where they left it, on the beach in the Ethiopian province of Eritrea. Which remains an Ethiopian province today, whatever those benighted savages may say. Our province, our beach, our coastline. *My* province, *my* beach, *my* coastline. On that day, the people of Abyssinia – my people – became the People of God. If anyone is to say what God wants, it is *me.*'

Ted finds something ridiculous about this short man, midget would be only slightly too unkind a word, puffed up like this and Barabbas looks as though he will strike him, too. But Haile Selassie, physically unimpressive though he may be, has more presence than any man Ted has ever seen and his cold eyes face the old terrorist down. Barabbas turns and stalks from the room, shoving Ted and Alex out of his way.

Dolan stands. 'We will take a short intermission while the floor is cleaned of this disgusting mess. Someone get these two out of here.' And off he goes, no doubt for another cigarette, while Haile Selassie fades back into the shadows, his eyes still on Ted. Hotel employees rush forward to help Betjeman to his feet. As they pass, slowly because Betjeman is white, shocked and hobbling, Ted puts out an arm to hold him.

'What a dreadful man,' Betjeman says. 'Quite without breeding of any kind. And as for Haile

Selassie...I wonder what all those Jamaicans with their knitted hats and their strange hair would say if they knew what their beloved Ras Tafar really thinks of them. You know he refused to think of himself as African? He thought he shared a continent with people who weren't really human.'

Yes, yes, thinks Ted, never mind all that. He says, 'You talk about church buildings as the embodiment of God. Do you actually believe in Him?'

'Oh, look,' he says. 'Man is a spiritual being. For all the crackpot lunacy of believers in intelligent design and those criminal madmen who think war between Islam and Judaism will lead to the Rapture and their ascent into Heaven, our need to believe in Him goes to the very heart of our human make-up. And as for Dawkins... If he had the brain he'd like us to think he has, he'd have taken a proper degree. The man's a biologist, for God's sake. That's one step up from an astrologer. Does needing to believe in Him mean He exists? How should I know? It doesn't mean He does not, you may be sure of that. Please excuse me. I need to find somewhere to lie down.'

Ted and Alex go back into the bar and onto the stage. Dolan's chair is still empty, so Ted sits in it. When he does, he finds himself grinning at the audience, ridiculously, childishly triumphant to be sitting there. Alex picks up the remote and presses a button and there on the screen is Ted and the man from the ministry. Though Ted didn't know that's who he was at the time.

He's speaking to Ted in French, and what he's saying is straightforward. 'Monsieur, you killed a man. We do not lack witnesses. Your life is forfeit.'

Ted holds out his hands, wrists together, and waits for the cuffs, but the man says, 'Do I look like a gendarme?'

'Then what is it you want?'

'Monsieur, we are going to take your forfeit life and lock it in a safe, where it will come to no harm. And you will be well paid. Better paid than you have ever imagined being.'

'Thank you. And in return for this kindness, you want…what?'

Now Dolan bursts back into the bar, sees Ted in his chair and Alex running the video and he is not pleased. 'Women!' he bellows. 'You have to control the remote, don't you? Give it to me. And *you* get out of my chair.'

Alex turns her back on him. 'Later. Perhaps.' Dolan is furious. He looks at the Lizard and at first it seems the Lizard isn't going to react, but then he detaches himself from the wall he's been leaning against and for the first time moves centre stage. He looks at Ted and though he doesn't speak, doesn't move, makes no sign whatsoever, it's clear that he wants Ted to go with him and Ted's body makes it equally clear that he has no choice.

Ted and the Lizard walk towards the gauze the Lizard conjured up to fill the hole in the wall and, although it looks completely solid and has shut out all the noise and all the light from the midway, they walk through it as though through gossamer.

Dolan is listening excitedly to his ear piece. He leaps out of the seat he has so rapidly retaken possession of, turns towards the arch and shouts...

'Ladies and gentlemen, PETER SELLERS!'

Peter Sellers? What on earth has Peter Sellers got to do with the story of Ted's life? And isn't he dead? And how does Ted know all this is happening, given that it's in there and he's out here? He looks at the Lizard, who points at one of the dwarves hanging about the edge of the midway and the dwarf scuttles up to them and says, 'There's two of you. One in there and one out here.'

'You've split me in two? Why?'

'We didn't split you. You've always been two people. That doesn't apply to everyone but it does to you. I assume you were meant to be a writer, but something went wrong. You wanted more money than a writer can earn, probably.'

Inside, the audience is stamping and cheering like a football crowd. And in through the arch walks this man whose face has been so many people. Chief Inspector Clouseau. Dr Strangelove. Clare Quilty. Chance the gardener. But never Richard Henry Sellers, which was the name his parents gave him. Alex whispers into Ted's ear, which is to say the ear of the copy of Ted that's still in the bar and not out there on the midway with the

Angels of Death, assuming that that's what they are, that this man will fit right into his story.

'Why is that?' asks Ted.

'Because some of what he says will be the absolute truth, and some of it will be as far-fetched as a bucket of shite from China as my father used to say, and we won't have a clue which is which.'

Ted would like to pursue that, ask why she thinks it applies to him and to this show, but Dolan is making a big production out of settling Sellers on the sofa.

Ted says, 'Would you mind telling me what he has to do with my life?'

'This is a chat show,' says Dolan. 'The audience demands variety, and we have to take care of our ratings. You'll be dead in a few minutes and I'll still be here, with a career to feed. You had no compunction about leaving me with those two barmy old men, did you?' He turns to his new guest. 'Peter. Your father was a Protestant and your mother was a Jew, but you were educated as a Catholic. Did you ever find that confusing?'

Something happens to Sellers's face. It's still the face it was a moment before, and yet it isn't. As though a new person has taken up residence in his body. 'It certainly had an effect,' he said. 'I was an outsider all my life and St. Aloysius College is where that started.'

'You thought of yourself as Jewish. Teachers there referred to you as "The Jew". Kenneth Tynan said that hatred of antisemitism was behind your ambition as an actor.'

'I thought a lot of Tynan,' says Sellers.

'Jews could be comedians. They couldn't be great actors. You were determined to prove that wrong. That was his theory.'

'I wouldn't mind seeing him again. Any chance of that?'

Ted feels like saying that one interloper is more than enough, and in any case why doesn't he answer the damn question, but Alex presses a button and there on the screen is a man with yellow hair and an air of astonishing self-belief. 'Peter, my dear boy,' he says. The others he ignores.

Dolan says, 'Kenneth Tynan. When you arrived at Magdalen College, Oxford...'

'It's pronounced Mordlin by those who know. Magdalene was a Jewish tart.'

'I should warn you that yours would not be the first career I've put an end to.'

'Oh, no! Here am I, dead only thirty years, and I might not have a career any longer.'

A thoughtful look crosses Dolan's face. 'You're dead...and Peter Sellers is dead...but you're both here. Does that mean you both passed through the darkness?'

'Not a logician, then? It means nothing. We might be in Heaven and we might not, but being the emanation of a dying killer's mind is hardly evidence. In any case, I'm not at liberty to say. Can we move on?'

'When you arrived at Magdalen College,' Dolan goes on, getting it right this time, 'you were dressed in a plum-coloured suit with a lavender tie and a ruby signet ring. This was 1945, when such things were not worn in England. Your middle name was Peacock. Were you trying to live up to it?'

'Ah, Peacock,' says Tynan. 'That name is where the similarity between me and Peter begins.'

'I don't see how that could be,' says Dolan. 'You made a life out of your own flamboyant individuality and Peter was a chameleon, always clothing himself in someone else's personality.'

'You clearly don't know where my name came from. Don't you have people to do your research? My father was Peter Tynan. Or so I believed as a child. In fact, Tynan turned out to be my mother's name. After my father died, I found out he was really Sir Peter Peacock. He had a wife and children back in Warrington. Warrington! I ask you. Do I look like a rugby league player? My mother had to give up his body so that his other family could bury him. And Peter wasn't Peter, but they called him that after his older brother, who was dead.'

'So you, too, were an outsider?'

'I detached myself from the umbilical cord of Birmingham. Wouldn't you? When are we going to get to this man's dealings with the female arse?'

'What?'

'Bailey.' He points at Ted. 'Him. He tanned a few. Didn't he?'

'For fuck's sake,' shouts Dolan, and then he blanches and he's listening to something through his ear piece and there's no difficulty knowing what's being said to him because he rips the remote from Alex's grasp and presses some buttons very hastily and the passage on the screen jerks quickly back and Tynan says, 'He tanned a few. Didn't he?' and Dolan replies, calmly and with complete self-possession, 'Would you mind awfully if we pursue the story in chronological order? Leaving out the bits we choose to leave out? Spanking may not even be mentioned,' and Tynan says, 'You think it was only spanking, do you?' and Dolan says, 'Is this some kind of obsession?'

'The buttocks are the most aesthetically pleasing part of the body,' says Tynan, 'because they are non-functional. Although they conceal an essential orifice, these pointless globes are as near as the human form can ever come to abstract art. Not that I ever penetrated them, of course. I would have found that unpleasantly close to homosexuality. I have no problem with queens, you understand, Heaven forfend and quite the reverse, some of my best friends *et cetera,* but it's such a dirty business. All that shit on the end of your knob. Flagellation, now. That was my thing. It would be nice if we could see a bit of that in this trial. If he spanked one or two before he tupped them. It would almost be worth coming back from the dead for that.'

Dolan pushes another button, and the screen goes blank. 'I really don't think that sort of talk belongs on a Dolan show,' he says. 'Peter, you started out as a drummer.'

'I actually started out as a janitor, at a theatre in Ilfracombe. In fact, if you go even further back, I was on stage at the Windmill with my mother at the age of five. But, yes, I played the drums for a while.'

'And then came the war. You joined the Air Force. Did you fly?'

'I could hardly *see.* That's a bit of a disadvantage in a pilot. And I was a corporal. I didn't get to be an officer in the RAF until Doctor Strangelove.'

'You saw active service?'

'I was in India and Burma.'

He still isn't answering the question, but Ted is as spellbound as everyone else.

'And after the war came ENSA. Where, in fact, you joined your father.'

'He was in it. We didn't work together. I'm bored with this, by the way.'

'Look, you just can't say that. This is turning into the worst show I've ever done.'

'Well, then, ask the right questions. Yes, I was in ENSA. As a drummer and as a comic. Then I did the Goon Show, I turned out comedy records, I did a damn stupid thing called *Goodness Gracious Me* that the PC brigade probably wouldn't let me get away with today. What I want to talk about is my serious acting.'

'Just a minute,' Ted says. 'Let's not write off the comic stuff. I was never a Goon Show fan, but *Fool Britannia* inspired sixth form boys across the land. That Profumo business. The late Minister for Whore...'

Sellers's face changes again. Without seeming able to prevent himself, he turns into Harold Macmillan. 'War!' he says. 'War has been declared. Don't forget I was the first to tell you.'

Alex's face is blank in that long-suffering way women have when the boys get going. Dolan looks as though he doesn't know what's going on. 'I never heard of this,' he says.

'When I said you'd never had it so good,' Sellers says, still sounding like Harold Macmillan, 'I didn't mean *that* good.'

Ted says, 'Gawd, it's like an oven in here.'

But the Sellers face is changing again, to a strangely Germanic man who has seen everything and doesn't think much of any of it. 'People think *Being There* was my greatest moment, but I never capped *Doctor Strangelove.*'

Ted says, 'The whole point of a doomsday machine is lost if you keep it to yourself. Why didn't you tell the world?' But Sellers is not to be tempted. 'Is that how I'm remembered?' he asks. 'As a set of voices?'

Dolan says, 'You had an interesting love life.'

'You only know what happiness is once you're married. But then it's too late.'

'You loved those four women when you were married to them?'

'I was never in love with any woman as deeply as I was with Sophia Loren. Who I never married.'

Like every other Sellers fan, this is something Ted has wondered about. 'Did you fuck her?'

'Sophia was a lovely woman, and a kind one, but she was married and she was faithful. I never had her. Nor did anyone except Carlo. Are you finished with me?'

'You can go,' Ted says, thinking that, really, he should never have been here.

Dolan says, 'This is my show,' but Sellers is already making for the arch and he doesn't look back. Dolan shakes his head. To Ted, he says, 'Someone was offering you more money than you'd ever dreamed of. Did you accept?

'I didn't think I had a choice.'

'What was it exactly he wanted you to do?' He presses buttons and the scene on the screen rewinds.

'Monsieur, we are going to take your forfeit life and lock it in a safe, where it will come to no harm. And you will be well paid. Better paid than you have ever imagined being.'

'Thank you. And in return for this kindness, you want…what?'

'Have you ever been to Côte d'Ivoire?'

Then Dolan switches off the screen. He looks at Ted and says, 'How's your other half doing?' The look on his face as he says it is as unpleasant as it's possible to imagine.

They walk past the place where the Lizard opened the man's cage and let the mob take him. The Lizard is serenely inattentive, but the dwarf feels Ted's unease. 'He was a rapist,' he says. Ted looks at him, uncomprehending. Of course, what the dwarf means is obvious, but the place they're walking through does not encourage quiet reflection. The mob is standing back, but it's the Lizard's presence that causes that. If he left, Ted feels he would be torn apart.

'We don't bugger every man who comes here,' says the dwarf. 'Any more than we fuck every woman. The one you saw was a rapist. He got what he deserved.'

A man steps forward from the crowd lining the route. He's stroking himself and he's looking at Ted. The Lizard frowns and the man steps back into the mob, but as they move along the midway he keeps pace with them in the crowd.

'And it doesn't last long,' says the dwarf. 'You probably think of this place as Hell, and you think of Hell as somewhere that goes on forever. It doesn't. Well, it does, in so far as there is such a thing as forever, but one person's torment doesn't. We get bored, and anyway we have other people arriving all the time. People don't come here until they're dead. Not since the Greeks, always nosing around, trying to make a name for themselves. Someone dies, they come here, we have a little fun with them, show them there is justice in the world, whatever they may have thought, and when we're done with them they're really dead. We burn them to get rid of the waste because we don't have space for so many dead bodies. The Other Place is probably empty from what you hear but we wouldn't have room to sit down if we didn't have a bonfire every three days, but that isn't part of the torment, the people we're burning don't feel the flames because they're gone, really dead this time.' He stops as though out of breath. Then he says, 'Clear?'

'Yes,' Ted says.' Thank you. Where are we going?'

The dwarf points at the lizard. 'He has something he wants you to see.'

They're getting into an elevator. Ted and the dwarf and King Tut. The Lizard stands back, watching them go. But something's wrong. The building they're supposed to be going up is next door. This lift is on the front of a tower that stands beside the building. It's a high tower and a high building, but they're not connected. How are they going to get across at the top?

There's worse. The lift is one of those that run up the outside, with glass walls so you can see the people and the traffic grow smaller as you ascend, and the landscape grow wider. Ted hates these. He was in one and when it reached the top he was on his knees, facing inwards, eyes closed. Sobbing. They'd seen it before, apparently. They brought him out in a service lift inside the building. Kept telling him not to feel embarrassed, that it took some people that way. He did, though. Feel embarrassed.

He's not good at heights.

He doesn't like crowds, either, and there is a crowd now and it's pushing forward.

What terrifies Ted, quite apart from the elevator, what really leaves him wanting to lie on the floor again and scream, is: what happens at the top? If the tower isn't connected to the building, *how will he get from one to the other?* And will he have to look down? And will he be able to stop himself?

He won't make it. He knows that, so he doesn't want to try. He's struggling not to get into the elevator, but the crowd is enormous and it's pushing and bustling and carrying him in there whether he wants to or not. The dwarf has him by the wrist and Tut is bobbing around a few rows back, taking care to keep him in sight.

How can all these people fit into one lift? And who are they? And why is Ted going where they're going? He doesn't know them. Doesn't think he knows them.

And now the lift is climbing, shooting up the outside of the tower at increasing speed. The car is full of people eating and drinking, sitting at nicely linened tables, crisp starched napery, silver bowls, cut glass. Eating and drinking. Attentive waiting staff. Red wine, fizzy water, rare beef. There's a cigar somewhere. Buzz of conversation. And Ted. He should be at ease in this environment. Man of the world, in his element in pampered luxe. Instead he's screaming bloody blue murder. And *no one's looking at him*.

How is he going to get across?

Oh, help him, Mother.

They're there. At the top of the tower. The crowd has strolled out and across, into the building next door. How? How did they cross? How the hell should Ted know? He couldn't watch. They're gone. What's left is people he was at school with, in the Scouts with, played cricket with. How, why, he doesn't know. And there, in the corner, trying to be invisible but never taking his eyes off Ted, is King Tut. Knowing that he's really Ras Tafar, Haile Selassie, Emperor of Ethiopia should reduce the fear of seeing him, but it doesn't. If anything, it makes it worse. The dwarf stands in the corner by the buttons.

The others are crossing now, all but the dwarf and Tut, who seems to be trying to creep a little closer to Ted, and Ted can't go with them. They're calling him, encouraging him, cajoling. 'Come on, Ted. It's fine, it's nothing. Just step over.'

But it isn't fine and it isn't nothing. It's a drop of hundreds of stories, thousands of feet, higher than the London Stock Exchange or the Gherkin, higher than the Empire State, higher than the Twin Towers of the World Trade Building.

And look what happened to them.

'Come on, Ted.' And he can't. Because he knows they're wrong. They've crossed over and for them maybe it really was easy but Ted can't do it. He can't. He's going to have to stay here. He lies on the floor. 'I'll stay in here. I'll go back down.'

'Come on, Ted.'

'You can't go down, Ted. The lift won't start till you get out.'

'For God's sake, Ted, be a man.'

And he's sobbing as though his little heart will break. Help me, Mother. Help me. Don't leave me stranded here.

And something strange has happened. Because before there was just the tower and the building and nothing between except blue sky and puffy white clouds. And now there's a platform halfway across. It's got cloud all around it, so he can't see where it goes, whether it's standing on the ground or what, but it's there and it looks solid enough.

It should help, there being a platform half way. But it doesn't. It makes it all worse.

'Stand up, Ted. Take a step onto the platform. Then hold out your hands and we'll haul you across. Safe as houses. Come on, Ted.'

Stand up. The man's an idiot. Always was, even as a child. He can't stand up.

'We're going to have to go, Ted. We can't wait for ever. We're going, Ted.'

So go.

'Ted! For fuck's sake, get on your fucking feet and step onto that fucking platform.'

Ted's the boy. Oh, Ted's the kiddy, all right. The athlete, hotshot cricketer who can't stand up for fear of falling. The master of a French whore, killer of villains and police alike who's too terrified by what he might see to open his eyes.

Now get you to my lady's chamber, and tell her, let her paint an inch thick, to this favour she must come; make her laugh at that.

Ted is the fellow of infinite jest.

What does my gorge rims at it mean? He probably couldn't write that line today. God, there's some dirty bastards around. Where be your gibes now? Your gambols? Your songs? Your flashes of merriment, that were wont to set the table on a roar?

He hauls himself to his knees.

'That's it. That's it, Ted. Now. *Over!*'

He's lying face down on the platform. If he'd thought he was scared before, he knew nothing. *This* is fear. This is cold terror.

He can't go forward and he can't go back. The lift has gone, taking the dwarf with it. Or maybe that should be the other way round. The outer door is still open, but all that's there now is an open shaft, waiting for Ted to fall down it. There's no one here but him and Tut, who crossed with him and is now so close he's almost touching Ted's spread-out leg.

He daren't look down. Look down? He daren't even open his eyes. How are they going to get him out of this? How can they send a rescue crew here? There's no ladder in the world long enough, he knows that, and he couldn't go down it anyway. Helicopter? How would they pick him up? Clinging to a net over that drop? I don't think so, pal.

He can't go forward and he can't go back and they can't pick him off. There's no way out. It's just him and Tut and the tower and the clouds and the wind. He hadn't noticed the wind. It isn't much, but it's there. Probably the sound of people drowned it out before. The people have gone.

He and Tut are alone.

Dolan is staring at Ted as at an exhibit in a zoo.

'What happened there, Ted?'

Alex kneels on the sofa beside him, her arms wrapped tightly around his chest, rubbing warmth into him. It's Lanzarote and Ted is freezing. There's the faintest of scents about her and Chanel it ain't. Musty soil. The fallen needles of old yew trees. Dead carnations in a jam jar of stale water. Rot and corruption. Oh, God. Ted looks over at King Tut Corner and there he is. Still watching with his hungry eyes. But there's no Lizard. Ted says, 'Where's the Lizard?' and Dolan says, 'He'll be back. Don't you worry. He'll be back and he'll be coming for you.'

When Alex kisses him gently on the cheek, it's the coldest thing Ted has ever experienced. He says, 'Can we call an ambulance? Is there a doctor? There must be a doctor.'

Dolan's smile is like a hangman's as he measures his victim for the drop. 'It's too late for that, Ted.'

'Why didn't you do it when you came? When you saw the state I was in, why didn't you get help? What kind of host are you?'

He's still smiling. 'You're beyond help, Ted.'

'You don't know that. They can do...'

'Far beyond.'

Alex's bony arms crush Ted's chest. She didn't use to be bony. Not back when they were romping in her bed in York. Not a bony woman at all.

She is now.

'It's all right, Ted,' she whispers. 'This is normal. Everyone goes through this.'

'Everyone?' asks Dolan.

'Everyone who hasn't had one of the biggies. If you're ninety and you're worn out by years of disease, it just might pass you by. But when it comes down to the short strokes, there aren't many people about to die who don't wish they weren't.'

Ted says, 'There must be something they can do.'

'There is no "they," Ted. This is it. The darkness is coming.'

'I'm frightened.'

'Of course you're frightened,' says Alex. 'How could you not be? Have another glass of Krug.'

'What do you want to do?' asks Dolan when Ted's glass has been refilled. 'Do you want to finish the story? In whatever time you've got left? Or are you ready to go? Let that poor girl up? Face the music?'

Ted steadies himself with a swig of champagne. The poor girl can fend for herself. Facing the music is the last thing on his mind.

Dolan says, 'We've got a lot still to cover. Why don't we cut to the end of your time in Marseille?'

Ramina slings her denim jacket over the back of a chair. 'You're going to have to sort these people out.'

'These people?'

'The others. Pierre was making a delivery today and they were there.'

'They threatened him?'

'They've gone past that. They took his drugs, they took his knife, they took his money. They told him if they have to stop him again they'll kill him.'

'What does Mahmoud say?'

'He wrings his hands. What does he care? He gets paid by both sides and as long as there's no trouble everything's fine.'

'I thought he was on our side.'

'Who told you that? He's on his side. You have to do something.'

'Like what?'

'Kill them.'

Kill them. Ted should kill them. *Ted* should kill them.

'Why me, Ramina?'

She doesn't answer. Her face says she doesn't understand the question, but she does. And Ted knows the answer, which is that Jean and Pierre, for all the money they are now making and the respect they have bought themselves, are still small-time crooks. Killing someone, other than in an unplanned brawl or by accident, is beyond them. It is not beyond Ted. He's the star of the show. Mister Big.

'All right. I kill them. All of them?'

'No, of course not all of them. Kill Roland and Martin and you won't need to touch the others. They'll come on to our side.'

'Until someone else spots the hole in the market. Then what?'

No one he's ever met could shrug the way Ramina shrugs. Not just her shoulders; her hands, her eyebrows, even her hair seem to rise.

'Then you do it again. That's how you stay at the top.'

'Ramina. We've made a lot of money. Compared to what they had, your brothers are rich men.'

'Yes? And so?'

'The longer we go on, the more certain it becomes that some of us will die. Maybe all of us.'

He isn't making any impact. He is preaching caution and forward planning to someone who believes that everything is decided by Allah. She waits silently for him to continue.

'Ramina, can't you see the sense of quitting while we still can?'

'You want to walk out on us?'

'You can be a very irritating woman, you know that? No, I don't want to walk out on you. I want you to come with me.'

'Where?'

'How do I know? Where we want. Paris. Spain. Morocco, even.'

Her lip curls.

'Montserrat, then. We have the money to go anywhere we choose.'

She stares at Ted in silence. Then she says, 'I'm sorry to be irritating. Of course, you must do what you want.'

'What's the use of that? You have to go with me, or it's pointless.' Her face is still blank. Ted says, 'I love you, Ramina. I don't want to be somewhere else unless you're there with me.'

Now at last her expression changes. 'You love me?'

'You know I do. Surely...'

'Really love me? Not just saying it?'

'Ramina. Why on earth do you think I live with you?'

'For the sex, of course. For the fucking.'

'Ramina. I love you.'

'I was a prostitute.'

'What's that got to do... Ramina. I love you.'

Alex says, 'You loved her. If I asked you to define love, what would you say?'

'After you.' He thinks about it. 'I was a young man. Ramina was right in a way; I was there for the fucking. That doesn't mean I didn't love her. For a young man, that's what love is.'

'Is that how it was with me?'

'You know it wasn't. But if I'd still been that same young man when you and I met, it might have been. When you see a man and a woman happy together for a long time, the credit belongs to the woman. If she's grounded, grown up, they have a chance. If she isn't, it doesn't matter how adult he is in man terms. They won't make it.'

'In any case, there was a drawback.'

'There's always a drawback.'

'When she realised you weren't just her man. When she realised you loved her.'

'I thought that knowing she was loved would make her feel secure.'

'But she thought being loved gave her power. Opened a door that had been closed.'

In bed that night, Ramina takes Ted in her pale brown hand. 'Men don't have brains, do they? Women have brains. Men have only this.'

'Is that what you think?'

'I could get you to do anything I want.'

'You think so?'

She strokes him gently. 'All I have to say is "No more of this, until you do what I say." And you'd do it. Wouldn't you?'

'I might.'

She takes her hand away. 'I want you to kill Roland and Martin.'

'I don't want to kill anyone.'

'I know you don't.' She replaces her hand. 'Which do you not want the most? To kill anyone? Or to say goodbye to fucking Ramina?'

'It's not a choice I want to make.'

'That's a pity, my little Teddie. Because it's a choice you're going to have to make.' And she turns on her side, her back towards him.

There had been a time, and it was not very long ago, when Ted would have accepted this. Not now. He hadn't been through everything he had, become what he was, to be cut off from what he wants at the whim of an illiterate Arab girl. The fabled English Gangster who walked the Arab Quarter with a gun in his pocket and shot a pimp in front of a policeman does not roll over and sleep because an ex-prostitute tells him to. A black-coated, Gauloise-smoking existentialist (though Alex was probably right about that. What *was* an existentialist?) who financed drug imports and risked his life whenever he went into the streets was not going to dance to the tune of the woman whose whole family depended on his money and his goodwill.

He took her by the shoulder and rolled her onto her back. She wasn't Carol, as he soon learned. By the time he mounted her, he was scratched and bleeding. But mount her he did.

Alex says, 'I'm calling a time out.'

'*You're* calling a time out?' says Dolan. 'Who the hell do you think you are?'

'You're not a BBC man, are you? Don't you have commercial breaks in your show?'

'This isn't that kind of...'

'So have one. Ted. Come over here with me.'

The screen, as they walk away from it, fills with a huge picture of a little boy peering into a cereal packet. He's looking for something. Ted feels like telling him he'll always be looking for something. Alex takes his elbow in her hand and leads him into the corner where King Tut is lurking. She waves him away and he goes, hissing at her like a snake disturbed in a dry river bed.

'I'm not a rapist,' she says. 'Do you remember saying that? It was right after you'd forced Carol, which we can just about accept because you're right, attitudes were different then. Your role as a man, the way people saw things, was to push all you could. Hers, if she was a respectable girl, was to resist. And she was expected to yield, if she was sure you'd do the decent thing, which by the way she was but you didn't, and as long as she'd held you off for long enough. But you can't say that about what we've just seen. That was rape, Teddie. You *are* a rapist.'

'God Almighty, woman. Didn't you say you were my defence counsel?'

'Well, make my life easier, Ted. All we've heard so far is the bad stuff. According to my notes, there's a fair bit to say on the other side of the ledger.'

'I'm only answering the questions *he* asks.'

'Ted. We all have a role to play. I have mine and you have yours. Tell us about the hospice. Tell us about the scholarships. Don't go down without a fight. And the fire. Those children would have died without you.'

Ted shudders. The flames. The little brother and sister. The terror he'd felt.

'That wasn't just instinct, was it?' asks Alex. 'A few years earlier you'd have let them die.'

Is that true? The parents were in such a state, already mourning for a son and a daughter who weren't dead yet. Would he really have ignored them? Left them to their grief? 'I don't know,' he says.

'It doesn't matter. You did what no one else was going to do. And you have a decision to make. About Arthur.'

'Arthur?'

'Are you going to use what he did to you as a defence for what you did to Carole and Ramina?' She held up her hand. 'Don't answer yet. You need to think it through.'

'I buried that memory so deep I haven't had to think about it for more than fifty years. Thank you for bringing it up.'

'You need to think about it now.'

'No I don't. Shit happens to everyone. Arthur does not excuse me, because there are no excuses.'

'We may as well give up, then. Come on. Let's get back.'

Dolan and the audience are watching a deodorant ad. Alex says, 'Let's get Tim Feather on the screen.'

'He was much later,' Ted says.

'Of course he was later. That's what happens, isn't it? You do what you do, you realise what you've become and you get the chance to redeem yourself. Most people don't take it. You did. Tim Feather, please.'

'But he hasn't called him,' says Dolan.

'*I'm* calling him. I want Tim Feather on that screen and I want him there now.'

Dolan looks at Ted. 'Well,' Ted says, 'I'd like to see old Tim again.'

And there he is, smiling from the screen. 'Ted.'

'Tim.'

'What the hell do you mean, calling me "old Tim"?'

Alex stands up and addresses the screen. 'Tim Feather. Would you mind introducing yourself?'

'Well, my name is Tim Feather and I was a social worker. And then I died.'

'You weren't always a social worker, though?'

'In a sense, I was. But what I think you want me to explain is that, before I was a social worker, I was a Catholic priest.'

'How did that happen?'

'Well, that's a funny sort of question. I went the usual route. Seminarian, curate, priest. But, once again, what I think you want me to explain is that I was one of eight children, Catholic father, Catholic mother, and I think they'd always had this dream that at least one of us would have a vocation, and it fell to me. And to one of my sisters, who became a nun. Which she remains to this day, by the way.'

'But you did not remain a priest.'

'I stayed in the job for fifteen years. After ten, I fell in love with a woman parishioner. I fought it and I lost. It wasn't a short fight. I was very aware of the vows I'd made, promises before God, promises *to* God. We didn't become lovers until I'd been a priest for fourteen years. But then there was only one outcome. The Vatican was a bit slow coming through with the dispensation, which meant I was already the other kind of father before I stopped being a Father.'

'Why did you become a social worker?'

'I suppose I wanted to help people.'

'What sort of social worker were you?'

'A good one, I hope.'

'That isn't what I meant.'

'I worked for a private charity. One that helped people with learning difficulties. Although we didn't use that term in those days.'

'And how did you meet a man like Ted Bailey?'

'He helped one of our clients.' He pauses and looks behind him. 'There's something nudging me in the back. Do you know anything about that?'

'You need to step out of the picture, please.'

And, right before Ted's eyes, Tim walks off the screen and stands beside it. Some nameless servant of the hotel hands him a microphone. Where he was standing a moment earlier is now a park which, though you can't tell from the screen, Ted could tell you is in Newcastle. There's a boy, a young man, it's always difficult to tell with those features because they make people look younger than they are.

There are two youths, two louts, and they've decided there's some entertainment value in tormenting this lad. They've taken his bag and they're pulling things out of it and chucking them around. He's crying, and that seems to encourage them. When he tries to get his bag back, they hurt him.

A couple walk past, see what's happening, and walk on. You can see them think about intervening but one of the louts snarls at them and on they go. Then a man on his own who keeps his head down, looking at the grass beneath his feet, and passes as quickly as he can. And here's Young Ted, walking in from the side. He looks about twenty-nine, thirty, which when he thinks about it would be about right. He picks a youth, walks up to him and drives his fist into his stomach. The youth lets out a whooshing sound and doubles up and Ted hits him on the side of the chin, a real haymaker, and down he goes.

It's amazing how quickly someone can go from prize bully to quivering coward. 'What do you think you're doing?' the other one wants to know. Ted puts his foot on the side of the face of the one on the ground and presses down. 'Same as you. Picking on someone smaller and weaker than me, and a hell of a lot less bright, and enjoying myself.' He waves at the things spread over the grass. 'Pick up all this kid's stuff, put it back in his bag and give it to him. Nicely.'

'Or what?'
'Or I'll rip your cock out through your nose.'
The youth isn't a complete fool and he doesn't waste time arguing or thinking about what he's going to do and pretty soon the lad has his bag back and he's stopped crying. Ted lets the one on the floor up and tells them both to clear off,

'Is that it?' says Dolan. 'Is that the case for the defence? He beat up a young thug who wasn't as big or as strong or as nasty as he was?'

'There was more to it than that,' says Alex.

'What? Is he supposed to get credit for coming to someone's aid? He helped Ramina when she was set on by three men, and look what came of that. Drug dealing and rape and murder. I'm sorry. You're going to need more than that.'

'If I can speak?' says Tim.

Alex nods to him. 'Go ahead.'

'Ted took the boy home and left. But the father had seen Ted in his cricket gear on the back pages of the *Chronicle* and he recognised him. He told me what had happened and I contacted Ted to thank him. That was how we met.'

'Yes?' says Dolan. 'And...?'

'We became friends. He never seemed to want to talk about what he did...'

'Really? You amaze me.'

'...but he was always interested in my job. Government funding was a big part of keeping us going and it was being cut back. We were going to lose our day centre, which was where people who were too old for school went, because we couldn't afford the rent and we couldn't pay the staff. A lawyer contacted us out of the blue and said an anonymous donor had given enough money to buy the place outright and pay people for two years. We never knew who it was. I didn't find out it was Ted until I was sent here.'

'Conscience money,' says Dolan. 'He could afford it. And he shouldn't have had it in the first place. Would you get back on the screen, please?'

Tim stays where he is. 'He also wanted to know about my time as a priest. He wanted to know what the most important rule of life was.'

'What did you tell him?' says Alex.

'Ask him,' says Tim. 'And I'll tell you something else. I had a colleague who ran a hostel for young people who'd been driven from their homes. Somewhere they could live, go to school, college, get a job. Put their lives back on track after they'd been abused or just not wanted. He never had enough money. And then he did. It came from Ted, although the lawyer who handled the payments never told him so. That's something else I only learned today.'

Dolan says, 'I'm not going to tell you again. Get back where you came from.'

Tim steps up onto the screen, and Dolan picks up his remote control and presses a button. The screen goes blank. 'I've had enough of that,' he says.

Alex turns. 'So, Ted. The most important rule of life. What is it?'

Ted shakes his head. 'I don't recall that conversation.'

'Ted. You're on trial for your life.'

Ted shrugs. He's spent a lifetime holding things inside. Some things are better there.

<u>*Chapter 14*</u>

Ramina won't look at him. He asks, 'Where have you been?' but she won't look at him. Walking around the apartment, it's as though the temperature drops wherever she is.

'Where have you been?' he asks again.

'Out. What do you care? Rapist.'

'Ramina. I'm sorry.'

'Sorry? You're sorry you raped me? Well, fuck you. You know? Fuck you.'

It was going to be a long haul. He'd seen her pissed off, but not with him and not like this.

'I didn't think of it as raping you, Ramina.'

'No? I say I don't want to fuck and you fuck me anyway? That's not rape? I nearly scratch your fucking ear off and still you fuck me? That's not rape? What the fuck do you call that if you don't call it rape?'

'I thought we were making love. I'm sorry.'

She comes very close to him. 'That's what making love means to you? You do what I don't want and it's all right, it's making love, because it's what you want?'

He picks up his coffee cup and hurls it across the room. It shatters against the wall. 'So what do you call love, Ramina? Refusing to come across because I won't kill two men for you? That's love?'

Whatever her face was saying, he couldn't read it. A small pool of coffee spread from the broken cup. She turned away as if to clean it up.

'Leave it.'

'Don't talk to me like that, Teddie.'

'I'm sorry. But leave it. Please. I made the mess. I'll clean it up.' He goes into the kitchen for a cloth and a bucket to put the pieces in. 'Where did you go?'

'Home. I went home. Where do you think I went?'

'You told your brothers what happened?'

'Of course.'

'And what did they say?'

She is silent.

'What did they say, Ramina?'

'They took your side. Of course.'

'What did they say?'

'I'm a woman. You're a man. If we fight, I'm wrong and you're right. They are men, too. I'm here for your pleasure.'

'They said all that?'

'They don't need to say it. I know what they think.'

'So what did they say?'

'They told me to come back here and tell you I'm sorry.'

'I haven't heard you do that.'

'No,' she spits. 'And you won't.'

He rests on his heels, the mess cleared away into the bucket. 'Well, I'll say it. I'm sorry, Ramina. I was wrong. I don't know what came over me.'

'You don't?' She fiddles with the flakes of croissant on the table. 'You want me to tell you? You don't control yourself,' she goes on when he doesn't answer. 'If you want something, you don't see why you shouldn't have it. You tell yourself the other person wants it too, really. Or you just don't care what the other person wants.'

'I'm sorry.'

'And usually I do want it. You're my man, I'm your woman. I want it to be the way it is. And I shouldn't have said no sex if you wouldn't kill them. I shouldn't have bargained with fucking. That was wrong. So I'm sorry, too.' She kneels down and places her hand on his forehead. 'But you have to control yourself. You said you loved me.'

'I do love you.'

She sighs. 'Whatever you say, Teddie.' She stands up. 'You want to fuck now? Want to try it standing up against the wall?'

'Standing up?'

'Sure. I can pretend we're outside and I'll feel like I'm a whore again.'

'Oh, God.'

'You know what else is wrong with you?'

'I know you're going to tell me.'

'You asked what my brothers said.'

'Yes?'

'You didn't ask about my sisters. Or my mother. You didn't want to know what they think.'

He sits down, looks out of the window. 'What do your sisters think, Ramina?'

'They're only women. They don't matter. What do you care what they think?'

He sits in silence for a while. Then he stands up, takes his coat off the hook. Ramina says, 'Where are you going?'

'Out.'

He walked for miles. Except as a tourist, he hadn't been inside a church since burying Bella, but that's where he ended up. He had no expectations, which was just as well, because no priest came to sit beside him, analyse his evident *ennui* and tell him how to sort his life out. Men in clerical garb bustled up and down the aisle but none of them looked at Ted; a woman shoved a mop so close to his feet she seemed to want him to leave; other women arranged flowers and dusted all the fiddly impedimenta of a Catholic Church in France. He left no happier than when he had arrived.

Not wanting to go straight home, he stopped in a café for a glass of wine, a cigarette and a coffee and watched the world pass by the window. A number of people seemed to know who he was and some of them nodded. Thinking he might be known to people unknown to him did not improve his sense of well-being.

When eventually he got back to the apartment, Ramina was conciliatory.

'Where did you get to, darling?'

'Oh, you know. Around.'

'You want to eat in tonight? Or shall we go out?'

'You choose.'

'Out, then.'

Something, he didn't know what, reminded him of a question he had asked just after she told him he would never be allowed to marry her.

'How old are you, Ramina?'

'You asked me that before.'

'You didn't answer.'

'I am older than you think I am, Teddie.'

'How old?'

'What does it matter? Why don't you go out, if that's what you want to do?'

'How many men have you lived with before me?'

She holds herself very still. 'Is that really what you want to know?'

'It's what I'm asking.'

'Maybe what you should be asking is how many men did I love before you? Because the answer is none. I thought you were different. Give me a cigarette, please. Thank you. I thought you loved me for me. No one ever did that before.'

'Your mother…'

'My mother made me a whore so my sisters could be virgins.'

So quickly a gulf can grow. All he could do was stare across it.

He lay that night as he always did, pressed against her, cradling her nakedness in his, his hand resting on her hip. From time to time he kissed her lazily, gently.

'We're all right, aren't we?' she murmurs.

'We're fine, darling.'

She moves over him, stares into his eyes. 'We are, aren't we? Really?'

'Stop fretting, Ramina. Everything's perfect.'

Alex says, 'It wasn't, though. Was it?'

'No. Love is so easy to lose. And very, very hard to win back.'

1970. A street in Marseille. Roland shoots Pierre in the fleshy part of the thigh. 'Tell your English branleur to leave, now. Tell him we will put his putain back on the streets where she belongs. If he stays I will stick my automatic in his mouth like a zizi and blow what brain he has through the back of his skull.'

Then, Roland having insulted his masculinity and his sister, Roland's partner Martin urinates on him where he lies sobbing with pain.

Indoors. Ramina doesn't look at Ted. She skirts around him in the apartment, solicitous as to an invalid, with sideways glances from lowered eyes. What she thinks, she does not say. What she thinks, he knows.

'Will you come with me to Martinique?'

'No. No, Teddie, I will not go with you to Martinique. I will stay here and let them make me a whore again. Give me a cigarette, please.'

'You know I can't leave you.'

'You can. It does not matter. I lived like that before. I had come to think…with you…but it does not matter. And I will have our memories.'

'All right, Ramina. All right.'

'Yes, my love, it will be all right. When will you go?'

He goes into the bedroom. When he comes back, Ramina stares at the gun in his hand. 'Will you take that to Martinique?'

'Don't push it, Ramina.'

'I don't understand.'

'Yes, you do.'

He reaches for his coat. At once, Ramina is on him, holding tight to his arms. 'Where are you going?'

'I'm going to shoot Roland and Martin. Where do you think I'm going?'

'You can't.' She won't let go.

He shakes her. 'Don't be stupid, Ramina. You've been manoeuvring and manipulating me into this ever since we started importing. Have the honesty to be open about it.'

'But not now, Teddie. Not like this. They'll be waiting for you.'

He stops trying to push her off. 'When, then?'

'Soon. I'll talk to my father. Soon, my darling. But not now. Put the gun away. Please.'

Next morning. He is going to buy breakfast. Mahmoud falls into step beside him. 'You are about to do a very stupid thing, Monsieur.'

'Buy croissants?'

'Do not pretend innocence, please.'

They walk in silence to the boulangerie. When he has his purchases, Mahmoud is waiting for him. 'Your woman intends to betray you.'

'She does?'

'Don't dismiss what I say, monsieur. Your woman intends to betray you.'

'Why?'

'You committed violence against her.'

'I did?'

'You did, you didn't. She says you did, and that is what matters. Her brothers are furious with you.'

'How do you know this?'

'Please, monsieur. These are my people. You are a stranger here.'

'So how will she betray me?'

'She wants you to shoot Roland and Martin. Yes?'

They walk in silence.

'You think Roland and Martin are the opposition. They are not. Ramina's brothers

want to work with them. To be one big firm instead of two small ones.'

'Roland shot Pierre.'

'A simple flesh wound. In the place that inflicts least damage. He will recover. Soon he will walk as he always walked.' Mahmoud turns to face Ted, holding his sleeve and preventing further progress. 'The shot was for your benefit. To make you think they were enemies.'

Ted looks at him in silence.

'You will shoot at Roland and Martin. They will let you shoot at them. So that they can then shoot you in self-defence.'

'If they're dead, how will they manage that?'

'When you shoot them, the bullets in your gun will be blanks. That is Ramina's task—to make your gun harmless before you use it.'

'I don't believe you.'

'Monsieur. Did you really think you could rape an Arab girl and get away with it? You know less about our people than I thought, if you believe that.'

It made sense. Ted knew that. "You've been manoeuvring and manipulating me." How she must have enjoyed hearing that. Knowing he had no idea just how far he was being manipulated—or to what end. The bitch. The evil, malicious, scheming bitch.

'Why are you telling me this?'

'I am a simple man, monsieur, and I like a simple life. I had one before you came. Now...' He shrugs. *'Disputes between my own people I can handle. You know in the eyes of the Government we are all French, but there are degrees of Frenchness. I am paid to keep things quiet here. If a dark-skinned citizen dies a violent death, no one minds. But if one of those same dark-skinned citizens kills an Englishman, there will be no peace. We have had it before. Your newspaper reporters will be all over Marseille. They will write stories about us. The President of the Republic will have to say something. Fingers will point, monsieur, and they will point at me.'*

'What shall I do?'

'You are angry, monsieur. I think if I tell you to go away, to leave France and never come back, you will not listen. You will say you will, to be rid of me, but you feel wronged and you will not go until you have been revenged.'

'You are right.'

'You know that leaving would be your wisest course?'

'I will not go.'

'But afterwards? If I help you have your revenge, you will then help me? By leaving France for ever?'

'There would be nothing to keep me here.'

'Forgive me, monsieur, but is that "Yes"?'

'If you help me, I will leave France.'

'You swear it?'

'I swear it.'

'Thank you, monsieur. Then I will help you.'

'How?'

Mahmoud looks casually up and down the street. Then he takes a gun from his pocket and slips it into Ted's hand. 'Hide that, monsieur.'

'What should I do with it?'

'They will arrange a meeting. You will be told you are to kill Roland and Martin. I have told you what they intend. They will believe that you have only your own gun, in which Ramina has placed the blank cartridges. You must let her see you take it, so they suspect nothing. But the gun you take out will be the one I have given you, and not your own. Do not use it on Roland and Martin. It is Pierre and Jean you must shoot. That will be your revenge.'

'What about Ramina?'

'That, monsieur, I must leave to you. If you spare her, I will see that she is well treated after you are gone. If you choose not to spare her…'

'I could not shoot Ramina.'

'I understand, monsieur. You may leave her in my care.'

'And the others? Roland and Martin? They are going there to shoot me, are they not?'

'It is they who told me of the intentions of Ramina's family, Monsieur. We made this plan together. They too like a quiet life.'

There has been an interesting change of atmosphere in the audience. Ted is a wronged man. The woman who claims to love him has been plotting his murder. Concern is in the faces turned towards him.

Dolan senses it, too. 'You'd been betrayed,' he says.

'So it seemed.'

'But we know Ramina didn't bring about your death, because you're still here.'

'As you say, Barry.'

'So how did you survive? Did Mahmoud's plan work?'

'If Mahmoud's plan had worked, I'd have been dead.'

'I don't follow.'

'I'll tell you what I don't follow, Barry. Sometimes, you seem to know exactly what happened next. And sometimes you don't. What's that about?'

Dolan grins. 'Ask yourself what it's about, Ted.'

'And if I can't answer?'

'Then you're not trying. This is your show, Ted. I'm not really here. Alex isn't really here. The audience isn't really here. You're me, and you're the audience. Although even you aren't really here. You're upstairs, lying on top of a young girl and too ill to get off her.'

'Sick unto death,' I say.

'It would seem so. How are you feeling right now?'

'Pretty groggy, since you ask.' He holds his hand in front of his face. 'Things get blurry. I have to fight to stay on top of it. The darkness is closer than it was.'

'You're getting ready for a long journey.'

'The champagne helps.'

'Champagne or no champagne, the Grim Reaper is leaning on his scythe, counting to however many it is he counts to. When he gets there it'll be "Here I come, ready or not." Are you ready?'

'As I'll ever be.'

'You don't think you should pop upstairs, look in on that poor girl? See how she's doing?'

'No, Barry, I don't. I don't think that's a good idea at all.'

'As you like. So. I asked if Mahmoud's plan worked, and you said if Mahmoud's plan had worked, you'd have been dead. You want to explain? Or shall we watch?' He turns to the screen.

When Ted gets back with the croissants, he can hardly look Ramina in the eye. He seethes with rage. In all the red mists he'd known, nothing was ever like this. He gave this woman his heart and she's planning to get him killed.

And he can't say anything.

'It's tonight,' she says.

'Tonight?'

She pours coffee for them both, half filling the large bowls. Ted adds hot milk to his and passes the jug to her. He breaks off a chunk of croissant and dunks it in his coffee.

'The boat will arrive at the quay at one o'clock tonight. My brothers will be waiting for it. They have made sure Roland and Martin know it is coming.'

'Their enemies Roland and Martin.'

'But you will also be there, Teddie.'

'And what will I do, my sweet?'

'Do? Why, you will kill them. You will shoot Roland and Martin.'

'Shoot them.'

'There will never be a better chance.'

'Then I had better do it. Have you checked my gun?'

'There is no need.'

'Perhaps I should check it myself.'

'By all means, chéri.'

He rips savagely at a croissant. 'Where is the boat to come in?'

'At the eastern end, farthest from the Grand Harbour. There is an alleyway behind the coastguard.'

'I know it.'

'You and I will be waiting there.'

'You are going with me?'

'Of course, Teddie.'

'You will wish to hand me my gun?'

'Why would I hand you your gun, my love? You will carry it, of course.' She rests her hand on his arm. 'And you will shoot these bastards, and we will be free of them. And we will come back here and you will take from me what my brave man deserves.'

He looks away. She shakes a Gauloise from its packet, places it between his lips, lights it for him. Her hand moves to his lap. 'Perhaps we need not wait till tonight?'

He brushes her hand away. He cannot bear this duplicity.

Time never stops. It doesn't stop for the condemned man, waiting to be hanged at dawn. It did not stop for Othello, or for Jesus in the garden. It does not stop for Ted.

He'd eaten lunch, walked the streets, dined lightly on an omelette and salad, slept. Time continued its inexorable passage through all this. Now it was midnight, and Ramina was shaking him awake.

'It is time to go, my Teddie.'

Ted splashes cold water on his face and begins to dress. 'Have you checked my gun?'

'You asked me that before. No, I have not checked your gun. You want me to check your gun?'

*He shrugs. She says, 'Perhaps you are right.'
She goes away, returns with his gun, hands it
to him. She says, 'It is fine.'*

'It is fine?'

'It is fine.'

How could she bear to look at him, this traitress? This woman who had shared the most intimate acts with him? This jezebel he saved from the streets, whose family he bankrolled out of their petty serfdom, who now smiling sends him to his death? This woman he loved, who said she loved him? This despicable cow?

He put on his coat. He could pretend no longer. From the pocket he took the gun Mahmoud gave him.

'Nevertheless,' he says. 'I think I would like to have back-up.'

She stares at the gun. 'Where did you get that?'

'This?' He waves it under her nose. 'From Mahmoud.'

'Mahmoud? Mahmoud gave you a gun? For what?'

'To shoot your brothers with.'

She covers her mouth with her hands. 'Shoot my brothers? I don't understand.'

'He has told me everything, Ramina.'

Her hands descend slowly from her face, come to rest on her hips. She shakes; with fear or rage Ted cannot tell. She speaks quietly. 'And what is everything, Teddie?'

'That you lead me into a trap. That you and your vile family wish to unite with Roland and Martin and be rid of me. That you have filled my gun with blanks. That when I shoot my worthless bullets, they will shoot back with real ones and I will die. That is everything. It is enough, I think.'

Tears fill her eyes, but she will not let them fall. She holds out her hand. 'Give me the gun. The gun I have filled with blank bullets. Give it to me.'

When he doesn't move, she rips the gun from his hand. 'Put it the other away. For this you need both hands.'

She flicks off the safety catch and returns the gun tenderly to him, fixing his hands firmly around the stock. She raises it till it points directly at her heart.

'Pull the trigger, Teddie. Let us see how well these blank bullets work.'

Ted stares at her, his fingers tight around the trigger. He has never seen fury like this. He tries to keep his cold smile in place. He can not.

'Pull the trigger, Teddie. Shoot me, imbecile.'

Still he stares, and still he cannot squeeze.

She slaps him, hard, across the face. 'Moron! Fool! English cretin! Pull the trigger!'

He stands motionless as she slaps him again, all the force of her overpowering rage and lost hope in the weight of the blow. 'Shoot me!'

He begins to cry. Slowly, he lowers the gun. 'Why would Mahmoud give me another gun?'

'How should I know? I am only a woman. I lack the subtlety of the male brain. You should go now.'

'He lied to me.'

'A policeman? Lied? I cannot believe it. Leave the two guns. There will be a train to somewhere.'

'I don't understand.'

She crosses to him, lays a hand gently on his arm. 'Teddie. My poor innocent. There is only one reason I know of why someone would want you to use a strange gun. He knows it has been used in another crime. You shoot my brothers with it and the police will arrest you for that, and for the other crime also.'

'The bastard. The treacherous bastard.'

'Except that they will not arrest you, because Mahmoud will shoot you. He cannot allow you to speak in court. But still you will take the blame. Go now. You have your money safe?'

'Why would he do that?'

'Teddie. You said once you thought Mahmoud was on our side. I told you he is on Mahmoud's *side. He thought at first to have two smugglers would be good. He would take two pay-offs. But it has become too troublesome. So he needs to eliminate one set. He chose us. It is fair. Roland and Martin were there first. And they have better protection. What are you doing?'*

'There is not much time. The boat docks at one.'

'It is a trap. Obviously. I will go and plead for my brothers. If we promise to go back to how it was before, they will let them live I think. Inshallah.'

She goes to the door. 'We will say goodbye now, Teddie. I do not want to see you again. And you should leave. In case things do not go well.'

He watches her go. From the window, her walk looks broken. Her shoulders hang. He picks up both guns and puts them in his pocket.

When he left the apartment there were still lights in some of the neighbouring windows, despite the hour. He was envious of people going about their normal lives. Whatever they were doing—reading; making love; arguing; eating a late dinner or finishing a bottle of wine—they were doing it free of danger or fear of the law. Nor were the roads empty and as he walked he watched people. Those two men smoking in a doorway;

were they sent by Mahmoud to arrest him for carrying a gun? The car that drove by too slowly and parked on the other side of the road a hundred yards away; was the driver one of Roland and Martin's men?

If he walked along the quayside they'd see him coming. It was dark where he chose to go because the narrow lanes behind the quay had been there for centuries, they didn't have street lights and if anyone was in those ancient grime-encrusted buildings at night they had reason to keep their presence secret. The evening was warm but that did not stop him shivering. The pervading smell was of day-old gutted fish. Where there is dead fish there are rats and where there are rats there are cats but these were feral beasts; dodging a particularly mangy animal, Ted banged his knee on a dustbin filled with stuff he probably didn't want to think about and had to grab it to stop it crashing to the ground and announcing his presence. He hobbled a few yards, shaking off the pain in his leg.

They were in the shade of the customs house. A drunk staggered into the area and looked uncomprehending at Ramina where she knelt, fellating Roland. Mahmoud made a gesture that could only mean "Move on, there's nothing for you here." The man may have been drunk but he wasn't stupid and he disappeared more quickly than he had arrived. Jean and Pierre shook with impotent rage as a smiling Martin covered them with his gun.

Ted was more nervous than the first time he stepped into the ring, more frightened than when Arthur threatened to set the dogs on him if he didn't undress, angrier than when Mr Walton collected him as calm as though the weekend of gay rape had never happened and he had not arranged it. Mahmoud said, 'It is better this way. We cannot go on with the Englishman. Marseille is not big enough for this trouble. We must not fight among ourselves.'

It was three to one just as it had been when Ted attacked Ramina's assailants and, now as then, surprise would be all. He stepped forward. He had to hold his wrist with the other hand to stop the shaking as he put a bullet into Mahmoud's forehead with his own gun. He turned it on Martin and shot him twice in the chest. With a cry of shock, Roland stepped away from Ramina. His cock was covered in her saliva. Had it not been, Ted might have...well, no. Ted could not let him live. He pointed both guns. 'Lie down.'

Roland sank to the ground. 'Don't shoot me,' he whimpered. 'Please don't shoot me.'

Ted wrapped Martin's lifeless hand around Ted's own gun, pointed it at Roland and squeezed till it went off. It took three shots before the man stopped twitching.

Ramina was on her feet. She watched without expression. When Ted opened his arms to her, she turned away. He said, 'You want me to go?'

'I have told you so.'

'Then I shall go.'

The two brothers watched carefully. 'Some of these drugs are yours,' said Pierre.

'I've had my money back. Many times over. You can keep them.'

He turned and began to walk away. At the edge of the square he looked back. A signal, any signal, would do.

But she gave none.

'Forgiveness would have been a lot to ask,' Alex says.

Ted nods. 'Too much.'

'You made a right mess of things.'

'And I cleaned it up.'

'You broke it, you fixed it,' says Dolan.

'Right.'

'Bit of a theme emerging there?'

'How do you mean?'

'I made the mess. I'll clean it up. It's what you said when you broke the coffee cup.'

'Do you analyse everything James Corden says?'

'Corden's a professional, Ted. He shows the audience what the audience wants to see. He doesn't trail his emotional baggage all over the set like a suicide bomber's tripes.'

'Thank you for that.'

'So. You left Marseille?'

'I left France. Went back to England. It was May. The cricket season was about to start.'

The German in the front row splutters. 'You'd just shot three men,' he says. 'And you went home to play cricket?'

Ted says, 'Keith Miller went home from bombing Germany, home being Australia, and he turned up in England and won the Ashes.'

'Ashes?'

'Len Hutton came back from the war with one arm shorter than the other and still showed the new generation coming up how it was done.'

Silence.

'Or was it his leg? I can't remember. The Battle of Waterloo was won on the playing fields of Eton.'

'Perhaps. With a little help from the Prussians. Even so…'

'Cricket isn't football,' Ted says. 'Cricket isn't a game. Cricket is a way of life.'

'Were they pleased to see you?' asks Dolan.

'Seemed to be. It was 1970, I was twenty-four and twenty-four is a good age for cricketers to show what they're made of. Two games in the seconds and then opening for the firsts. Until my moment of glory, that is, when I was picked for my county.'

'A minor county.'

'Yes, Barry, a minor county, but still a higher standard than anything you ever played, I think.'

'How did you manage to combine county cricket with working for the French?'

Ted bought an old cottage on the road up from Hexham to Wall, farmland behind and no house on either side for at least a mile which was an isolation that suited his mood perfectly. If people asked, he said he was looking after it for a friend and his wife he'd met on his travels. And if they wanted to know how he supported himself, he explained that he was a consultant, promoting sales of French companies' products and services and paid by one of their ministries. That had the advantage of being true. Sort of. The Frogs had been happy to see him go back to England but they hadn't let go of his collar. The French Ministry for Trade, if that was really who he was dealing with, had given him a passport, identical to the one he already had except that it was French, gave his name as Edouard Bailey, and contained stamps from countries he had never visited.

<u>Chapter 15</u>

The capital of Côte d'Ivoire is Yamoussoukro, but Abidjan is where all the business is done. The plan as originally outlined was that Ted would be there as bodyguard to a French businessman called Charles Lyon. It hadn't worked out like that.

He'd had two questions when this deal was first put to him by the man who said his forfeit life could be redeemed. The man who called himself Michel. The first was: Why me? And the second was: Why would you pay a bodyguard so much money? The answer to Question One was: "You can use a gun and we know you will if you have to. And you can pass as a Frenchman, which we need you to do, but you're not one and if it all turns to rat shit you're deniable. We never set eyes on you." As it turned out, that was also the answer to Question Two. And they didn't really care how much they paid because they were in the Ivory Coast as sellers, not buyers, and it's never the seller who pays. But Ted didn't understand that yet. Like so many other people, he had this picture of corrupt western businesses going round the world saying, "Let me give you some money." As the Managing Director of one of those companies said to him once, "Why would we do that?"

It was Marie who put him straight.

1970. It's hot and it's wet. The dry season in Abidjan lasts from December to April, but dry season means the time when it doesn't rain quite as much as it does the rest of the year. Ted is there in July. Abidjan is twinned with San Francisco. They are not alike. There's a lot of waste land in Abidjan and although it looks deserted each stretch has the same message stencilled on a wall in black paint: *Do not piss or shit here*. It's in French, but the message is the same as the one he'd see in English when he went to Lagos. Marie met him when he got off the plane at Abidjan.

Michel had told him what he said was her story. Twenty-eight years old, third generation Ivorian, the granddaughter of a Frenchman who'd come out in the early years of the century to administer duties and taxes on behalf of the Government in Paris. Civil servants were expected to pocket a share of the money and he did so. He'd intended to go home when he'd made his pile, maybe buy a chateau somewhere and live like a marquis, but the temptation to add just a little more was always too great and when he died in Man, where he had gone for the cooler respite of the mountains, he left his son, Marie's father, a rich man. The son moved to Cape Town and married a woman of Lebanese descent but never felt comfortable among the Anglos and the Afrikaners and hated the cold, damp winters. Marie was born after they moved back to the Ivory Coast. When the Lebanese woman returned alone to South Africa, Marie was raised by a black nurse of prodigious size and, later, by the Poor Clares in Abobo.

The screen is live once more.

Marie says, 'There's been a change of plan.'

'Oh?' The people around them in the airport car park are black or tanned to a deep brown

but Marie's skin is pale and her hair and eyebrows bleached almost to whiteness. She's slim; in her blue knee-length skirt and white blouse she could have been a bank teller; she has the neatest, sweetest little buns Ted has seen in years.

'Charles Lyon couldn't make it.'

'Charles Lyon?'

'The businessman you were supposed to protect.'

'There's no point in my being here, then. If there's no one to protect, there's no need for a bodyguard.'

'Let's talk about it over dinner tonight.'

Ted gets into the back of the car; Marie sits up front beside the driver. She stays long enough at the hotel to be sure check-in goes smoothly. Then she says, 'Why don't you rest for a few hours? I'll pick you up around seven.'

When Ted gets to his room and unpacks, he finds in his case a revolver that hadn't been there when he left home, and twenty rounds of ammunition.

Night comes early on the equator and Abidjan looked more friendly. Stores were open and the pavements full of people, most of them with nothing to do but talk to each other. The men were tall and, mostly, thin; the women equally tall but more forceful.

'The ones you have to be careful of,' says Marie, 'are the tall women with high cheekbones.'

Ted raises an eyebrow.

'They are Muslim. Get the menfolk of one of them on your case, you'll need that gun we put in your bag.'

The restaurant is almost full. No one shows them to the empty table and Marie does not explain how she knows it is for them. No one comes for a while to take their order, either, and it takes Ted a while to realise that the party at one table is the owner and his family and that the waiting staff are eating at another, getting up from time to time to attend to customers. Marie smiles when she sees him watching them. She smiles a lot; private smiles that keep Ted at a distance rather than sharing the pleasure of the moment.

It's Ted's first time in Africa and he probably expected to be stared at but it isn't so; they are noticed no more than the wall coverings. Conversation is loud and animated, some of it in French and some in languages Ted knows nothing of. Marie lights a cigarette. When she offers the pack, he shakes his head.

'I've got a story for you, Edouard. Like most of our stories there's no truth in it. I can tell it to you, if you like? Or we could go for the facts.'

Alex says, 'Of course, there's a problem there.'

'I saw it at the time.'

Dolan says, 'She has a prepared story for you; she tells you it wouldn't be true; and then she offers to tell you a story that is true.'

'So why should I believe the second story is any more truthful than the first would have been? As I said, I saw it at the time.'

'I'll take the facts. Starting with who you work for.'

'You know that. I work for the French Embassy here. My job is making trade easy for French companies and difficult for everyone else. So. The facts. Charles Lyon, the man whose bodyguard you were meant to be, was never going to be here. I don't suppose he even exists.'

'There's no trade deal?'

'I very much hope that there will be a trade deal. And you will make it.'

'I'm not a salesman. I've never made a deal in my life. And what am I supposed to be selling? Shouldn't I understand the product?'

The smile is still in place and it still excludes Ted.

'It's more important that you understand how international trade works. First of all, people have to be paid off. Not a single deal takes place in Africa worth more than, say, five hundred dollars without someone taking a cut. I don't suppose things are any different in the Middle East or Asia, but my patch is Africa. It can look complicated, but at the root of it all is a simple transaction. The seller and the buyer agree what the buyer is going to pay. How much money has to end up in the seller's bank account, if you like. Then they agree how much the seller will add to the invoice. Let's say the sale itself is worth one hundred thousand dollars and the buyer wants twenty thousand dollars in return for choosing this seller rather than another and making the deal happen. Then the seller gives the buyer an invoice for one hundred and twenty thousand, the buyer pays in full and after the cheque has cleared the seller pays twenty thousand dollars into whatever bank in whatever country the buyer tells him to. See?'

'No, I don't see. A bribe should be paid by the seller, but what you're describing is a bribe paid by the buyer, which the seller then pays back. What's the point of that?'

'Oh, Ted. I hoped you'd be smarter than this. Look. Let's say you work for the Government. The Government pays you, but you don't think

it's enough. You're married, you have children, you have the his-and-hers Mercedes, the five bedroom house with razor wire on the wall, the servants, the children in private school. Your salary as a middle ranking civil servant won't buy those things. But the Government has lots of money, and you want some. Your job is to buy something. Tractors, perhaps. The people who make the tractors tell you they'll fill a ship with tractors, they'll pay the freight and the insurance and get the whole lot to dockside at Port of Abidjan. All for a million dollars, US. They're not completely stupid, so you either have to pay them cash up front or get a Letter of Credit from a bank that their bank trusts. With me?'

Not much caring for the way she is talking to him, Ted allows himself the smallest possible nod.

'Good. So you say, "Invoice us for one point two million." They knew you were going to say that, they were waiting for you to say it, they may not like it but they know if they refuse there'll be a German tractor manufacturer or an Italian tractor manufacturer or an American tractor manufacturer only too happy to oblige. So they invoice your Government for two hundred thousand dollars more than they need and when they've been paid they transfer the extra two hundred thousand to an account

in Switzerland in your name that you hope your Government knows nothing about. So the bribe is paid and it's the buyer and not the seller who pays it. Or, rather, the buyer's employer. Understand?'

Ted nods again.

'I used that example because in fact on this trip it is tractors you're going to be selling. There are forty of them and the amount we need to see in our account in France when the dust settles is three point two million dollars. But you'll probably have to round that up to four million dollars to meet the buyer's PFA.'

'PFA?'

'Personal Financial Aspirations.'

'That's eighty thousand dollars each. What are these tractors made of? Gold?'

'It is a lot of money for a tractor. But tractors is what the documentation will say. Some of the buyer's eight hundred thousand dollars will go on the Customs man who signs that what was in the crates was what it said on the paperwork and not what it actually looked like, and on stevedores to keep their mouths shut. Your share will be five per cent of the three point two, less ten per cent of the difference between that and the price you actually agree. You're looking blank again.'

'Who wouldn't?'

'Ted. If you sell for three point two million dollars, you get one hundred and sixty thousand dollars commission. But you have no chance of doing that because then the buyer doesn't get a kick back so why would he agree? If you sell for four million you get one hundred and sixty thousand less eighty thousand, which is still a lot of money for a week's work in the sun. But the higher you let him drag you, the less you earn.'

Dolan is walking around like Perry Mason. 'How much did you earn?'

'I found out I was a good negotiator. We settled at three point six million, so I got a hundred and twenty thousand.'

'For a week's work.'

'Two days, actually. But let's not get carried away. A dollar was worth less then than it is now.'

'So when it was over you got…how much?'

'Fifty thousand pounds.'

'Twenty-five thousand a day. And you didn't even ask what was really going to be in the crates. Would you like to see what was in them? And how they were used?'

'No, I think I probably wouldn't.'

'Watch anyway.'

He turns to the screen, but the screen stays blank. Alex has her hand up. Dolan presses the button several times, but nothing happens. Alex says, 'You can press that as often as you like. It isn't the prosecutor who decides what evidence is admissible, it's the judges. I've appealed to one of them and he has upheld my objection.'

'Well, isn't that typical,' says Dolan. 'How are we supposed to try the man if we can't see the evidence?'

'My client is on trial for what he did,' says Alex. 'Not for what other people did. People have died in huge numbers in Côte d'Ivoire but Ted didn't kill them.'

'He has blood on his hands.'

'Bullshit. Ted, you'd earned fifty thousand pounds for that trip. How many more were there?'

'I lost count. By the end of the following year I was a millionaire.'

'What did you do with all that money?'

'I bet he didn't pay tax on it,' says Dolan.

'I played cricket. I bought my E Type. I took little holidays in places most people never see. I ate in restaurants my parents could only have dreamed of. And then I met Aitch, walking through the Bigg Market.'

Dolan presses a button and all turn to look at the screen.

HB is short for Head Banger. He was probably not the only son of a career criminal ever educated at Heaton Grammar School, but he's the only one Ted knows. Grinning happily, he hails Ted with a four-letter word shouted across fifty yards of populated space. Ted grins back, ignoring the shocked faces of the passing shoppers. They shake hands. Then they head for the Burgoynes, an old pub knocked down long since, where they lunch on hot meat pie and brown sauce washed down with pints of Exhibition. Ted asks how Aitch's life is panning out.

'Great.' The grin spreads wider. 'I'm a stockbroker now.' He peers closely into Ted's face and laughs. 'Everybody does that.'

'Does what?'

'Tries to cover up their amazement. Like you just did. Don't deny it, man. I'm not blaming you.'

'What's it like, then? Being a stockbroker?'

'You mean, how did a thick Geordie lad fall into that?'

'You were never thick, Aitch. But I always thought stockbrokers lived in Surrey.'

'Aye, well. They have them here, too. A couple of little firms like the one Ah'm with. Me dad asked us to help in the family business, but Ah'm not him.' He shrugs. 'He's back inside. He wanted us to look after things while he's away, but he'll be there a long time. Ah mean Ah like a fight, but not for me life.'

'That bad?'

'You've got the paddies from Gateshead and out the west, and the bliddy Lascars trying to muscle in from down Shields. And all the amateurs. Me Dad could keep them out, but Ah'm not me Dad. Me brother, Billy? He was

no help. Stayed at school, now he's at college, says he's going to get a job. So I decided that's what I should do.'

'But a stockbroker? Isn't that a bit boring?'

'Didn't someone tell me you used to be an estate agent?'

'You've got me there. So what do you do?'

HB's accent changes. Not in a big way, but the alteration is there. He can do the vowels when he wants to. 'I'm in the research department. Well. I am the research department. I go out, talk to businessmen, find out what they're doing. Where the opportunities are. Who's growing, who's about to win a big contract. And who's putting on a brave face, pretending things are fine when they're sliding down hill.'

'Sounds interesting.'

'Aye, it can be.' His face clouds. 'I sometimes wonder why they took us on, though.'

Ted raises an eyebrow, and waits. HB will tell his story in his own way. Or he won't.

'They knew who me Dad was. I think they thought I'd bring them something I can't.'

'What? Float a criminal gang on the stock exchange?'

'No, man. Drugs.'

'Drugs? What would stockbrokers want drugs for?'

'Clients, man. They want to grow. The old man, that's the boss, he's about a hundred but he went to some do a year or so back. Somebody trying to sell him something, I don't know what. But they had girls there, which he'd seen before, and people smoking pot, which he hadn't.'

'I'm surprised he didn't call the police.'

'It was business, man. The boss thinks the police should spend their time arresting thieves and hoodlums. Not interfering with business.'

'Did he use the stuff himself?'

'Apparently. There he was, down in an armchair you'd have needed an army to get him out of, nice young tart on her knees sucking him off and somebody hands him a joint.'

'You seem to know a lot about it.'

'He told us, man.'

'About the girl?'

'He's been a widower for years. Who's he hurting? He's proud he can still get it up. So they give him this joint, and he tells them he doesn't smoke. And someone says, this isn't like smoking, and someone else says draw it in and hold it down. So he does. It's a wonder his bliddy heart didn't pack in.'

'Hold it down?'

'Have you not done any drugs?'

'I'm an athlete, Aitch.'

'Course you are. Anyway. One joint and he's a convert. He's off in the war. In Africa, driving a tank with the rest of the Desert Rats. But he's not dreaming it, he's there. He had a long conversation with his wireless operator, which is a bit amazing because his wireless operator was killed in Holland in forty-four. Pot'll do that, sometimes.'

'Interesting he talked to his dead tank buddy and not his dead wife.'

'That's what these old men are like, man. The war's far more important to them than anything else.'

'And if he fought in Africa, he's not a hundred. Not even fifty, probably.'

'Fifty, a hundred, what's the diff? He's an old man, man.'

'Makes you wonder what his wife died of.'

'I've no idea. Never asked.'

'My dad fought in the war. So did yours, I should think.'

'Probably spent it in the glasshouse. I know he never talks about it.'

'Nor does mine.'

'They called up my cousin. Sent him to Korea. He was one of them never came back.'

'That's tough.'

'Me aunty's not been right since.'

'So has he asked you about getting drugs?'

'Aye, has he. Not straight out, mind. Comes at it sideways, like.'

'What do you say?'

'I dodge the question. I'm still hoping me dad can help us out. But drugs are new since he started. Drugs are American. Gene Krupa and Kerouac. Me dad's more Vera Lynn and Ann Shelton. Gambling, girls and protection. He has no contacts.'

'They have betting shops now.'

HB smiles. 'Aye, well, bookies still need to be looked after.'

'I can get you some drugs.'

'You? How?'

'What's so difficult? What do you think you need to buy drugs?'

'Well. Money. Obviously. You need money to buy anything. And then contacts.'

'I have both of those.'

'I'm talking about real money, man.'

'So am I.'

'Where did you get it?'

Ted felt no need to mention Henderson Wilde and the old ladies' houses. HB probably had a mother of his own. Nor did he say anything about earnings deposited by the French into a Swiss account. He told Aitch about Ramina, and her brothers, and the drugs. He didn't mention Abdul, or Mahmoud, or Roland, or Martin, and the end they came to.

HB is watching Ted carefully. 'This is true, isn't it?'

'True as I'm sitting here.'

'Bugger me. You're one of us, man.'

'So. Are you interested, or what?'

'Even split?'

'Even split.'

HB sticks out a hand. 'It's a deal.'

Things were simpler in those days; there were no magnetic stripes on passports, and no computerised databases to check them against even if there had been. Ted's French passport probably had some mark he wasn't aware of to alert French passport control to who had just entered the country so he used his British one to be safe. He told himself that the stare the immigration officer fixed him with was the same as he used on every Englishman. There was nothing he could do about it, anyway. The E-Type handled beautifully on the French roads. So beautifully that in the pleasure of driving he almost forgot his nervousness over what lay ahead. He had left Marseille in 1970 when he was twenty-four; he was heading back there in 1971 when he was twenty-five. Put like that, it didn't seem a huge difference, and yet it felt enormous. He was making more money than he knew what to do with and yet, just to do a favour for an old school friend, he was on his way to see people who may be alive or may be dead; who may have what he wanted or may be once again relegated to serfdom; who may welcome him or may wish to kill him.

And, of course, there was Ramina.

It is eleven when Ted arrives in Marseille. He drives to the Andalucia and parks right outside. When he enters, there is total silence. He takes a seat facing the door. He is the invisible man. No one offers to serve him. No one even looks at him. He lights a cigarette and waits.

They have sent a messenger, as he knew they would. Pierre arrives with a strut and a coat of epic expense. He sits opposite Ted, shakes his hand, speaks rapidly in Arabic. Coffee is put in front of both of them.

'It's good to see you,' he says.

'You too. You're looking well.'

'Is this a friendship visit? Or do you have business here?'

'I want to buy drugs.'

Pierre raises his eyebrow. 'To sell where?'

'In England.'

'Not here?'

'In England.'

'Then we can do business. What are you looking for?'

'What have you got?'

'The usual.'

'Then that's what I'll take.'

Pierre spreads his arms. 'Simple!' He drinks his coffee, drops too much money on the table and stands. 'Let us talk to my father. We will go in your car that is so beautiful like a woman. A woman shaped like a big zizi. Who thought of that, do you suppose? A car shaped like a woman shaped like a zizi. The English are very clever. And filthy in the mind.'

As Ted drives, Pierre says, 'I like your style, Tedward.'

'Ted. Or Edward. But not Tedward.'

Pierre shrieks with laughter and slaps him on the back. 'Edouard.' He laughs again. 'Still, I like your style.'

'You do?'

'Of course. Not once have you mentioned Ramina.'

'Is she well?'

'She is. And pleased you are here.'

'She knows?'

'Of course. She was there when the message came. She has missed you, I think.'

'She told me to go.'

'I know this. But still, she misses you. She does not work now. Of course, she cannot marry, but she no longer brings disgrace on the family. She is, how do you say? Retired. We give her everything she needs. I think she still loves you. You still love her?'

Ted doesn't answer.

'Of course not,' says Pierre. 'Love for men is not how it is for women. For us, when it is over it is over. For them... Ramina told you to go. She was angry with you. Now the anger is gone and the love remains. You must have a very big baguette, I think. You will not tell Ramina you no longer love her?'

'How can I not?'

'Lie.'

'I don't want to lie to Ramina.'

'God means us to lie to women. If He did not, He would not have made them stupid.'

Ted was calm when he walked before Pierre into the cramped family home. Perhaps the next few minutes would decide whether he lived or died. He should care. But he did not.

As usual, the men gather in one room while Pierre's mother serves coffee and sweetmeats. Ted can't see Ramina but she is there, a shadow in other shadows, a sensed presence just out of sight.

Pierre explains the reason for Ted's visit. Ted says, 'We'll never be big business for you. We're not looking to build a drugs empire. It's a question of businessmen, and meeting their needs when we know what they are.'

'Still,' says the old man, 'it is a chance for us to repay our debt to you. Will you collect from here, or do you want us to deliver?'

'If I can take some with me? And then come back every couple of months, when we know what we use?'

'Pierre will show you what we have. Later. You would like to see Ramina?'

The shape that has been lurking in the corridor emerges from the shadows. 'Of course he would like to see me. Hello, Teddie.'

The old man stands and motions to his sons. 'We will leave you.'

Ramina pushes the door closed behind her retreating menfolk. 'So, Teddie. After all this time, are we pleased to see each other?'

'Of course, Ramina.'

'You do not seem so sure. But we will see a lot of each other if you are to return in two months.'

'I look forward to it.'

'Do you? Do you, Teddie? Perhaps we could go to Nice. I could pleasure you again at the Negresco. We could eat chocolate and prunes in Armagnac in our room, and drink champagne. Or I could visit you at your home in England.' She moves round him, examining. 'Relax, Teddie. I do not have a passport.' She takes his hand in hers. 'I should not have sent you away. I have regretted it often. Have you regretted it, too?'

'How can you ask?'

'You could have written. Or come; you could have come here.'

'I am here now.'

'At last. Perhaps things will be all right between us again. Do you think that?'

'Ramina, I...'

She comes very close. 'Is there something you wish to tell me, Teddie?'

'Don't bully me, Ramina.'

'Hah. The man says this to me. Do you remember, Teddie, when I told you you could not marry me? Do you remember that?'

'Of course I do.'

'I told you then if you ever wanted to take another woman, I would cut off more than just the little piece of skin at the end of your magnificent baguette. Do you remember?'

'How could I forget?'

'I was lying, Teddie. If I ever found you had taken another woman, I would not harm you. I would not harm my little Teddie with the astonishing zizi. But the woman? I would find her, Teddie, and I would cut out her thieving black heart. Whatever it took.'

She takes his lapel in her hand, stands on her toes and kisses him on the cheek. 'Do we understand each other, Teddie? Do we understand each other?'

Ted was more relaxed on the journey home. Which was surprising, really, given what he carried with him in the car.

Drugs were not yet the demon they would become, but they were illegal. Mick Jagger had gone to jail for possessing them. Breaking a butterfly on a wheel it may have been, but if someone as prominent as Jagger went down then so could Ted. And the Stone did not also have a gun that he had killed with. And yet Ted was unafraid.

There is something to be said for fatalism.

Dolan says, 'You were buying drugs for HB's boss. You still haven't said how Alex and you got together.'

'HB's firm threw a party. I'd contributed what HB's boss thought the most important thing, so I was invited. Alex was there because she was the boss's daughter.'

Richard Grainger is the man of whom it is said that he found Newcastle of bricks and timber and left it in stone. When Ted was a boy there were four hundred and fifty buildings in Grainger Town, and two hundred and fifty of them were listed. The offices of stockbroker Jeremy Hughes occupied the middle floor of one of them. It wouldn't last because the city fathers were intent on knocking down buildings that should have been preserved but at that time, just as the Sixties turned into the Seventies, it was still one of the finest architectural areas in Britain.

'May I ask you a personal question, Mister Hughes?'

'Jeremy, please. What do you want to know?'

'How old are you?'

'My, my, that is a personal question, isn't it? Why do you ask?'

'Just curious.'

'You'll have to stay that way, I'm afraid. Let's say I belong to a generation that put boundaries around what to discuss with young whipper-snappers.'

Later, though, Alex, told Ted her father was forty-six.

'That's a strange question to ask, isn't it? At this juncture? Before I've even had time to button up?'

'I'm sorry. You were finished, weren't you?'

She stops what she's doing and stares at him. 'I do hope you're not going to turn out to be a funny bugger, Ted Bailey. I have enough of them at work. Yes, if that's what you're asking, you rang my chimes. I'm fully satisfied. Nicely post-orgasmic. I still think it's a strange question.'

'Aitch said he was about a hundred. Where is this work where you meet the funny buggers?'

'Leeds University.'

'What do you do there?'

'You're expecting me to say I'm a secretary, aren't you?'

'I'm not expecting anything, far as I know. What do you do?'

'Well, before I left this afternoon I was preparing a seminar on the inadequacy of glottochronology as a means of tracing common ancestry among languages.'

'It's inadequate?'

'Not if you want to compare it with cladistics, I suppose. But it hardly competes with the comparative method, wouldn't you agree? I mean, you wouldn't rate Starostin's work against Saussure's. Now would you?'

'Are you taking the mickey?'

'Why would I do that?'

'So what are you? A professor?'

'One day, I hope. For now, I'm a humble lecturer. Shall we rejoin the others?'

'What's Leeds like? As a place to live?'

'I wouldn't know. Terrible, I should think. Living in Leeds would keep me close to my fellow academics, which no one in her senses would want. I have a flat in York. Overlooking the river.' She touches his hand to her lips. 'Where I hope, given your recent performance, you'll want to visit me. Soon.'

'I hope so, too.'

Whatever Ted had told himself about not being spotted when he entered France, the Frogs knew where he'd been and what he'd been doing there. It strengthened their hold. They already had him for multiple murder and now they'd watched him drive through France and England buying and delivering drugs. A phone call from Michel demanded his appearance in Paris.

'How do you think the British Police would react if we gave them the film we have?'

Ted sighs. 'Am I going to face this every time I do something that excites you people? You have something on me. Use it or shut up about it.'

Michel stares at him. Most people, while they're thinking, talk as well. It's as though they can't simply cerebrate in silence; they have to let you know they haven't switched their brains off, and to do that they need to let you hear something coming out of their mouths. Not Michel. He did his thinking and then he delivered the results. Ted met other security officers after Michel and a lot of them were like that.

When he's finished cogitating he makes a short note on the pad in front of him. Then he says, 'I'd like you to talk to someone.'

'Who?'

'She'll tell you who she is.'

She turned out to be a psychiatrist. Or maybe a hypnotist. Because first she hypnotised Ted and then she psychoanalysed him. He didn't know he was being hypnotised and he wasn't very happy when he realised what she'd done. That didn't trouble her.

'If I had not hypnotised you, I would not have found out what I did.'

'Which is?'

'Edouard, it is the psychiatrist who asks the questions and the client who answers them. Not the reverse. That is the trouble with you English. You have no intellectualism. Just like Americans. Everything for you must be practical. If I even mention anomie, do you understand what I mean?'

I shake my head.

'No. And you do not have anomie, my friend.'

'Is that good? Or bad?'

'It means you could not be a spy.'

'Good, then. Because I don't want to be a spy.'

'The Directorate thinks they might wish to use you that way. But I must tell them they cannot. Let us speak of the very first job you carried out for the Directorate.'

'Tractors to Côte d'Ivoire.'

'Côte d'Ivoire, yes. Tractors, no. That ship carried eight tractors, just for the look of the thing. The rest of the hold was filled with guns. Guns our government had officially refused to sell to Côte d'Ivoire. Guns Côte d'Ivoire said it didn't need. You arranged a reward for the buyer equal to four hundred thousand American dollars. You will have been told that some of that money would be used to keep the customs officer and the dock workers quiet?'

'That's what Marie said, yes.'

'People who import guns to kill their compatriots do not waste money on customs officials and stevedores. They have other ways to shut people up. Those men died, Edouard.'

'I'm sorry.'

'You feel responsible?'

'I...No! I arranged the sale of some tractors. If there were guns I knew nothing of them, so why should I feel responsible?'

'Good. Good. Arthur.'

'I don't want to talk about Arthur.'

'Arthur is relevant to the questions the Directorate asked me.'

'You had no right to take me back to that time.'

She smiled, as though the concept of right amused her. Ted had had no experience of hypnosis. He didn't know how the hypnotised person experienced things, or what he could remember afterwards. He was appalled to find that a memory he had thought buried was now once more fresh in his mind.

They don't want to mark his face. That much is clear. At the end of the weekend, Charlie Walton will come back to pick him up and take him home, and they know he won't tell people what they've done. Know because they've done this before. As they tell him. He hadn't understood the meaning of gloat. He does now.

So, because they don't want to mark his face, they take their time about making him undress.

As for what happened next, as Alex said when he went home with Ramina after he'd bankrolled her brothers, we don't need to see it.

The psychiatrist had seen it, though.

'You didn't fight,' she says.

'Didn't I?'

'You were fourteen when that happened. You're twenty-five now. And for eleven years you've wondered, deep inside you, whether the fact that you didn't resist meant that you were gay.'

'Have I?'

'Would you like to know what I think?'

'Is there any way I'm not going to?'

'You're not gay. You were outgunned, and you were a sensible enough boy to know it. Arthur was a monster, physically as well as morally,

and he had the dogs. When he brought them into the kitchen and held them on the leash a foot from you and told you again to take your clothes off he had you beaten and you knew it. That's why he did it. And making you put on the girl's underwear. He was telling you: We're men and we're going to treat you like a girl and you will submit because in our way of living that's how it is between men and girls. Sometimes, the girl's life is ruined. Yours wasn't, because you didn't let it be. Why do you resist the tears?'

Because he was English, and a man. But he kept that to himself.

'Being gay wouldn't be a problem. Being submissive would. You could do the work the Directorate wants you to do as easily whether you loved men or women, but if you gave in to what other people want you'd be useless. You've never wanted to do anything about Arthur?'

'Like what?'

'You have a gun. You've had one for a while.'

'No. No. I've never wanted to do anything about Arthur.'

'Good. You know, we French have given many good things to the world, but it may be in philosophy that we have scored highest. You have read Camus?'

Ted shakes his head.

'Sartre?'

'I'm afraid not.'

'A pity. The Anglo-Saxons believe that suffering justifies redress and sorrow for oneself. What Sartre and Camus told us is that you start from where you start from, that your duty is to fulfil yourself and nothing excuses you from trying. So many of your countrymen would treat Arthur as justification for a lifetime of self-pity. You do not. You are one of us, mon brave.'

Alex is looking upset. 'This was 1971. You were seeing me by then. Why did you never tell me about Arthur?'

'What you didn't know couldn't hurt you. Or me.'

'But I thought you loved me.'

'I did love you.'

'Loving someone means telling them your secrets.'

'For a woman, maybe. Not for a man. And certainly not for me. I had secrets I could never talk about. To you or anyone else.'

'Yes. I'm finding that out.'

In 1971, that sense that the future would be better than the past began to die. Newcastle was put firmly in its place when Londoners were cast as the Geordie villains in *Get Carter*. Elsewhere in Britain British Leyland replaced the successful Morris Minor with the diabolical

Marina, decimal currency took over from the pounds shillings and pence Ted had grown up with and the political elite persuaded the people that the European superstate they were planning to join was an innocent free trade area.

But none of that mattered to Ted, because he was twenty-five, he was playing cricket for a good club and he was in love for the first time since Bella had taken him away from Carol.

That the summer of 1971 was warm and sunny helped both of those things.

It also helped the feeling of being in love to spend so much time in York. The racecourse was almost in the centre of town and provided wonderful walks. The Minster was stunning—one of those churches Betjeman used to define God's essential Englishness to Barabbas. Most of all, though, Alex and Ted loved walking by the river, and talking, and what they did afterwards.

Alex knew Ted was involved with narcotics because that was how they had met. She also knew Ted had other interests that often took him abroad, but she never asked how he came to have so much money. Nor did she want to know where he had learned to do the things they got up to in bed and Ted certainly didn't mention Ramina, or the fact that he still took her to the Negresco every second month on his drug collection trips.

Growing up, Ted had understood that men and women had their defined roles in life. They did different jobs, and it was men's work that was serious. Men were the breadwinners; if women worked, it was either for something called pin money or to fill the time till Mister Right came along. Men did not clean house, cook, wash clothes or dishes or change a baby's nappies. Women did not drive if their man was in the car and nor did they express opinions that clashed with those of the Master of the House.

It was hard to sustain those beliefs in Alex's company. She had a better brain than he did, and it was trained in a way his had never been. She, though, had been brought up with the same ideas about gender roles. She'd ask what Ted thought even when it was clear that she knew more about the subject, and she did not think his place was in the kitchen. That was a problem because he'd learned to cook in Marseille and enjoyed it. If he'd relied on Ramina to feed him he'd have starved, and Alex was little better. In the end they came to an agreement: Ted could cook for Alex as long as he didn't try to wash up afterwards. There were still difficulties because to Ted cooking was part of cherishing someone while to Alex food was fuel and time spent preparing it was time that could have been better employed on something else. When she saw him making mayonnaise she reacted as though he did it to spite her; what was wrong with Heinz Salad Cream? He was learning that relationships did not come without effort and compromise.

Ted was English. Fish had never been a big part of his diet. He started to eat it while he was in Marseille. The Gulf confirmed him as a fish lover.

Qatar became independent in 1971 and Michel's bosses decided that they had business there. According to Michel, that meant Ted had business there, too.

'You had better travel on your British passport. But you will be representing French interests.'

'I've never heard of Qatar. What's there?'

'Conflict. Potentially.'

'Oh. Is it safe?'

'What is "safe", Edouard? Manchester is not safe. London is not safe. Reporters justify their expenses by making you think how brave they are. You go to some place in Africa, the Middle East, forty-nine times out of fifty it's nothing like you've heard. People are supposed to be killing each other for sport and it's just like Monte Carlo.'

'And the fiftieth time?'

'The fiftieth time is worse than anything you could possibly have imagined. Don't think about it.'

'So what am I going to be selling in Qatar?'

Alex says, 'You never seemed to like going to Qatar.'

'It isn't my favourite place. Saudi Arabia with alcohol.'

'Did you know this time what you were selling?' says Dolan.

'There was no need to keep it secret. Qatar had just become independent. They didn't want to be part of Saudi, they didn't want to join Abu Dhabi and the other emirates and they didn't and don't like the Bahrainis who once ruled them. On the other side of the Gulf they could see Iran. Which terrified them. Still does. Then there's the internal threat. There are only two hundred and fifty thousand Qataris and the total population of the place is eight times that. What happens if the Indians rise up? The Bahrainis? The Iraqis? Of course Qatar wanted arms. Who wouldn't in that situation? And they had the money to pay for them.'

Dolan says, 'I don't see why the French needed you, then.'

'They needed me because they were competing with every other arms manufacturing country in the world and I'd shown I could negotiate with greedy people. So much oil and not many locals means there's no one richer than a Qatari and yet the place illustrates a fundamental rule: the more you have, the more you want. And that goes double for the ruling family.'

'Surely the king has all he needs?'

'Not him. His family. Cousins. Nephews. Hangers on. He gives them enough but they want more.'

'You must be an expert on arms by now.'

'I know nothing about arms. The technical boys would go in and show how they met the spec. But so would the Russians, the British, the Americans…when the technical stuff was settled and we needed to spread some money around, that's when they sent for me. What you have to do, you have to see who really is a player and who is trying it on. Any time you want to sell something in the Gulf, you're surrounded by people who have the ear. Every one of them is married to a woman whose brother is the ruler's right-hand man. When the ruler wants to take a piss, this man's cousin holds his dick for him. No one else can open the doors he can. The stories I've been told…it's bullshit. Obviously. Men meet you in expensive hotels, they insist on picking up the tab, they're beautifully manicured, expensive suits, cohibas, you want to go somewhere they'll send their driver with the Lambo or the Ferrari to pick you up, yours for the day. You want a woman? Nice Moroccan girl, more beautiful than you ever dreamed of? Just give him your room number and she'll be there this evening, nine o'clock on the dot, everything paid my friend, you don't so much as need to tip her, a good Moslem girl who won't even raise an eyebrow when she finds out you're not circumcised. And the fact is they haven't a pot to piss in and if they don't persuade you or someone like you to pay them a retainer, and soon, they'll miss a payment, be arrested and simply disappear. But you can never lose sight of the fact that one of these people really is the one who can open the door and your job is to identify him, get close to him, *buy* him.'

'What do you think made you good at that?'

Ted shrugs. 'I can come up with the same theories as you can. What does it matter? I've made a life out of hearing the things people don't say. Looking into their eyes and knowing when they lie and when they tell you the God's own truth. When I was growing up, selling was one career choice I never considered because salespeople have to be extroverts, everyone knows that, and I wasn't one. It's nonsense. The best salespeople are introverts who've learned to present as extroverts. Because if you don't know what's going on in your own head, what hope do you have of understanding what's happening in someone else's?'

'In any case, you did the deal.'

'I did.'

'You made a shitload of money.'

'Guilty.'

'And people who disagreed with the government went on disappearing. And the guns that killed them were your guns.'

Alex says, 'If they hadn't been Ted's they'd have been someone else's,' but the faces of the people in the audience say they aren't persuaded.

1972. Qatar. An exhibition. Outside, the sun bounces off white buildings and white sand in a way that hurts the eyes. In this hall, the aisles between exhibitors' stands are carpeted in blue and the temperature stays at a steady twenty degrees Celsius. On the stands, electronic devices, almost all grey; those that aren't grey are buff.

The products on Ted's stand are computers. Process computers; computers that control the action in a kiln or a mixer that turns out pharmaceuticals. Or control other things. Very versatile, a process computer.

Ted knew no more about computers than he did about arms; he'd been called in at short notice because the man who should have been there had broken his leg in a skiing accident. Or so they told him. 'You won't have to talk about the equipment, Edouard. Just be there in case someone needs to discuss finance.' Who in Qatar would need to talk about money?

Visitors. That's who.

The man tells Ted his name is Pavel and he is from Czechoslovakia. Pavel is sharply dressed. He comes straight to the point. 'Can you sell this computer to Czechoslovakia?'

The price of the computer is sixty thousand dollars, and the wording of his question is significant. Not, "We'd like to buy this computer." "Can you sell this computer to Czechoslovakia?" Because they can't. The computer contains chips and other parts made in the USA, America has a list of countries those things cannot be sold on to and Czechoslovakia is on that list. But no one has told Ted.

Ted says he doesn't see why not and Pavel leaves, promising to return the next day to sign the order. Ted tells one of the salesmen on the stand what he's done and the salesman tells Ted the facts of commercial life. Next day, Pavel comes back and Ted says he's sorry, he can't sell it to them after all. Pavel does not look surprised. He says, 'That's a pity, because we'd be prepared to pay one hundred and twenty thousand dollars for it.' He says this in English, which he is speaking to Ted for the first time. His English is very good. He hands Ted a business card and says, 'A one hundred per cent mark up. Sixty thousand dollars, cash in someone's pocket. Think about it.' Ted starts to say he's sorry, there isn't anything he can do but Pavel says, 'I'll call you,' and walks away. Ted doesn't see how Pavel is going to do that; Ted hasn't given him a card because he doesn't have one and nor has he given his name, but what does it matter? The French have had an opportunity to sell a computer and turned it down. No skin off Ted's nose.

Love. At the time the audience sees on the screen, Ted was in his twenties. He's seventy-three now and he thinks he's begun to work out what love means to him, though he has no idea whether it's the same for others. Why do you look at one woman and think she'd make a good friend, flee from a second but see a third and know you'd like her in your life for ever? What he did know, back then, was that he'd fallen in love with Alex. Whatever that meant.

He was still living near Hexham and she was still in York. He'd driven a hundred miles to pick her up and another forty to Rosedale Abbey. The summer of 1972 was far wetter than 1971 had been but the pub they had booked into did not encourage guests to stay in during the day so they put on their walking boots and waterproofs and headed out onto the moors. "Moor" in North Yorkshire means heather. Miles and miles of it in undulating waves. Lovely when the sun shines, but not so good in the rain so they went back to the pub, checked out and drove to Helmsley where they found a more welcoming hotel.

By the time they'd had lunch the rain had stopped and they walked all afternoon, arriving back at the hotel in time to get into the large bath together. While soaping each other, Ted asked the only question that seemed to make sense: Would she marry him?

Yes, she said. She would. She might be crazy, but she would. There was a condition. He had to give up dealing. She wasn't going to marry a man who might be arrested at any time for importing drugs. They talked it over, at dinner and later in bed, and came to an agreement. Even when he was out of the drugs business, HB and Jeremy would still need their supplies. Ted would make one more trip to Marseille and this time he would buy enough to keep them going for a year. That would be the end of his involvement.

He knew that what he had with Ramina must also end. He was in love with Alex and they were going to marry. There could be no other women. Whatever else love might mean, it meant that. He told Alex about Bella, and that they had planned to marry, and that she had died. He didn't mention Ramina.

Alex's closest friends from school — Claire; Elyse; Marianne — were scattered now around the world. As an academic, she had Arpanet; none of the others did, and there was as yet no internet. When she wanted to communicate with them, she wrote.

Elyse was married to a French diplomat. Still junior himself, he was the third generation of a diplomatic family and he knew who to speak to. The people now at the heart of government were the men he had called

Uncle as a child. When Elyse, glowing with delight, looked up from her Paris breakfast to tell him that they would be invited to a wedding, that bride and groom were English, that the groom was a stockbroker but had lived in Marseille and had connections helping French companies to sell their goods abroad, Elyse's husband took careful note of Ted Bailey's name.

Pavel had said he would call. In fact, he turned up at the cottage near Hexham. 'So,' he said. 'Did you think it over?'

Ted hadn't given it a moment's thought. If Pavel couldn't buy the computer, he couldn't buy it. Pavel explained how these things were done.

Dolan says, 'You're skating over things a bit fast here. Let's fill in the gaps. With the help of this Czech, you set up a company to buy and sell computers. Buy them in France, at least at first and until you expanded, and sell them in countries that weren't allowed to buy them.'

'Yes. That's what I did.'

'You were breaking the law.'

'Oh, for fuck's sake. Last year I bought some thermoplastic for road marking and sold it to Iran. Iranians die in road accidents just like anyone else, but they're embargoed. The means to prevent people from dying exist, but America says it's illegal to supply them. Some laws are made to be broken.'

Dolan is enjoying himself. 'So you're a good Samaritan? A Robin Hood? You go through the world doing good?'

'I go through the world making money. It isn't a crime. Whatever you may think.'

Alex sighs. 'Barry, it isn't my job to help you, but before you go too far down a dead end can I point something out to you? Ted is on trial for his everlasting life. He won't lose it because he broke a human law. Men's laws have changed year by year since we came out of the trees. God's haven't.'

She takes the remote from Dolan's hands and Dolan does not resist. She points it at the screen, runs a finger down the buttons, chooses one. Onto the screen comes a large house, viewed from an equally large garden. A veranda with a wrought iron railing stretches all the way round the ground floor.

'For those who like to know where and when,' she says, 'the month is September, the year is nineteen seventy-two and the place is York. Ted is twenty-six and so am I. This house is eighty years old, built by a husband and wife who had retired to England in the eighteen nineties after thirty years in Malaya. They built it to remind them of the place where they'd buried all three of their children and they called it Kota Baru. Within a year of moving in, they were both dead, too. Ted and I knew nothing of that and we expected this house, which by the time we bought it had changed its name to Number Three, to be the place where we would lead long and happy lives. As it turned out, that was not going to happen.

'Ted paid cash for the house but put it in my name. He was the one with the money and the house was to be my insurance. We were going to have what in those days was called a trial marriage. We'd live together, doing everything married men and women did except have children so that we'd know whether marriage worked for us. The Pill had made that possible. You never hear about trial marriages anymore, but our parents' generation thought we were immoral. Who cared what they thought?

'Ted bought a partnership in my father's firm. He was a stockbroker now, the most respectable occupation he's ever had, before or since, but he still worked for the French and he was building his illegal trading company. He didn't tell me about those things and I didn't ask. We thought we'd probably marry the following June, but I wasn't going to commit to anything until he'd been to Marseille and ended his involvement with drugs. There was something else he intended to end while he was there. I knew nothing about that, either.'

She presses another button and the screen changes. 'Marseille. November first, nineteen seventy-two.' Then she says, 'Ted?'

<u>*Chapter 17*</u>

Ted has seen Ramina in many moods, but never one like this. She paces the floor, forwards and back, eyes rolling, hands reaching out, fingers fluttering. Her pale, coffee-coloured skin is mottled and patched with red.

'Why did you tell me this?'

'I thought you should know.'

'Know? You thought I should know you had found another woman?'

'Yes.'

'I did know. Imbecile. How could I not know? But why did you have to tell me?'

'How long have you...'

'When you came back, that first time. What do you think? I am so stupid I cannot tell when the man I have loved to distraction has met someone else?'

'I'm sorry. But then why...'

'Because having some of you was better than having none,' she screams. *'I'd found out what it was to live without you. You were back. If I had to share you, I'd share you. If she had most, I'd let that be.'* She turns away, her voice dropping to a whisper. *'Every three months, I see you for five days. In a whole year, less than three weeks. And now you come and you bring me here.'* She stabs at the Negresco's luxury

drapes. 'You bring me here and you tell me all my sacrifice is not enough. I am not even to share you. You will go away and I will never see you again.'

'It's best, Ramina.'

'Best! Best for who? Not best for me, Teddie. Don't do this, Teddie, my sweet love. I have shared you with another woman. I will share you still. Please don't leave me. Please.'

Ted turns away. 'I'm sorry.'

'But why, Teddie? Why?'

'Because I intend to marry and I don't want to be unfaithful to my wife.'

'Is she pregnant?'

'No, Ramina. She isn't pregnant.'

'Then why? Why, Teddie? What is so suddenly different?'

He knows as he answers that what he says is not enough.

Dolan tilts his head. Listening to his producer on his little earphone, no doubt. He says, 'How exactly did Ted dumping Ramina get you killed, Alex?'

'Oh. Well, I didn't know this then, of course, and I don't think he did, either. Poor Ted. You were really rattled when the police pumped you. Weren't you? You knew you must be involved, but you didn't know how.'

'Still don't, really,' Ted says.

'Would you like me to tell you? When you saw how Ramina reacted,' she says, 'you knew you couldn't go back there. That part of your life was over. But you still needed the drugs. And Ramina helped you. Didn't that make you suspicious?'

'I thought she'd accepted the inevitable.'

'For a man who's had so many women, you're a hell of a bad judge of them, you know that?' To Dolan she says, 'They go back to Marseille and Ramina, all bright and bubbly and accepting, tells Pierre what's happened. And Pierre agrees Ted really can't keep going back, rubbing his sister's nose in her shame, but Ramina says she still loves him and he needs a whole year's supply to take back with him, so he has time to sort out new arrangements. She knows that'll take a few days to pull together, which gives her time for what she means to do.

'So Pierre's out there collecting the gear for his old English buddy, and his old English buddy is visiting his old Marseille haunts.'

'Breakfast of champions?' asks Dolan.

'Yes, I stood at the zinc a couple of times.'

Alex says, 'Pierre was doing his thing, and Ted was doing his. Which left Ramina free to do hers.'

'And that was?'

'Ted had killed Mahmoud. But there's always someone who wants to be the new Mahmoud. I don't know his name. Call him Mahmoud Two. So Ramina goes to see him. She'll give him Pierre and Jean, her brothers who care more about this Englishman who's destroyed her life than they do about her. She'll tell him where they keep their stash, and when the next shipment is in so it'll be full. He can turn up, find it, and then he's got the pair of them exactly where he wants them. He can start exacting tribute, just like Mahmoud used to. And she tells him what she wants in return.'

'Which was?' Dolan says again.

'A man to do her bidding. An Arab Frenchman with a passport and a criminal background, something hanging over him that Mahmoud Two can use as a lever. He has to have a car, or know how to steal one. He has to be violent. Oh, and he has to be deniable if it all goes wrong.'

'And he found one for her?'

'No shortage of people like that in Marseille,' says Ted.

Dolan asks, 'Did you know about this?'

'I'd guessed the outline, but I've never known the details.'

'Come on, Ted. Not a word is said in this room that didn't come out of your head. We've been through this.'

'Anyway,' says Alex, 'this guy, who by the way is to know nothing about Ramina, what he has to do is follow Ted home, identify the woman who's taken him from Ramina and ease her passage into the darkness. I really think the poor cow thought Ted would go back to her once I was out of the way.'

1972. An apartment in Paris. Elyse and her husband.

'We will not be able to attend the wedding.'

Elyse looks at her husband in horror. 'I think you mean that you will not be able to attend the wedding. My best friend from school is to marry and, believe me, I shall be there.'

'I shall forbid it.'

'I shall ignore you.'

And then the stilted formality breaks up as both are convulsed with laughter.

'Listen to us,' he says. 'We will not be able to attend the wedding. I shall forbid it. I sound like my great grandmother when she learned that her daughter Hortense had been sporting with a coachman.'

'Really?' Elyse's eyes shone. 'I never heard of this Hortense.'

'They married her off to an army man. He had the grace to die in battle, bravely and without purpose. Hortense raised the child in seclusion in the Vosges. They sent the coachman there with her. To transport her, you know. When she required it.'

'And was she transported?'

'It would seem so. She had three more children and he was the only man on the scene. Seriously, darling, there are things you should know about this man your friend Alex has found. He is not of our class. He fathered an illegitimate child on a shop girl. And he was engaged before, but the girl died.'

Elyse raised her hands to her mouth. 'But not at his hands?'

'I have no idea. It was a car crash, and a car crash can mean anything. But we know that in Marseille he shot three people, one of them a policeman, to further his drug dealing.'

'If you know it, why was he not brought to justice?'

'The people he killed were of no account. Including the policeman. And the Directorate used his guilt to recruit him as a freelance. A very well paid freelance. And they have fooled him, or at least they believe he was fooled, into selling things to people who should not be allowed to buy them.'

'How did they do that?'

'They sent one of their own, masquerading as a Czech. Now your best friend's fiancé has a company in the Dutch Antilles that he believes was set up by the Czechs but in fact it was our people.'

'You do not like dealing with the Directorate, do you?'

'There is nothing to like. And I will be forced to have more dealings with them when they discover we are at his wedding.'

'But we will go.'

'Of course we will go.'

Alex's eyes have filled with tears. Ted places his hand on her arm but she shakes it off. 'I'd known Elyse since we were both new girls at the same school miles away from home. She was my best friend. She was going to be my maid of honour but that didn't happen because I was dead before the wedding could take place. God, I wish the dead could cry. Carol was right; you've wrecked people's lives and you don't know you've done it. I love you, Ted, but I wish I'd never set eyes on you.' She walks to the back of the stage, away from the audience, away from Dolan, away from Ted. She stares at the wall. Then she comes back. 'I never saw her again.'

'I'm sorry, Alex.'

'Yes, Ted. I know you're sorry. Sometimes sorry isn't enough.' She looks at Dolan. 'Press the button. Let's get on, for God's sake.'

Fame is such a fleeting thing. In his heyday, there can't have been anyone in Britain who wouldn't recognise the man who has appeared on the screen, and now Ted can't even remember his name. He was a newsreader—Ted knows that—but maybe he only knows it because that's what he's doing. He's reading the news. On a screen behind him, a farmer has left his car's engine running while he relieves himself by the side of the road. He looks up to see the car being driven off. He runs, then walks as fast as he can, then hobbles into Chapel Haddesley, where he calls the police.

The screen changes from fields to city streets. 'When the stolen car is stopped on the outskirts of Nottingham, the driver is seen to be drenched in blood.'

A man steps out of the car carrying an old khaki rucksack from which he takes a revolver and shoots one of the two policemen dead. Then he puts a bullet into the hip of the second. He gets back into his car and drives off without haste. Close up on a phone box in which an appalled passer-by calls the police and tells them what has happened.

'A police helicopter soon picks up the stolen car, which is then shadowed as it heads south. It runs out of petrol near Leicester.

'The killer has no idea that British police aren't armed. He would laugh at such a concept. He assumes that British police and Marseille police have the same motivations and the same ethical standards. He isn't going to be taken back to Marseille to face the rage of Mahmoud Two, and nor is he going to allow the British police to capture him after he has shot two of their colleagues. In his revolver he has four more bullets.'

The man's gun blazes away three times at the ring of police cars that fence him in. He stands up and steps forward, offering himself as an unmissable target. With only one bullet left and

*no attempt to put him out of his misery, he has
no choice. He puts the gun in his mouth, pushes
it as far in as he can and pulls the trigger.*

'The blood on the dead Frenchman's clothes, hands
and face belongs to the same group as Alex's. His
fingerprints are on the handle of the knife that killed
her.'

The newsreader disappears along with his screen, to be
replaced by a shot of Ted answering the front door. A
uniformed policeman is telling him that Detective
Inspector Saville and Detective Sergeant Hedley want to
see him. He rings Tony Webb who says he doesn't do
criminal cases but he'll have a man called Sean Jarvis
meet Ted at the station. 'He has some way to travel.
Don't say a word till he gets there.'

Criminal cases?

*Jarvis lets Hedley know he can't get to York till
morning. When it becomes clear that he won't
speak in his absence, Ted is driven home and
told to be back the next morning at nine. Jarvis
drives him there. 'Some of the questions they
ask will have answers they can check. And
some will have answers they already know.
Don't lie, or they'll find out and they'll want to
know why.'*

'Suppose I can't answer truthfully?'

'Look at me and I'll intervene.'

'What if you can't?'

'Just hope that doesn't happen. Another thing. If you're talking and I come straight up in my chair, that means I want you to stop. Immediately. And now I suggest you tell me all the stuff you won't want to tell them. Don't worry. This conversation is privileged.'

Saville is a firmly upholstered man in a well-fitting grey suit whose eyes convey friendly calm. 'Pleasure to meet you,' he says. 'I saw you carry your bat at Scarborough last year. What was it you got? Hundred and three?'

'Hundred and eight. I'd offer you an autograph but I don't want it turning up at the bottom of a statement.'

Saville and Hedley laugh as though this is the funniest thing they've ever heard. 'Marseille,' says Saville without further preamble.

'Yes?'

'How well do you know it?'

'I lived there.'

'How did that come about?'

'A woman I was engaged to died in a car crash. I didn't want to stay in England after that. I went to France, drifted, ended up in Marseille. Liked it, so I stayed.'

'For long?'

'Quite a while, yes.'

'What did you live on while you were there?'

Ted glances towards Jarvis.

'Inspector,' says Jarvis. 'I've assumed we're here to talk about the death of Alexandra Hughes?'

'Among other things, yes.'

'How does knowing what my client lived on in Marseille advance that inquiry?'

'Just looking for the background, sir. Of course, if Mister Bailey doesn't want to answer, he doesn't have to. At this stage, anyway.'

'Mister Bailey,' says Jarvis, 'is worried that what he says might incriminate him with the French tax authorities.'

Saville smiles. 'And how might that happen?'

'It's my understanding,' says Jarvis, 'and Mister Bailey will correct me if this is wrong, but it's my understanding that Mister Bailey supported himself by teaching English to French people.'

The smile now covers the whole of Saville's face. 'Is that so, sir?'

'As you will understand,' says Jarvis, 'an itinerant English teacher in France doesn't earn a lot of money.'

'About enough to cover my rent,' Ted says. 'And enough food to stay alive on.'

'Not enough spare cash to trouble the tax man with,' says Jarvis. 'I'm sure you understand that.'

'Of course,' says Saville. 'Not enough spare cash for a lot of things. Not enough to travel down the Riviera to Nice, for example. Not enough to stay in the Negresco. You have our sympathy, Mister Bailey. A copper's salary certainly wouldn't run to a place like that, either. Would it, Sergeant?'

Ted's whole life was unravelling in front of him. Jarvis stepped smoothly into the breach.

'Ah, the Negresco. You've learned my client's secret.'

'Secret? And what would that be?'

'Mister Bailey is a man attractive to women, Inspector.'

'Is that so?'

'It is. And that is no crime, if I may say so.'

Saville's huge smile says he is enjoying this immensely. 'And some of these women are rich, Mister Jarvis? Is that what you are going to tell me?'

'Indeed. One of the people to whom my client taught English was the wife...the very lonely, neglected wife, if I may say so...of an extremely wealthy man.'

'And it was she who paid for the Negresco.'

'Just so, Inspector. She paid for the Negresco, she paid for my client's expensive clothes and she made him a gift of fifty thousand pounds when he left France.'

'A very generous mistress indeed. You must have something very special to offer the ladies, Mister Bailey. May we have this kind benefactress's name?'

'No,' says Jarvis, 'you may not. She is a married woman, as I have told you. Mister Bailey will not divulge her identity, under any circumstances.'

Hedley frowns, but Saville throws back his head and roars with laughter. 'Mister Bailey's discretion does him great credit. And you, Mister Jarvis, have helpfully answered in advance some further questions we might have had. Like: where did he get the money to buy his house and his partnership?'

'I'm pleased to have been of service. May I take it we can go now?'

'Perhaps not just yet. I said you had answered some of our questions, not all. Mister Bailey, tell us about Ramina.'

Ted's head rolls on his neck. How much more of this? 'Ramina?'

'Ramina. Surely you haven't forgotten her already?'

'No. No, of course. Ramina.' He looks helplessly at Jarvis, who merely nods encouragement. *'Ramina. Ramina was the woman I lived with. In Marseille.'*

'I see. Didn't she mind your little trips to Nice with your rich mistress?'

'I...no.'

'Indeed, she made some of those trips with you herself. Is that not so?'

'Yes.'

'What did Ramina do for a living?'

'Ramina?'

'Ramina. How did she support herself?'

'She...she was a prostitute.'

Saville's eyes go mockingly big. 'A prostitute! She had sex with men for money?'

'I believe that's what a prostitute does, yes.'

'And did she give that money to you?'

'Are we trying for living on immoral earnings now?' asks Jarvis.

'Is your client guilty of that?'

'If so, he is guilty only in France.'

Ted says, 'Ramina was a traditional sort of woman.'

'Yes?'

'She had some old-fashioned ideas. I was her man, so I should have the money she earned.'

Sergeant Hedley speaks for the first time. 'How about her brothers? What did they do for a living?'

'I really have no idea.'

'No? No idea at all?'

'That's what he said,' says Jarvis.

'When did you last have sex with Ramina?' asks Saville.

'Eh? With Ramina?'

'With Ramina. How many women have you been having sex with?'

Jarvis says, 'That was uncalled for, Inspector.'

'Nevertheless, I'd like an answer. Mister Bailey?'

'About three weeks ago.'

'In Marseille?'

'In Nice.'

'What were you doing there?'

'Seeing Ramina.'

'For sex.'

'No. Yes. But mostly to tell her it was over between us.'

'Really?'

Hedley says, 'Did you tell her before you had sex? After? Or during?'

'Really, Sergeant...' says Jarvis.

Ted says, 'It doesn't matter. I picked her up in Marseille, we drove to Nice, booked in at the Negresco. We had dinner, then went to our room. Where we made love. Then I told her it was the last time.'

'What had brought you to that decision?' asks Saville.

'I had become engaged. To Alex Hughes. I didn't want to be unfaithful.'

They look as though they are weighing this, though what is actually going on behind their coppers' eyes Ted can't tell. Hedley says. 'When you broke it off with Ramina, how did she take it?'

'Sweetness and light.'

'Really?' says Saville. 'Of course, we can't check that.' He leans forward and stares hard at Ted. 'Not with her being dead.'

Ted stares unseeing at the two policemen. His voice when he speaks is an almost silent croak. 'What do you mean, dead?'

Hedley says, 'According to the Marseille police, she was beaten to death by her two brothers.'

'But why?'

Hedley shrugs. 'The French gendarmes don't know. They don't seem to care very much, either.'

'Of course. Why would they bother themselves about a couple of Arab drug dealers and their prostitute sister?'

Jarvis comes upright in his chair and Ted realises what he has said.

'So,' says Hedley. 'You did know how her brothers earned their living.'

Jarvis says, 'I really think my client needs a break.'

'Not yet,' says Saville. 'You see, Mister Bailey, how this might look to us? You are having sex with two women. Now both of them are dead. One killed by a man who came from Marseille on the same ferry as you.'

'You can't possibly know that.'

'We most certainly do know that. And the other killed by two men with whom you had a business relationship.'

Jarvis holds up his hand. 'No such relationship has even been hinted at, let alone proved. Any accusation of such a relationship is grotesquely false and will be strenuously denied. Mister Bailey will answer no further questions.'

'And then there's the drugs,' says Hedley. 'There are allegations that drugs have been consumed at customer events held by the firm in which you are a partner. Did you supply those drugs?'

'Mister Bailey will answer no further questions,' says Jarvis. 'If there were drugs at any such function, Mister Bailey knew nothing about them.'

Ted looks at Jarvis. The man is not only relaxed, he is smiling. 'This isn't funny, Sean.'

'It is to me,' says Jarvis. 'I appreciate you've never been questioned by the police before. You'll probably never be questioned by the police again. So you don't need to know what tricks they get up to. But I do. For the record, and for the benefit of these two officers as well as you, it is clear that they have no evidence that any drugs have been supplied to anyone, and so no suspicion can fall on you.'

'Evidence has been laid before us,' began Hedley.

'No, Sergeant. Rumours and tittle-tattle have reached your ears and you wish to turn those into evidence. A court would see your vengeful spirit for what it is, should my client ever find himself in front of one. Which he won't.

'Second, Ted, no evidence has been produced that you had any relationship, business or *otherwise, with the brothers of the dead French woman.*

'And, third, the fact that Alex Hughes's killer came to Britain on the same ferry as you is the most tenuous link to a murder I've ever heard. I wonder how many other people travelled on the same boat? Did anyone see you speak to this man? No. Is there any evidence you even knew he was there? It would almost be worth encouraging the police to charge you just to see what the kind of barrister your money would command would do to such a piffling case in court. But they're not going to charge you, because they know who killed Alex, and you're not going to answer any more questions, so we may as well leave now.' He stood up. 'I take it you have no objection, Inspector?'

Saville laughs. 'None at all, Mister Jarvis. We may need to talk to Mister Bailey again.'

'You have only to call me.'

Hedley walks out of the police station with us. On the steps outside he asks, 'How well do you know Roy Meredith?'

'I've never heard of him.'

'You work with him,' says Hedley. 'He does your research. Supposedly.'

'You mean Aitch? Aitch Bee? Is that his name?'

'You were at school with him, weren't you? You must have known his name.'

Jarvis intervenes. 'If you know Ted was at school with this man, and you know they work together, you know how well Ted knows him. What's the point of the question?'

Hedley goes on talking to Ted. 'His father has a criminal record as long as your arm. He's in prison right now as it happens. Due out in a few weeks, I do believe.'

'I knew he'd been inside.'

Hedley says, 'It's the drugs. They must have come from somewhere. If not from Ramina's brothers by way of you, then maybe Meredith can help me.'

'So ask him,' says Jarvis. 'No, Ted, say nothing. Sergeant, this is disgraceful. Mister Bailey will not say another word and, if you don't want to find yourself in trouble, I suggest you follow his example.'

'You all treat it like a game,' Ted said when they were in Jarvis's car.

'Because that's what it is, Ted. A game where the regular players know the rules. People like you wander in from the edge of the court and people like me have to show you how to hold your racquet. People like you who can't afford people like me go to jail. Those who can, don't.'

'I could see you were good.'

'I'm the best. As you will understand when you get my bill.' He touched Ted on the arm. 'Ramina.'

'Yes?'

'You're either a consummate actor or you didn't know she was dead.'

The tears returned. 'I didn't know.'

'I believe you. More to the point, so did they. How are you feeling?'

'Wretched.'

'I'm sorry.'

'What about Aitch?'

'Mister Bee? What about him?'

'Hedley was as good as telling me that if I don't admit supplying drugs to old man Hughes he'll get Aitch for it.'

'Let him try.' Jarvis took a card from his pocket. 'Here. Give your friend this. Tell him to call me if he hears from the police. I take it you'll pay his bill?'

'What? Oh. Yes, of course.'

'He's got nothing to worry about, then. Has he?'

Jeremy Hughes is grey. 'I curse the day I ever met you,' he says. 'That's right. Hang your head. Let it wash over you. Look at your feet and wait for it to pass. That's what children do, Bailey. Are you a child?'

'I don't really know what I can say, Jeremy.'

'Do you take no responsibility?'

'Do you?'

Hughes steps closer. 'What did you say?'

'You wanted drugs. You only hired Aitch in the first place because you thought he'd get you some. He couldn't. I did, and you were like a dog with two dicks. This is where it's led.'

'You are despicable.'

'What else did he say?' asks HB.

'He's selling the firm. Says he has no appetite for it anymore. He's staying on, though. There's no room for me. He wanted me to resign. I told him the new owners can buy me out. My initial stake plus fifty per cent.'

'Who are they, do you know?'

'Some London firm. It's the accounts they're after. London's taking over. They reckon there'll be no brokers here in five years.'

'He fired me. Told me to take him to court if I had the guts.'

'Another firm would give you a job.'

'I don't think so.'

'You're through with stockbroking?'

'I think stockbroking's through with me. Hughes will see to that.'

'So what will you do?'

'I'll find something. The old man's due out soon. I'll probably end up in the family business after all. What about you?'

The room has disappeared. The stage, the camera, the screen – all gone. Alex, Dolan, the audience – vanished with the props. Darkness is everywhere and yet there is light. Someone is talking to Ted but Ted can't make out the words and can't see the person. Is this death? The finality of his last moments?

Something is materialising but he doesn't understand how. And it isn't something; as the mist clears and the shapes swirling before him begin to coalesce, it's a person. Someone instead of something.

And then whoever it is fades back into nothingness as the room comes back into focus. Alex and Dolan and the audience are there; the stage is there; the cameraman switches from Dolan to Alex and back again. Alex is speaking and you can hear every word because the whole room is focused on what she's saying. Ted understands why when he realises she's talking about a subject the whole world cares about. Heaven. She's talking about Heaven. 'It isn't like that,' she's saying. 'You can walk for miles without seeing anyone.'

'Walk?' says a querulous old man in a white jacket who looks like Mister Whippy. 'You said the dead have no bodies. How can you walk without legs?'

Alex covers her irritation, though Ted can see it all right. 'Okay, so walk was the wrong word. But you do move. Seem to move. Through space.'

'And you say this space is empty?'

'In the sense that there aren't many people in it, yes. Ah, Ted. You're back with us.'

'Never mind him,' says a plump woman in unsuitable pink that matches what the sun has done to her face. 'We've had enough of this man's philandering. This space that there aren't many people in. What's it *like?*'

'It's not like anything. Just before I was sent here I was in a room, a meeting room with a big table and chairs but usually it's empty space. Even that isn't true because you can't call a garden empty space and there's grass there and it stays tidy although nobody cuts it and there are flowers and bushes and trees and the leaves never drop and the flowers are always at their peak and there is the song of birds although you never actually see a bird. It's full of light, all the time. It's blue, all the time. Robin's egg blue. And yet it's also white.'

'And your loved ones,' says another woman. What is it about false teeth? They've been able to make good ones, natural looking ones, for more than forty years to Ted's certain knowledge because his father had some. And yet people persist with artificial choppers that anyone can see are man-made the moment they open their mouths. Why? This woman is expensively dressed, clearly not short of money, she wears glasses that have everything. Tinted varifocals, lovely thin lenses, polarised. She didn't get those for a penny under five hundred quid and she'll change them after a year, like as not, while her teeth – which are permanent, as such things go – look like a row of identical plastic knobs. 'You do meet your loved ones when you pass over?' she wants to know. 'They are there waiting for you?'

'I've never met a single person I knew in this life,' Alex says.

The pink woman clearly finds that answer unsatisfactory.

'And I'm not sure how happy I am,' says Alex, 'with that expression, "Pass over." I experienced it as going through the darkness.'

The pink woman mutters something to her neighbour. 'I've been to séances,' she says. 'I've talked to my late mother. She told me the first thing that happened when she passed over was that her mother and father were there waiting for her.'

'I don't know who you talked to,' says Alex, 'but I promise you it was not your mother.'

The pink woman is going to cry. Mister Whippy shouts out, 'Have a bit of sense, woman. When you're dead, you're dead. There is no life ever after. There's only here and now.'

Now the pink woman really is crying. She points a trembling hand at Alex. 'So where did she come from, then? Eh? Answer me that. Where did she come from?'

Another woman has her hand up. 'Hymns,' she says.

'What about them?' asks Alex.

'You spend all day in almost unendurable light which is the presence of God, singing unending hymns of praise.'

'Not me,' says Alex. 'I didn't sing hymns when I was alive and I don't sing hymns now I'm dead. And there are as many Jews and Moslems there as there are Christians. Do you really expect them to be singing *Onward, Christian Soldier?*'

'Jews and Moslems?' asks a voice. 'In Heaven? That's ridiculous.'

'It's how it is. And if I've been passing my time in the presence of God, I haven't noticed it. Not that time exists where I am.'

Mister Whippy is delighted. 'Silly cow,' he shouts. 'Where would be the room for all those dead people? Where would they all go?'

'She's obviously a charlatan,' says the hymn woman. 'She's no more dead than I am.'

'So,' Dolan says. 'Since we're clearly not going to agree on what happens in the land of the dead, perhaps we can come back to someone who is still alive. However barely.'

'That,' Ted says, 'or I'll send this lot away and get a new audience.'

'No point staying here anyway,' says the hymn woman. 'Charlatans and pornographers.' It isn't clear who she means by the last, but she's making her determined way to the door so they're not going to find out.

'Where were we?' asks Dolan. 'Ah, yes. Aitch wanted to know what your plans were. Presumably the French had something to say about that?'

1972. Elyse's apartment in Paris. Elyse's husband says, 'I have done what I can. Even to get this far, I had to call in favours. Alex died because of this man's history. She is not the first he has on his conscience.'

'And he is to get away with it?'

'I told you; I have done what I can. His French passport has been taken from him. He has been

told we will never use him again. The Directorate knows that if they do, and I find out, the Press will learn some things that will end senior careers.'

'You said he had murdered a gendarme. He cannot be prosecuted for that?'

'I do not say that he cannot be. But he will not be.'

'Huh.'

Dolan says, 'Did you know before then that the Frogs and not the Czechs had set up your company?'

'No. It came as a shock.'

'So that was the end of your illegal trading career?'

'Why should it have been? I'd been introduced to a nice way to make money, I already had some contacts and I knew the kind of thing people wanted to buy. And the French hadn't cut me off entirely, whatever Elyse's husband might think. Setting up a new company to do what I wanted to do was easy enough.'

'But not in this country.'

'Of course not.'

<u>*Chapter 19*</u>

1972. Michel visits Ted in York.

'Spain?'

'Why not? You have to go somewhere. It's sunny. You'll soon pick the language up.'

'Do they play cricket there?'

'How should I know?'

So Ted went to Marbella. He liked it there. It wasn't what it would become. He bought a villa with a pool and the sort of garden that can survive long periods of drought. He hired a local man, thin to the point of gauntness with a tanned brown face and a cloth cap forever on his head, to keep the garden in check and the pool clean, and a plump local woman, Marianela, to clean the house and wash his clothes. Cooking he did himself. The staff lived out.

He enrolled in Spanish lessons. He joined a golf club and took lessons from the pro. He also started to drink.

Dolan says, 'Before you went to Marbella, you'd been a social drinker. Nothing more. And now you were putting it away on a big scale.'

'It took a while, but the day would come when I'd realise heavy drinking is something I only do when I'm unhappy.'

'Most people would think you'd given other people more to be unhappy about than you had.'

'My past was catching up with me. I was realising how great the gap was between how I thought of myself and the life I was really living. I drank to dull the awareness. Scotch, brandy, other things. Wine. Too much of all of them.'

'And you met Sarah.'

'I'd noticed her before, but she'd had that taken look.'

The street outside a restaurant in Marbella. Ted is about to enter when his arm is held by a woman. Her nose and eyes are reddened by weeping, though he still finds her attractive. Slim, but with curves, so what Ted sees as slimness is in fact flat-bellied fitness. Smartly dressed. Carefully tended hair that really could be auburn, though Ted thinks it's probably dyed. He says, 'You're one of the owners, aren't you?'

'I was. I should be. Those bastards...'

The other owner, who Ted had always thought was her boyfriend, appears in the doorway. 'Is this woman bothering you? You want me to call the police?'

'I don't need any help from the police, thank you. Or you.'

Ted gives him the look he'd perfected in Marseille and, whatever he was thinking of doing, the man changes his mind.

'I don't want her in here. She's a trouble-
maker.'

'You want to go in?'

'I'd rather go somewhere else.'

'Okay. You choose.'

'I haven't got any money.' She points at the
boyfriend, already retreating into the bar. 'He
took it all. Him and his Spanish whore.'

'That's okay. I can stand you a drink.'

'I really need something to eat. Please.'

'Sure. Why not?'

As they turn away, a bag is flung from the door.
Sarah picks it up. Ted takes it from her.
'Please. Let me.'

She leads the way to a seafood restaurant. 'Is
this okay? It isn't expensive.'

'It'll be fine.'

The waiter brings aioli and bread and a bottle
of tinto. Ted lights a cigarette, pours them both
a glass of wine and picks up the menu.

Sarah says, 'Will you choose for me?'

'You afraid of ordering something too pricey?'

She nods, blushing.

'The money's not a problem.' He holds out his
hand. 'Ted Bailey.'

'I know who you are. Sarah Lavenby. If the money's not a problem, can I have one of those?'

He pushes the cigarettes across the table. 'Course you can. Lobster?'

She laughs, blowing smoke down her nose. 'That's the most expensive thing on the menu.'

'As I said, the money's not a problem. Gazpacho to start. Okay?' He puts down the menu. 'So. Tell me the story. Starting with how you know my name.'

Her head moves rapidly as she speaks. She knows who he is because she's heard customers talk about him. Then she tells her story. She'd come to the coast from Andover three years earlier to run a bar with her boyfriend. Now the bar is thriving but the boyfriend has found a local woman. She had thought the papers she signed at the outset protected her and the ten thousand pounds she put into the venture. That ten thousand was all she had from the breakdown of a previous marriage. She was devastated to learn that she had no way to recover it. The boyfriend gave her a thousand pesetas, worth about seven pounds in Andover money, and told her to make her own way back there. The local woman laughed.

They empty the bottle, Ted drinking most of it, and he orders another. Slowly, the fire of anger in her eyes is replaced by the intensity of interest in the story she is telling and the person she is telling it to. A smile plays on her lips. Then a laugh.

Of course, needs must. Of course it was the bar owner's schtick, seeming to care about the customer because she has to. Probably that's what it was.

Or maybe he'd been without a woman for too long. It didn't matter. One good push and he'd be gone. Sliding once more over infatuation's cliff to the rocky shore below.

When she went to the bathroom, Ted watched her full hips sway invitingly. He liked full hips, loved that swell of the waist into the business end of a woman, that soft flesh that said, "I'm fecund. Make me fruitful." Though, since Alex, he hadn't answered that siren call.

When she comes back she looks into Ted's eyes. 'This is very kind.'

'I'm enjoying it.'

She holds his gaze. 'I haven't anywhere to sleep tonight.'

'You've been here three years? Have you no friends?'

'Bar people don't make friends. Only customers.'

Ted leaves his hand on the table. Hers is very close. He says, 'You can stay with me if you want.'

'Have you got a spare bedroom?'

'I have. But that isn't what I'm offering.'

She's thinking about the offer. But whether on moral or practical grounds, Ted can't tell.

'Is this a one night stand?' she asks. 'Will I be on my way again tomorrow?'

'I don't know. How can I tell? I haven't fucked you yet.'

She puts her hand over her mouth. She starts to laugh. Every time she lifts her eyes to his she goes off on another peal. Ted orders a cognac to round off the meal.

When they get back to Ted's place, Sarah excuses herself to take a shower. Ted stands by the pool and smokes a cigarette. Then he showers in his turn. When he comes out, she's in bed waiting, her long hair unpinned and spread across the pillow.

'I took this side of the bed because you seem to leave your stuff over there. Is that all right?'

Next morning, the sun is streaming through the blinds. Marianela is moving in the next room. Ted gets up, puts on a dressing gown and goes into the kitchen where he turns on the coffee maker and lights the first cigarette of the *morning. Marianela doesn't reply to his "Buenos días."*

He finishes the cigarette and takes a mug of coffee to Sarah. She has the sheet pulled right up to her nose, only her eyes and some hair showing above. 'Is she angry?'

'What?'

'The fat woman. The maid. She peeked in here before you got up. Is she angry?'

Ted couldn't answer because Marianela was gone when he got back into the kitchen. That didn't happen immediately because there were things he and Sarah found they both wanted to do in bed and it was eleven before he was showered and fixing breakfast; not late by Spanish standards but long after his normal time, and he decided to go straight for brunch. A huge omelette with potatoes and chorizo and onion, baked in the oven. Hot chocolate. Bread. A bottle of wine. Another cigarette.

The question of Marianela's possible anger is resolved at half past twelve when her husband comes to the door. He looks embarrassed, explains, knows that things are different in England, wants to be understanding, live and let live, but Marianela is a good Catholic, he believes Ted knows that, she thought him an English gentleman, can't be herself in this different moral setting. If Ted will just let him have the money that's due?

So of course he did, adding some extra for Marianela's faithful service and to make up for her affront. Marianela's husband said thank you and left. He knew Ted would find someone else, but Marianela...Ted understands?

He did.

'What was that about?' asks Sarah.

'You've been here three years and you don't speak Spanish?'

She shrugged. Never needed to. Charlie does. Might have been better if he hadn't, she supposed now. Most of their customers? English, Irish, Australian, American, the odd Kiwi? South Africans? Not many Spanish people. They have their own places.

So what now, she wanted to know.

What indeed?

'I think you should move in.'

'Permanently?'

'Indefinitely.'

'Is that the same thing?'

'Won't it do?'

She lays her hand on his. 'Do I please you?'

'Don't you know you do?'

'I think I do. I need to be sure.'

'You can't be sure. There is no certainty. There are no guarantees.'

'But as far as you can tell?'

'I think you should move in.'

<u>*Chapter 20*</u>

Ted drove to the bar alone. The lunchtime crowd was gathering, but he cornered the local woman. 'I've come for Sarah's things.'

She points with her chin. Outside the back door, scattered across the small courtyard where cats forage among the empties, clothes and handbags and tights of no account among the rubbish. 'Help yourself.'

'Get something to put them in.'

She's ready to argue, looks to Charlie for support, sees she isn't going to get any. She begins to gather boxes. Ted lights a cigarette.

Charlie says, 'Actually, this is a no smoking area. If you wouldn't mind moving over there?'

Ted stays where he is and goes on smoking. He drops ash on the clean floor.

The local woman has collected enough boxes. 'Fill them. Carefully.'

The local woman is swearing under her breath. Charlie looks at Ted's car parked on the pavement, right in front of the door, so close people have difficulty entering. He sees more than one couple approach the door, size up the situation, then move off to find somewhere more welcoming. Charlie says, 'Nice car. You must have a good thing going.'

'I do all right.' To the woman he says, 'The boot's open. Put them inside.' The woman's rage is flaming, all of it directed at Charlie. 'My latest investment is this place.'

'What?'

'I've bought Sarah's stake. I'm selling it back to you. Twenty thousand pounds.'

'You're out of your mind.'

'The price goes up a thousand a day.' He drops his cigarette into a bowl and lights another as Charlie rushes to scoop the burning fragment from among the highly flammable dried flowers. 'Or some of my friends could drop by? Then we'd both be out of luck.'

'Do you have any idea how many protection men there are on this coast?'

Ted puts his face right into Charlie's. 'They're all retired. I'm not. Twenty thousand. Today. Or take the consequences.'

'Look. Come on. I haven't got that kind of cash.'

'Raise it. Do you have any idea how many money lenders there are on this coast? And I want it in cash. No cheques.'

'You can go to hell.'

'Okay. We'll do it your way.' He looks round the bar. 'Pity.'

Ted called Michel. When Charlie came downstairs next morning to open up he found an enormous jerry can full of petrol standing in the middle of the bar. Attached to it was a single match and a note saying, in English, "Next Time."

At lunchtime, Ted drives Sarah to the bar. The local woman tries to bar their entrance but desists at a word from Charlie.

'What's the paella like here?'

Sarah says, 'You're better with British standbys.'

Charlie comes to the table with a canvas bag. 'I've got your money.'

'Give it to Sarah. I take it the extra thousand is in there?'

'It's in there.'

'Good boy. Actually, British standbys aren't what I fancy. Shall we eat somewhere else?'

We're back in the car and Sarah has counted her money twice. 'How did you do that?'

'Appealed to his better nature. Where do you want to eat?'

'Somewhere very expensive.'

'It shall be done.'

Word travelled. Ted got a phone call from some guy he'd never heard of who said his name was Rob Dobell and invited him to a round of golf. Ted met him at the golf club, a fit man in his early sixties with no spare fat and no signs of excess, though Ted couldn't warm to his bright yellow and crimson shirt. 'Call me Rob,' he said. They shook hands like old friends.

'I worked it out the other day,' says Dobell. 'I reckon I must play golf two hundred days a year. Surprised we haven't met before, really,'

'I don't usually play this club.'

'No? You new to golf, Ted? Mind if I give you a bit of advice? Vary your course. Newish player, handicap like yours, you must have talent. Well, you would have. You wouldn't have been the cricketer you were, otherwise. You won't make the most of your ability unless you take on new challenges. I'll be interested to see what you make of this place. You want to try the practice greens, or shall we go straight to the first tee?'

'Why don't we just tee off?'

'Good choice, Ted. It's just a par three, nice short starter hole.'

Dobell watches Ted's drive fly high and straight down the fairway. 'What did you say your handicap was?'

'How did you know about the cricket?'

Dobell places his tee carefully. Without looking at Ted, he says, 'We checked you out. Of course.' A solid swing, head staying down at the finish, a good drive that ends up a bit further on than Ted's. He picks up his tee and they start to walk.

'We?'

'We. Isn't that what you wanted?'

'I'm not sure I follow you, Rob.'

'No? Listen, Ted, what I'm going to do here, I'm going to be absolutely frank with you. If everything I say comes as a surprise, I'm sorry. But I don't think it will and, anyway, I'll still be glad we had this talk. Okay?'

'Sounds good to me, Rob.'

'Okay. That's your ball, isn't it? Let's get up on the green and finish this hole, shall we? Then we can carry on with our chat. And I'm going to give you a tip on this approach shot. You see that sand trap between you and the green?'

'I see it.'

'We're close to the beach here, and there's a wind. Nine times out of ten, the wind is blowing off the sea. Like it is today. What you learn when you play this hole is, if you play to miss the bunker, you end in the rough off to the right. So what you have to do is play right at the bunker, as though you were planning to go into the sand, but give it just enough to get over the top lip. Then you'll find you're nicely placed. Give it too much, you'll overshoot completely* *and you'll really be in trouble. No way out. You got it?'*

He stays to watch Ted follow his instructions to the letter, lifting the ball just enough to clear the sand and carry steadily on to the edge of the green. 'Good, Ted. A little bit more would have got you down in three, but good anyway.'

Dobell takes the hole by a stroke.

'You can think of that hole as a bit symbolic, Ted. Minding the traps, giving it just enough to get what you want but not overdoing things. And the venue, Ted, that was symbolic, too. Nice easy course to start off with. If there's a next time, we'll play somewhere good. But we've started with something easy. Somewhere there's not much chance of going seriously wrong. You know what I mean, Ted?'

'I'm not sure I do, Rob.'

'Well, let's talk it through. I won that hole, Ted. You want to tee off from here? See,' he said as Ted placed his ball, 'what do you reckon you know about me?'

'Nothing. I know nothing about you.'

'Okay, know was the wrong word. What do you think you might be able to guess about me?'

The conversation went on over five holes, after which they chatted golf and generalities till they reached the eighteenth and the bar. It can, though, be boiled down to this:

Dobell says, 'I'm an Englishman living in Spain, don't work, no obvious means of support, play a lot of golf. I've got a nice house and I drive a nice car, except that usually I don't. Usually it's driven by another Englishman, always wears the shades, bit of an affectation that, Ted, the shades, and he looks as though he can handle himself. Anyone looks at Tracey, my wife, she's a good looking girl, Ted, younger than me, hasn't let her figure be pulled out of shape by having children the way my first wife did, anyone thinks about offering her a little cheek, little impertinence, he's going to look at my driver and probably decide to take his impertinence somewhere else. You know what I mean, Ted?

'You ask people what they think about me and they're going to say, "Rob Dobell? Dunno, mate. Minds his own business, stays out of trouble. Retired crook, probably."

'Ask the English police what they think and they're going to tell you, "Rob Dobell was a blagger. Rob the Robber. Robbed banks for a living. Post offices, sometimes. Security vans. Went in mob-handed and tooled up. Wasn't above seeing someone get hurt when he did it, badly hurt sometimes, hurt dead more than

once." That's what the police would tell you, Ted.

'In fact, it's what they told a jury. Twice. And the jury didn't believe them. Either time. Which means I don't have a criminal record but that doesn't stop the police saying nasty things about me and making my life shit when I go home. So I don't go home. Tracey goes back and forth between here and England but me, I never go there. Never.

'There's quite a few people like me here, Ted. Not as many as the Daily Mail likes to claim, but a few. No extradition, see? But I'm sure you know that. We meet sometimes, play golf, have a drink, party in each others' houses. Not eat, Ted. Wives can't cook worth a shit and somehow they always piss the help off. If we want to eat, we go to a restaurant. You've seen us, sometimes, if you've been watching. Sitting there with your Penguin Classic, eating the paella, having a little drink if you don't mind me saying so, but looking around, Ted. Noticing things, I would say.

'And then you pulled your stunt at the Manville. Stupid name for a bar, that, idiot's idea of British class. Manville's more like some dive, cellar of one of those old Victorian four storey jobs down near the Angel, know what I mean? City Road? Spitting distance of Pentonville, which isn't a bad idea at all? And *don't ask what goes on on the top floors. But there it is. And there you are, waving a big flag and shouting "Look at me. I'm a BAD man." So we did look at you.*

'One of us, might be me, might not, has a friendly copper back home who told us some juicy stuff about you. Woman dead in York. Drugs. Sounds interesting. But you didn't kill the woman and the drugs weren't proved. Never went to trial in fact, and if it had it probably wouldn't have been you in the dock. Interesting, Ted, but it could all be genuine or it could be got up for the Press. And for us. There's some stuff about France, but that's all hearsay and suspicion, as far as we can tell.

'Anyway, the jury's out. There's three possible verdicts. One, you're one of us, a straight-up guy and all you were doing was making the twat who'd dumped your new woman pay what he owed her plus a bit more for your trouble. I like that. Shows style. Two, you are *a bad man but you're also a bloody idiot who likes to make a noise. And, three, you're an undercover cop trying to get yourself accepted so you can snuffle out information and send it home.*

'Those are the possibilities, Ted. And someone had to come and meet you to sort out which one is the right, true verdict. And that someone is me. Because it matters, Ted. The sentence for verdict one is, you're made welcome, live here

as long as you like, no one troubles you. The sentence for verdict two is, we ask you to leave Marbella, move west along the coast where they don't mind loudmouths. But the sentence for verdict three, Ted, is death. We haven't done away with the death sentence here. Not among ourselves.'

'So what are you going to do? Set me a test?'

Dobell says, 'You're angry, Ted. Anger isn't good. It clouds your judgement.'

'Angry? You think this is angry? So you have the death sentence. Big fucking deal. I've killed four people. A pimp, a cop and two drug dealers who thought they could take my turf. How many have you done, Rob?'

Dobell holds up his hands. 'Ted. Relax. I'm telling you how it is.'

'Yeah? Well, there's two versions of how it is. Now you know mine. About which I will tell you a little more. Four people are dead at my personal hand. And unlike you I've never been put in front of a jury. I'd see that as a mistake. A confession of failure. Know what I mean, Rob?'

'You didn't think that was risky?' asks Dolan.

'My whole life was risky. If Dobell wanted a fight to the death, he could have one.'

'Interesting, that. You never feared death. And now you're terrified of it. What happened to all that courage? Does age take it away?'

'It isn't death I'm scared of. It's dying. Someone takes a gun and blows your brains out, that's it. Over. The Big Sleep. But that isn't how I'm dying, is it?'

'So what happened? What was the verdict and what was the sentence?'

'I was admitted to the Elect. A straight-up guy. Played golf with some heavy hitters. Sarah and I drank in their homes. They drank in ours. We dined together in restaurants that weren't quite as good as most of the diners thought they were.'

'So Sarah and you really were an item?'

'Oh, yes. Oh, yes.'

'You're going to tell me you loved her?'

'How often do you find love? Real love? I liked being with her. That's enough in my book.'

'And Michel?'

'I made some sales for him. Along with my own business. But he let me go.'

'This was the drink? It had made you too much of a risk?'

'That's what I thought at the time.'

The tall blond foreigner leans across the gap between two tables. In formal, carefully enunciated English he says, 'Would you mind not doing that?'

'Not doing what?'

'Smoking,' says the foreigner. 'The smell is not nice.'

Ted takes the cigar out of his mouth. He puts it back, draws deeply and blows a cloud of smoke in the foreigner's direction. 'You want lebensraum? What am I? The fucking Sudetenland? Fuck off.'

The big blond sighs. 'I am not German. I am Swede.'

'Great. Another country with a fine wartime record. Built great wide roads through your neutral forests so the Krauts could use them for runways.'

'The war is over.'

'The Danes hate you fuckers. You know that?'

'It's been over for nearly forty years. When are you English ever going to let go?'

'Our finest hour, mate.'

Sarah stands up, gathers her bag and her beach towel and her sunglasses. She walks away without a word. Ted draws heavily on the cigar before releasing another cloud of smoke towards the Swede. He lifts one buttock and farts. Loudly.

The Swede rises to his feet and moves to another table at the opposite end of the bar. The young man sharing his table follows him.

'When I first met you,' says Sarah, 'I thought you were a gentleman.'

'Who told you that?'

'Why are you behaving like this?'

'Get off my case, Sarah.' He pulls the cork from a bottle of Armagnac. Sarah takes the bottle out of his hand and replaces the stopper. 'You can't go on drinking like this, Ted. You'll kill yourself.'

He lights a cigarette.

'Weren't you a cricketer?' she says. 'An athlete? Did you smoke then?'

'I need a piss.'

If he's honest with himself, which at that time he was increasingly rarely, his walk to the bathroom was less than steady. He dropped the scarcely smoked cigarette into the pan where it hissed and went out. Sarah hated to find cigarette ends floating there. So did he.

He had to steady himself against the wall while he urinated. He managed to get most of it inside the porcelain.

Ted washes his hands and returns to the kitchen. Sarah has made a pot of tea. She pours a mug for him.

'It's five in the afternoon, Ted.'

'What are you? The Speaking Clock?'

When he woke, the lights were on and he was lying on a lounger by the pool. From inside the house came the smells of cooking. He sat up—slowly, because it hurt to move quickly.

'Sarah, how about this for a deal? I live my life and you live yours?'

'As I said, I want a...'

'You can't divorce someone you've never...'

'You know what I mean, Ted.'

They stare at each other. 'You mean,' Ted says, 'you want a settlement.'

She nods.

'Money.'

'Please.'

'You know your problem, Sarah?'

'I'm a human being, Ted. I'm sure I have many.'

'You want the advantages of being in a relationship without any of the drawbacks.'

She turns and walks into the house. Ted follows. When he reaches the kitchen, Sarah is scraping paella into a pedal bin.

Ted is waiting for Dolan to say something. Ask why he was drinking, was he an alcoholic? That sort of thing.

He doesn't speak.

It takes a while to realise. How long a while is, he couldn't say. Might be seconds, might be days. He's drifting. Everything goes so slowly, takes so long.

But the crucial fact, the bit that matters. They've gone again. Nobody's there except Ted and Tut. He's left his corner now, come out into the open and what Ted sees on his face is greed. He knows what he wants and he thinks it might be getting closer.

The room is dissolving.

Or Ted is.

Everything he's trying to do, say, get said, is becoming an impossible struggle. But he wants to get it done.

That night. Late. Three in the morning sort of late. Ted is propped up on a wall. How he got there, or why, he doesn't know. Perhaps the young woman leaning against him can help.

But he doesn't care enough to ask.

'Have you got any money?' the woman asks.

'Loads of it. Masses. Unbelievable riches.'

'But have you got any here?'

'Oh, here. Dunno.'

He takes the wallet from his pocket and fans it out. The woman takes it and peers inside. 'Do you want me to suck your cock?' she asks.

'How much?'

'You can afford it.'

'Okay, then. Sure. Go ahead.'

The woman takes some banknotes from the wallet. Then she puts two back. She kneels in front of him. 'Do you need to pee, first?'

'What?'

'A pee? Only I met a guy once, as drunk as you are, and he did need one. And he did it in my mouth. Before I could get him hard.'

Ted is laughing. Laughing so hard, tears are rolling down his cheeks. 'Oh, God. Oh, that is disgusting.'

She takes him in her hand and moves her face to one side, pointing him at the ground. 'Just see,' she says. 'If there's a pee coming.'

There is.

When it's finished, she gets to work.

At which point, headlights go on and the scene is lit as brightly as at siesta time.

Ted called Sarah, but it was Dobell's driver who came. Eight in the morning and not a particularly bright day, but the shades were firmly in place. Ted got into the back of the Jag. The driver handed him a flask of coffee and a packet of bacon sandwiches and set off on the eighteen kilometre drive home.

This is not how Ted wants it to end. Obviously. He didn't call all these people together so he could tiptoe quietly away. He wants the big finish, Dolan on his feet holding out both arms, "Ladies and gentlemen, **Ted Bailey**!" and the audience stamping and cheering as Ted walks out of the door and into the darkness.

A few screams, even. Like people do when *The One Show* has a pop singer or a soap star on set.

Not this silence.

Dobell is waiting at Ted's house. Sarah is not.

'She's staying with us for a few days, Ted.'

'With you?'

'Tracey and Sarah always got on. You noticed that? You didn't notice it. Come on in.'

Ted almost thanks Dobell for inviting him into his own home.

Dobell pours beer into a glass, so cold it's opaque. He holds it out. 'Hair of the dog?'

Ted sucks four inches off the top.

'San Pedro de Alcántara, Ted? What the hell were you doing there?'

Ted shrugs. He finishes the rest of the beer in one long pull. He puts the glass down and walks through the sitting room onto the patio. He sinks onto a lounger.

'You look done in,' says Dobell.

'I'm knackered.'

'You want to grab some zeds?'

'Wouldn't mind.'

'I'll stop by about midday. We'll have some lunch together. Okay?'

Midday turned out to mean two o'clock in the afternoon. When Dobell arrived, Ted was showered and shaved and dressed in crisply pressed linen shirt and shorts. He was drinking orange juice.

'You smell a bit better,' says Dobell. 'Fancy a steak? Always good for a hangover.'

'Sure.'

Dobell's driver leaves them outside Rankin's. Ted says, 'What does he do? While he's waiting? When does he eat?'

'You're talking about my driver?'

'Yes, I'm talking about your driver.'

'Does he look as though he's starving?'

The interior was air-conditioned, cool and dark. Rankin's specialised in booths, space between tables, discreet service, quiet. It was a place where deals were done. No one knew who Rankin was, or might have been.

Ted orders his steak rare; Dobell wants his well done. Dobell orders water and a jug of Bloody Marys. 'Nothing like it when you're hung over.'

'What's today? National Hangover Cure Day?'

'You owe me a hundred quid.'

'What for? Nursemaid service?'

'In a way. That's what I paid the civiles to forget about what you got up to last night.'

'Oh. Right. Thanks.' He pulls out his wallet.

'Pay for this meal and we'll forget about it.'

'Cheers.'

'Good job it didn't get up to desk level. That would have cost a lot more. Public nudity, Ted. Sex acts in the open air. This is Catholic Spain, for God's sake.'

'I'm not proud of what happened.'

'You ever think you might be drinking too much?'

'You just ordered enough vodka to float me for a week.'

'I'm your mate, Ted. I'm not your keeper. You want to kill yourself, I'll keep you company for a while and then wave you goodbye.'

The steaks arrive. Ted cuts off a piece and puts it in his mouth. He picks up the salt and sprinkles it lightly over the rest.

'Sarah says you drink because you're unhappy.'

'You talk to Sarah about me?'

'Sarah talks to Tracey about you. Tracey talks to me. Is it true, do you think?'

'Is what true?'

'Don't be an arse, Ted. Do you drink because you're unhappy?'

'About what?'

'Well, shit, Ted, that's for you to know, isn't it? Not me.'

Ted finishes his steak. 'You got a ciggie? Thanks. When did we start smoking American cigarettes?'

'The power of advertising, Ted.'

'When I was a kid, where I grew up, we called them tabs.'

Dobell laughs. 'Yeah. I know. We had a Geordie boy on the team. He always said tab when he meant fag.'

'I used to smoke French cigarettes.'

'Too smelly. Shitty Gitties, we used to call them.'

'There was a guy came to see me a few months ago. Irishman.'

'Yeah?'

Ted waves for coffee.

'The Irishman?' says Dobell.

'It isn't important.'

'The forging, was it? Or did he want guns? No, it wouldn't be guns. Paddies can get all the guns they want. Buy them from Gaddafi. But forgery, now. Printing British bank notes. That's an IRA speciality.'

'Who said he was IRA?'

'Did you get involved? Is that why you're on the piss all the time? Are you scared who might be looking for you?'

'I've never been scared in my life.'

'That's a stupid thing to say.'

'You want any pudding? I'm just going for coffee.'

'I'll have an ice cream. They do good ice cream here. You should have got in touch. Villains like that around, you need help.'

'It's okay. I dealt with it.'

In fact, Ted had told the Paddy to fuck off. Said he wanted nothing to do with him or his proposition. He might be a bad lad but he was a British bad lad and proud of it. A patriot, him.

Apart from which, where did he come from? How close was the relationship between French Intelligence and the IRA? Between Michel and this anonymous Irishman, with his offers of untold riches for a bit of treachery? Was he IRA at all? Was he even Irish? Who do you trust?

This is what Ted wants to be telling Dolan. But Dolan isn't here. So he's talking to himself. They're never going to write his biography, there'll never be a film of his life, so this has got to do. Someone has to hear it. Or what's it all been for?

He looks around. There's no one there – no one to hear what he wants to say. So he decides to speak the words anyway. As if Dolan was present. Or Alex.

And then there's the jury. Alex has told him he's being judged, and before he can be judged he has to speak. So he speaks.

'I met my great-grandmother. Not that I remember it, but I know I did because there's a photo. It's her eightieth birthday, there's a huge family party and I'm down the front, a little boy of five. A slightly overweight little boy. I hadn't discovered cricket then. Didn't spend all day running, batting, catching.

'My great granny had had an interesting life. It interests me, anyway. She was a bastard, to start off with. Her mother, who was called Eliza, was born in Lancashire. (How do I know all this? Because I looked it up. I did a search on a website called ancestry.com and I found some nerd who'd put his whole family tree on line. More like a family forest, really. Acres of it. So I emailed him the photograph and he replied with the whole story).

'In 1863, Eliza married a Welsh miner called Enoch Williams. They married on the 6th of July, if you're interested, and their first child, Thomas, was born on the 8th of September that year, so Eliza would have been pretty chubby when she walked down the aisle of Haigh Parish Church. That's near Wigan and you pronounce Haigh as "Hay", apparently. Still,

at least they did marry. As far as the nerd could tell, Eliza's mother Jane had never bothered but Eliza wasn't short of brothers and sisters. Or siblings, as the nerd insisted on calling them.

'Eliza had two more children and then Enoch got himself killed underground at the Bridge Pit in Haigh. The nerd sent me a copy of the death certificate, which says he died from "Injuries by a fall of stone and dirt upon him in a coal mine." That was on the 11th of July, 1867. Agnes—my great granny—wasn't born till the 29th of June the next year, so she clearly wasn't Enoch's.

'We'll never know now whose she was. Or how she came to be. Maybe the father told Eliza he loved her. Maybe it was a purely commercial transaction, entered into (please excuse me) to put bread on the children's table and a roof over their heads. Who knows?

'Eliza eventually married another miner called Marsh and when they stopped mining coal in Lancashire the family moved to County Durham and on the 26th June 1886 Agnes, who knew herself as Agnes Marsh, married John Burnett. If you're still with me, their first child, who would one day be my grandmother, was born on the 1st of November that year, so Agnes followed in the family tradition.

'(And guess what? When my grandmother's first child – my Uncle Jack – was born, she and Granddad had been married all of three months).

'Anyhow, now that you know all that you'll be delighted to know none of it is the point. What is the point, or at least might be, is that Agnes's life wasn't a total bust. Okay, she was born a bastard to a woman who already had three children she lacked the financial resources to bring up. All right, when Enoch died the colliery gave Eliza no compensation and one week to get out of the house. Yes, things must have looked pretty bleak.

'But John Burnett became a Colliery Deputy. And, as people in Durham mining villages used to say when Durham had mining villages, in them days a Deputy was a Deputy. He'd have worn a bowler hat and carried a silver-topped cane and, when he walked through the village, men would have saluted and women would have bobbed a little curtsey.

'There's another picture of Agnes, taken about the same time as the eightieth birthday party. Taken the same weekend, I shouldn't wonder. She's at home, in her sitting room. There's a nice modern electric fire and she's resting her toasty-warm slippers on a fitted carpet. There weren't many of those in working class homes in the late nineteen forties.

'So Agnes did all right. She came through.

'And she and John were ambitious. Their children didn't get many years at school, but those they did get had to be used. "Work hard or you'll end up down the pit." It could be done. We're going to have a Queen of England, if that's the sort of thing that interests you, whose great grandparents came from the same sort of place and did the same sort of thing. And so did mine, to the point where my father didn't need to go down a pit the way his forefathers had and neither did I. Which was useful, given what Maggie T did to them.

'Why does this matter? It didn't, then. Agnes ended up having a far better life than could have been forecast at the start of it. She would have been happy. She was *happy*—you can see that from her expression in the photographs. Though smug might be a better word.

'But she wouldn't be happy today, because not enough people knew how her life had turned out and what hurdles she'd had to jump over to get there. The neighbours knew, some of it at least, and in Agnes's time that would have been enough.

'It isn't enough today. Is it? Today she'd have wanted Hello writing up her eightieth birthday. Today she'd have wanted to be on television, with glassy-eyed nonentities telling the *audience how wonderful she was and people applauding.*

'I want it, too. Not the glassy eyed nonentities. The celebrity. That's what I want. I've lived a hell of a life and the people who stayed home while I was leading it don't know about me. Don't know enough about me.

'It doesn't have to last. Who knows where Julia Carling is now? Who gives a shit? Really?

'And there's some stuff I wouldn't tell. Because you're not supposed to.

'But I want my fifteen minutes. Before I go into the darkness, I want people to know who just passed.'

What Ted would have told Dolan about, if his imaginary molecules had still been there and not evaporated into the make-believe ether, was the demons. Or Demons – they really deserve a capital D.

And how it all catches up with you.

Chapter 21

Ted was dreaming. He was aware, at some level, that Sarah lay rigid beside him, too terrified even to move. She'd had a chaotic and sometimes precarious life but nothing had prepared her for the possibility that a human being might ever be in the grip of something like this.

Bella was in his dreams. Of course. And so was Ramina. Bella looked as beautiful as ever she did, but Ramina's face had been pulped.

Ted stepped out of the shadow of the Customs House and gunned down two drug dealers and a bent cop.

He shot a pimp dead.

Alex died at the hand of a French Arab.

But these weren't passive dreams. Ted wasn't watching dead people act dead. The dead talked to him. And what they said wasn't nice. Out of twisted, gumless mouths in agonised, sometimes fleshless faces, the dead cursed him.

And there were the others. The ones Ted hasn't mentioned to Dolan, and Dolan hasn't mentioned to him. The boy, for example.

God spoke to him, too. He wasn't happy. This was not what He wanted.

So maybe Ted was drinking too much.

Who wouldn't?

He'd begun to hate himself. In another century he'd have welcomed that as the first step towards redemption. People were so primitive in the old days.

But now, it seems self-hate leads only to drink.

'Mac,' says Dobell.

'Mac?'

'You haven't heard that name?'

'Uncle Mac? Mack the Knife?'

'Mac whose been digging your potatoes.'

'What?'

'Trampling on your vine.'

'He's been shagging Sarah? On my time?'

'You want him done?'

'Whoa. Whoa whoa whoa. Let's just step back a bit here. What do you know?'

'Like I said, Sarah and Tracey talk to each other. Mac is some guy she met somewhere. While you were pissed, probably.'

Ted felt as though someone had opened the top of his head and poured in something he couldn't absorb. Sarah had been seeing another man. He took her in, made a home for her and she was cheating on him. What the hell was going on?

'She's been unfaithful to me? Sarah?'

Dobell shrugs. 'I can't believe you don't know.'

'She said she wanted a divorce.'

'I didn't know you were married.'

'That's what I said.'

'Women, eh?'

'I used to work with an Arab guy who said God means us to lie to them. It's why He made them stupid.'

Dobell smiles. 'What line of work would that be?'

'Import and distribution.'

'You did do some of that, then?'

Ted shrugs.

'Well, you know,' Dobell says. 'If we could climb into that strange place, the female mind, and take a look round, what would we think? Would we ever be the same again?'

Still, Ted was shaken. Groggy. He would never in a million years have believed this would happen to him.

'You passed over the woman on the wall a bit quickly,' says Dolan.

'Barry! You're back!'

He's a bit fuzzy round the edges, though. Transparent, sort of. It feels like Ted can see straight through him. There aren't so many people in the room. And Alex has gone. Which means, he supposes, that he doesn't have the energy to summon her up. Or them. It feels like he's used everything he's got just to get Dolan back in front of him. He looks around. Is the German still here? And the Lizard?

They are.

And Alex isn't gone after all. She's over in the corner, talking to someone. Tut has slipped back into his corner.

'The woman on the wall,' says Dolan. 'That was Michelle. Wasn't it?'

'I didn't know that then.'

'No. That came later. Why don't you tell us about the boy, Ted? Or have you got an alternative version for him, too?'

Ted looks at Alex. 'No,' she says, 'I'm afraid you're going to have to hold your hand up to the boy, Ted.'

And there it is. The boy. Ted's shoulders slump and all he can do is stare at Dolan, who must see despair in that look. He picks up his remote and points it at the screen.

Ted had been planning a trip to England, to visit his parents and watch some cricket. Dobell said there was a job going down he might be interested in. The people pulling it needed money and Ted would get a great return if he decided to invest. Ted didn't need the money and should have declined. Boredom and the thrill of the game drew him in. He'd regret it for ever.

On the screen we see the inside of a club. Close-ups of gambling, drinking and, on one of the floors, women with men doing what men do with women. Then we're approaching a door, in front of which is one of the biggest bouncers Ted has ever seen but he isn't wearing anything under his shirt and mere size is no defence against a pistol. He goes down on his back with blood spouting from his chest and five men step over him and go crashing through the door into an office. The man behind the desk is scrabbling in a drawer for a gun of his own but the girl kneeling between his legs prevents him by slamming the drawer shut on his hand and they shoot him dead, too.

Part of the deal, the part that made it attractive, was this girl. She leaps up from where she's been fellating the club owner, runs to the safe and taps in the combination. One of the intruders, who is in fact her brother (and Dobell's nephew), pushes her out of the way and scoops the contents of the safe into a bag. There's a lot of money there, but there are also photographs and video tapes of well-known men in intimate acts with women other than their wives. And, in two cases, with boys.

There's a lot of yelling and bouncers are converging on the office. The five men have to shoot their way out of the club. One of them takes a bullet in his hip and the others drag him with them. Shooting is still going on as they run out of the building into a waiting car that roars away from the kerb. A few yards away, a woman is crossing the road with her son, a boy of about eight. The driver swerves, avoids the woman but hits the boy square on, tossing him over the car's roof. A doctor will say later that

*he was dead before he hit the ground; but
that's what they always say. It's kinder to the
family left behind. The car disappears round a
corner in a great slide that leaves rubber all
over the road. The screen goes blank.*

'Well,' Dolan says. 'That was really choice.'

'Fucking A,' whispers Ted.

'You and Dobell didn't actually take part in the raid.'

'Dobell wasn't even in the country.'

'Nevertheless, you killed that boy.'

Ted doesn't answer.

'When you put up the money, you bought his death.'

Ted still doesn't answer.

'Whatever else you think you can wriggle your way
out of, you can't avoid this. You killed an eight-year-old
boy.'

'Yes.'

'You do well to whisper that word. And you
destroyed a family.'

'Yes.'

Dolan's contempt is plain. He presses the remote,
and onto the screen comes a woman who looks seventy
but who Ted knows is not yet fifty.

'This is the boy's mother,' says Dolan.

'Yes.'

*The woman speaks in halting sentences. 'We
were a good family. A happy family. There was
me, my husband, our daughter, and Lenny.
We'd named him that after his grandfather,*

who was called Leonard. And then these men killed him.

'We were doing fine. We didn't have a lot of money, you don't when your children are that age, but we did things together. After Lenny died, my husband went to pieces. He started drinking. He hardly spoke. Marriages don't survive a loss like that. Ours didn't. We were divorced within eighteen months. Two years later, my husband killed himself. When she reached her teens, our daughter got in with the wrong people. She started taking drugs. I hardly knew her. She did what you can imagine to finance her habit. I haven't seen her for ten years.'

She starts to cry.

Dolan lets it go on for a while, and then he turns the screen off.

'You want to defend yourself?' he asks.

Ted shakes his head.

'Did you even make any money out of it?'

'It was blood money.'

'Something you'd already had experience of, when you killed Ramina's pimp.'

'I gave it to a children's hospice.'

'What about you?' he asks Alex. 'You got anything to say?'

Alex says, 'I'll leave it for the summing up.'

'I don't think a summing up is going to save him. Any more than this business with Michelle can.' He presses the remote and they're back in Marbella.

It was two days before Ted realised that the girl on the wall was still in jail. Dobell had bailed him out, but not her. He didn't want to go down there again, but *noblesse oblige*.

> *She's in a terrible state, weeping on Ted's shoulder the moment she's brought into the visiting room. The wardress eyes her with disgust. 'Tammy,' she sobs. 'They won't tell me where they've taken Tammy.'*
>
> *'Tammy?'*
>
> *'My daughter. She's ten months old. How's she supposed to manage without her mother?'*
>
> *'You have a child?'*
>
> *She nods, her mouth smothered by tissue, unable to speak.*
>
> *'What the hell were you doing offering to suck me off on a wall?'*
>
> *The tissue comes away from her mouth. 'Tammy has to eat!' she screams. The wardress steps forward, hand raised in warning. 'So do I,' she says more quietly. She clutches Ted's wrist. 'Help me. Please.'*

Ted looked into the eyes that stared into his. They spoke of bottomless agony. A woman was in trouble. A woman needed help. Money would do the trick. And Ted had lots of money.

Just at this point the German in the front row speaks. He wants to know what happened to Sarah.

Ted likes Germans. He finds them congenial company. But they can be very pedantic.

'She wanted a divorce,' he says. 'I gave her one. I paid her ticket home to England and told her she could find a house and I'd buy it for her.'

'Before you went to see this woman in the jail? Or after?'

'Before.'

'I don't get it.'

Ted sighs. 'Dobell bailed me out. I went home. Dobell and I talked in Rankin's. He told me what Sarah was asking for. I said she could have it. I'd buy her the home she wanted. I told him to bring her round to my place so she could pick up whatever she still had there and get out of my life forever. A deal she subsequently failed to keep. As you know.

'The next evening I was having a beer and I felt horny. I remembered I was supposed to get my cock sucked, in fact I'd already paid to get my cock sucked, and it hadn't happened. That started me thinking about the girl and whether she'd still come across if I found her. And then I wondered who'd got her out. And I rang the *civiles,* and they said no one had. Does that make it clear?'

'Yes. Thank you. We Germans, you know. We like things to progress in order. Beginning. Middle. End.'

Ted was back at the jail two hours later. He sat in his car outside while lawyers took his money and did what they had to do.

Then he sat in the back of the courtroom while they did it again.

Someone—what is she? A social worker? A nurse? A policewoman?—brings little Tammy into the courtroom. The judge addresses Ted directly. 'You are taking responsibility for this woman?'

'Yes, sir.'

The judge stares over his spectacles at this foreigner's insufficiently respectful form of address. He decides to let it go. 'She must leave mainland Spain within twenty-four hours. If she does not do so, you will be held personally responsible. The penalty will be heavy. You understand that?'

'Yes, sir.'

The judge pulls his papers together and, without another word, stands and leaves the courtroom. A lawyer takes Michelle by the arm and leads her to Ted. The undefined woman brings the screaming Tammy and places her into Michelle's arms. Michelle presses her tight against her and, slowly, the screams subside into snuffling sobs. Each sob shakes the tiny body from one end to the other. Both lawyer and woman look at Michelle as at

It was an obvious question, but she didn't ask it until they were under way that afternoon. 'Why are you doing this?'

'I was bored.'

She stared at him. 'Bored. God, the times recently I'd have so loved to be bored. You've got the money for this boat and your villa. How can you be bored?'

'I bore easily.'

The next question was pretty obvious, too. 'What do you want in return?'

'Nothing you don't want to give.'

'I may not want to give anything.'

'Then that'll be what I want.'

'Actually, I owe you a blow job.'

'Yes, I guess you do.'

She put her hand on the front of his shorts. 'Would you like it now?'

'No, thank you.'

'What can I do for you, then?'

'You could go into the galley and make us both a sandwich.'

'Sure. I'll check on Tammy first. Make sure she's sleeping okay.'

'Fine.'

'What are you smiling at?'

'I've never had responsibility for a child before. It seems strange having her on the boat.'

'Strange?'

'Nice. Now you're smiling.'

'Well. I would, wouldn't I?'

'You fell in love with her,' Dolan says.

'Yes, I suppose I did.'

'That was the second time you'd fallen in love with a prostitute. What do you think that says about you?'

'Michelle wasn't a prostitute.'

'She had sex with men for money. That's how you met her. She was going to have sex with you for money.'

'She was feeding her child.'

'By having sex with men for money. By working as a prostitute.'

Ted opens his mouth to speak. He closes it again. He shrugs. What would once have caused broken bones is now not worth fighting over. Ted is going into the darkness. It's here.

'You didn't think of her as a prostitute?'

He holds a microphone close to Ted's lips. Ted's voice is fading, with everything else. Slowly, as if every word could kill him, he says, 'I thought of her as a sweet, intelligent, educated, loving young woman who'd had a hard time and was ready to put it all behind her for me. She'd been through hell with her previous man and still she was prepared to reach out to me.'

'To your money.'

'To me. She really loved me. Not at first, maybe, but it came. And I loved her.'

'All right, she loved you. She didn't do badly out of it, though. Did she?'

'Neither did I. I stopped drinking.'

'You what?'

'I don't mean I stopped drinking. I mean I stopped drinking. Got it under control. Sarah had been right. I'd been putting it away because I was unhappy. And now I wasn't.'

'And you put that down to Michelle? Not just to a change of scene?'

'Oh, getting out of Marbella was good. No question. I went back a couple of times to sell the villa and the car and generally tidy up. I didn't miss the place. Or the people. But mostly it was Michelle.'

It's coming and going. He thinks he can't get another word out, and suddenly the energy flows through him again. 'Some women are a bloody trial to live with. You know that? And some seem to carry an air of calm with them wherever they go. That was Michelle. I loved the sound of her voice. I loved her straightforward common sense. I loved her.'

'And she was good in bed.'

'She was spectacular in bed. We were like kids with each other. When Little Ted got together between the sheets with Little Michelle, the angels in Heaven sang Hallelujah.'

'So what went wrong?'

'Looking back...' It's gone again. 'I'm sorry, Barry...I'm struggling to...'

'Take your time.'

'I didn't want to do something she wanted me to do. It turned out to be more important to her than I'd realised. She left me.'

'What did you do?'

'Said I was sorry and I'd do what she'd wanted me to do. She said it was too late. She was implacable. It was over. Oh, shit.'

'What's the matter?'

'Oh, God.'

'Ted?'

'This...I think this...Oh, God, it's cold. It's so, so cold. It was before that. Before she wanted me to...I think...I think she started to have...to have doubts when...oh, it's so cold...'

'Get Ted a brandy, please.'

'Doubts...when...'

'When she found out how you made your money?'

'Thank you. Yes. I was...so cold...Aitch...Oh, Mother, please. Help me.'

It's cold. So cold. And dark. He's in the darkness. It can't be the end, can it? If he knows where he is? That has to be good, doesn't it? Something to give him hope?

He was laughing, up there in the corner, looking down on his body in the bed. He doesn't seem to be laughing anymore. And, oh, that poor girl.

What did he say? He said it wasn't all darkness. There was light somewhere. Just a little light, and far off, but bright.

Is there light now? He can't honestly say there is. There's the idea of light. But light itself? No.

And he isn't up in the corner any longer. He's in a passageway. It's a level passageway, so no clues there. Might be going up, might be going down.

Might not be going anywhere.

There isn't a lot of room, he'll say that. His arms are a bit tight by his sides. He's never liked that. Never cared for it as a feeling. Ted was never the man you wanted to be trapped with in a broken down lift.

It's getting colder. The idea of light is fading. But he knows where it would be. Which way it would be, if it was there. He can feel that.

He tries to push himself forward, but nothing's working. He isn't going forward and he isn't going back.

I'm sorry, God. Please don't turn your back on me. Please, God. It was my fault. It was all my fault. I know that. I made the choices. And I'm sorry.

Don't desert me now.

His legs want to move, but they don't. They can't. He doesn't know what he's supposed to do. Do you have to get yourself through the darkness? Does someone come to meet you? Or does it just happen?

There's no one here. Except the Lizard and King Tut, if you want to count them. Ted doesn't want to count them. It's so quiet. And so cold. And it's getting colder.

Oh, Mother, help me.

Alex stands up. 'I'll do my summing up now. It won't take long.'

Dolan sniggers. 'I bet it won't. What is there to say in defence of this piece of work?'

'This. And, Ted, this is my moment. If I ask you a question, answer it. Otherwise, keep your mouth shut.' She takes the remote from Dolan and presses it. Onto the screen comes a narrow street in a small village close to the sea. It could be anywhere in the Canaries, but it isn't anywhere, it's very close to the place where Ted lives.

The pictures bring smell with them as well as sound. Fire stinks. Fire terrifies. Fire excites.

All of those things are evident in the crowd huddled in the lane in front of the house – a lane too narrow for any fire engine. Water is being sprayed from a hose brought from around the corner. The hose is not long enough, the pressure is too low, and most of the water is falling short. It's going to take a long time to get the fire out this way.

A screaming woman is being comforted by several others. Two *civiles* stand as close as they dare to the burning house, but they aren't thinking of attempting a rescue. A priest makes his way to the grieving little knot of people and the women make room for him. Alex says, 'No one doubts that her children are doomed – dying or already dead. She will need a great deal of comfort in the weeks and months to come.'

The camera picks Ted up as he circles the people. Alex says, 'Ted knows, if there's going to be a rescue, it has to be now. He is as frightened of fire as everyone else here. The idea of dying in it, the pain, the agony...but through the centuries, men have seen fire as cleansing. What Ted is thinking is that, if he can save the children, drop them from an upstairs window and then let the inferno take him...that will be an end to grief; an end to dreams of Ramina and the boy and all the other lives he's blighted. Including mine. Atonement.'

The camera closes on Ted as he moves alongside the man standing slightly apart from other men. The man whose tears are unstemmable. The father.

'How many children?'

The man looks at Ted without speaking.

'There isn't much time. How many children?'

'Two,' says the man, without hope. 'A boy and a girl.'

'Which room?'

The man is staring at him. 'Señor...'

'Which room?'

Wordlessly, the man points at the upstairs window above the door.

'Give me the key.'

And hope appears on the father's face. He hands over a key, pats the back of Ted's hand, begins to speak but Ted has no time to listen.

The fire must have started in the kitchen, which was at the furthest point from the door. The stairs were passable. Hot, singed, about to burst into flames but passable. Ted jumped them two at a time, skipping because of the intense heat that threatened the soles of his shoes. Now it became harder, for air through the opened door had fed the flames as though the house were a blast furnace and they were playing around the landing. The floor began to give way beneath him. Standing on that landing, the fear was overwhelming. Ted was terrified. And yet, he felt that peace was so close. Rescue the children by dropping them from the window into hands waiting below. Then die in the blaze. A perfect end to an imperfect life. The door handle burnt his hand. He crashed the door open with his shoulder and stepped into the room and, oh God, oh no, the bedding was already catching fire.

They may already have died in each other's arms.

Ted moves quickly to the window. He can't open it.

He tries harder. He can't open it.

Now the bed is on fire, and the end tilts as the floor, the joists burned through, begins to give way. Another minute and the two children will be tipped into the deadly blaze below. Ted jumps onto the bed, grabs them both, turns his back to the window and runs backwards, hurling himself at it.

The glass shatters.

Ted is flying, a child under each arm, his hair singed, his shirt on fire. He keeps the presence of mind to hold the children up so that when he crashes to the ground they are not crushed beneath him.

One of the civiles *thrusts his gun into Ted's burnt and filthy face and tells him he's under arrest for assaulting a police officer. The mother's hugs threaten to squeeze the life out of her children. The women are screaming. The father is sobbing. The priest stands over Ted, making the sign of the cross. But Ted is unconscious. He hears nothing.*

The screen goes blank. Alex puts down the remote. The German says, 'What happened to the children?'

'They lived. Ted was in hospital for weeks. It took months before he was well. Someone had the sense to drop the charges against him. I don't believe he ever forgave himself for surviving.'

'If the windows had opened, he would not have done so.'

'Which is why they did not.'

'They were jammed deliberately?'

'Coincidence is a tool that is not favoured where I live now.'

The audience is silent, but Ted is sobbing. 'I didn't want to live. I didn't want to live. I wanted to save the children and die.'

Alex says, 'There are so many other things I could tell you. About donations and help, anonymously given. But I don't think anything compares with what we've just seen.'

It's over. Something swells and bursts inside Ted. All those years of suppressed emotion and pretending that nothing mattered – what a waste. And how pointless to realise it now; to recognise what he could have been when the time to be anything is passed. It isn't sadness, though, that is making him cry. He's crying in relief, crying because he'll soon be out of it and it's time. The audience is beginning to move. A woman comes up onto the stage and touches his tear-streaked face with her hand. 'God bless you, Ted Bailey,' she whispers. Then she joins the others, and they drift away. Soon there's just Tut in his corner, and Ted, and the Lizard, and Dolan, and Alex—and she's standing up, getting ready to leave. And he spoke too soon when he mentioned relief because he's scared.

'Where are you going?' he asks Alex.

'I have a meeting I have to attend.'

'Is it about me?'

'Yes, Ted. It's about you.'

'Is it important?'

Now she just stares at him. Ted says, 'Can I go with you?'

'No, Ted. You can't go with me. Go back into your tunnel, or wherever it is they're holding you, and wait.'

He doesn't want to ask this, but he has to. 'Is it going to be all right?'

'I'm sorry, Ted; I really don't know. If it is, you'll find out. If not...well, you just won't come out of your tunnel.'

'Not even to go to Hell?'

'There is no Hell, Ted. No Hell and no Purgatory. There's where I am, and there's what comes after that, and otherwise there's nothing. Nothing is where most people end up, if you want to know.'

'How do you rate my chances?'

'Ted. I don't even know how *I* made it. The only thing I'm reasonably certain of is that, if you're sure you're coming through the darkness, you won't.'

'If I end up with nothing, how will I know?'

She jerks her head in the direction of the Lizard. 'That will be for him to decide. Now go back to your tunnel and wait.'

He isn't going to make it. Throughout his life, he's been the lucky one and now his luck has run out. He watches Alex go in the knowledge that he'll never see her again.

And then she turns back.

'Ted?'

'Yes?'

'You do realise that Michelle played you for a mug?'

'Did she?'

'She wanted your money, she asked for it and you gave it to her. So did Sarah, if it comes to that.'

'Come on,' says Dolan. 'All through his charmed existence he's thought he could pay for the wrongs he did by writing a cheque. You can't blame his women for taking him at his word.'

'Is that how you see it, Ted?'

'Money was all I had. I created mayhem in people's lives, I destroyed them without even thinking about it, and money was the only way I had of making amends. If I lived another ten lives, I couldn't make up for the hurt I created.'

'You'd do it all again,' says Dolan.

'No. No, I'm very clear about that. If I had my life to live again, I'd live it the way I once expected to.'

Dolan snorts. 'That isn't going to cut much ice with God. You're doomed.'

Alex says, 'As I said before, Barry, this idea you have of God is the one the world has. And it's wrong.' And then she vanishes. She doesn't walk away, doesn't go through the arch, doesn't go up in a puff of smoke. She simply disappears.

Dolan's face is a sneer. 'You're nothing but a piece of shit, Bailey.'

'I know that.'

'And, whatever she says, there *is* a hell. And you're going to it.'

Then he, too, disappears. The darkness has reached Ted. It's lapping at his feet. It billows up from the ground. He's surrounded by it, enmeshed in it. It's colder than he could ever have imagined.

But, even now, the *Dolan Show* has one more surprise to give because there's a noise off-stage and then a big man with headphones and a clipboard is barring someone's way through the arch. 'You can't go in there,' he says.

'Get out of my way,' says a female voice and onto the stage strides a woman in her thirties pulling a man by the hand. Behind them come two beautiful little girls. She walks right up to Ted, ignores the darkness and throws her arms round him.

'Tammy?' he says. 'Tammy!'

And he starts to cry once more, but this time they are tears of happiness. He never thought he'd see her again.

'Hello, Dad,' she says. 'Dad, this is my husband, Luis. He has something to say to you.'

'Mister Bailey.' He's speaking Spanish and Ted is delighted that Tammy has gone back to the country where they were so happy to find a mate. 'Mister Bailey. Meeting Tammy changed my life. It made me a human being. Because Tammy knows how to love without reserve, and she taught me, and we've taught our daughters. And Tammy has told me her whole story, and I know that the person who taught her to love was you.

I'll never be able to tell you how grateful I am.' He puts out his hand and Ted shakes it. Then he is hugging Ted, too, along with Tammy, and the little girls wrap themselves around the adults' legs, and Ted is crying even harder, but the tears are tears of unconfined joy.

And then the four of them fade into nothing. And Ted is not afraid any longer. What will be will be. Doomed he may be, but he's left one good act behind him. One family at least remembers him with kindness.

He turns to where Ras Tafar has stepped up onto the stage and he raises two fingers. 'You,' he says, 'can fuck off.'

Peter says, 'We'll hear from you when you're ready, Alex. There's a few things we haven't seen yet. We'll watch them now.' He doesn't say "Okay?" or "All right?" They don't. Everyone turns to look at the screen.

Ted is visiting his parents with Michelle and Tammy. They think Tammy is his and Ruth Bailey is delighted with what she believes to be her grandchild.

She has other things to be delighted about, too.

'You remember I mentioned in a letter about Ellie Mason, Ted?'

'Ellie Mason?'

'You do. She had a little girl. Born with a heart problem. What do they call it, Charles?'

'A congenital defect,' her husband says.

'That's it. They needed fifty thousand pounds to send her to America for treatment.'

'Oh, yes,' says Ted.

'I did tell you. I know I did. Anyway, the little mite's been over there and she's back now and it's all been fixed. She can run and play just like any other bairn.'

'Oh, good,' says Ted.

'Yes. A lawyer wrote to Ellie and her husband and told them to go and see him. Where was it, Charles?'

'Grainger Street. Grey Street. Collingwood Street. How should I know where it was, woman?'

'Anyway, she went to see this lawyer and he gave her all the money. Every penny. Said one of his clients had donated it.'

'Amazing,' says Ted.

'And he wasn't allowed to tell her who it was. It was a secret. She still doesn't know.' She looks at Michelle. 'Isn't that wonderful?'

'It is,' Michelle agrees. 'To think there are people that generous.'

'Tony Webb,' says Charles. 'That was the lawyer. Didn't you know him, Ted?'

'I played cricket with him.'

'I knew I remembered the name.'

'Do you want me to call him and ask who Ellie's benefactor was?'

'He wouldn't tell you,' says Ruth. 'Not allowed to. Doing good by stealth, they used to call it.'

They're still in the Canaries. They live on Fuerteventura now. They've bought a villa and Tammy's been going to school in Corralejo. She's a little Spaniard, a little islander, completely bilingual. Ted is the only father she's ever known. She calls him Daddy, and sometimes Papá. They go for walks together. He teaches her to cook. She sails as though she'd been born on the water.

Ted thinks life is perfect. Tammy would probably agree, if people her age thought in those terms. Michelle does not.

'She's growing up, Ted. I want her to go to school in England. I want her to be English.'

'What on earth for? Have you looked at the English lately?'

But it doesn't rest. She comes back to it. It becomes a sore between them.

'You are so selfish,' Michelle says. 'You don't think of anyone but you, and what you want.'

Ted's been away on a short trip. Only three days, but he's looking forward to being at home again with his people. Michelle, whom he loves. And Tammy. His little princess. What he feels for Tammy goes way beyond anything the word "love" can encompass in his mind.

They're not there.

But there is a letter.

> Dear Ted
> When you get this, I'll be back in England. I've decided to end our relationship. I'll be very happy to discuss this with you, as long as you understand that my mind is made up and it isn't going to change. We can talk about what contact we're going to have in the future, if that's what you want, but our relationship is over and that is not up for discussion. Please accept it.
> I'd be very grateful if you could see your way to continuing to support me financially. Committing to you has meant cutting myself off from opportunities I might have had to build a career and an income for myself. I know that was my choice; looking back, it wasn't a good one.
> Look after yourself and go well.
> x
> M

Ted opens a bottle of brandy and takes it onto the balcony. He sits and stares out to sea. Hours pass. Night comes, the stars rotate in the heavens, the moon rises, passes across the sky and sinks once more into the sea. He doesn't think about what's been done to him, or where he stands, or what he wants, because he knows that if he did he would not be able to stand the pain. The only thing he lets himself think about is fatherless Tammy.

In the morning he reads the letter again. She's written a phone number, which he knows is her parent's house. He is shaking when he calls. Michelle's mother answers. Her tone is warm; she's always liked Ted.

Michelle comes on the line.

'First of all,' Ted says, 'of course I'll go on supporting you both. How could you expect anything else?'

'I didn't. You've always been a decent person, I know that. And supporting me is the decent thing to do.'

He notes the switch from his "you both" back to her "me" but decides not to make an issue of it. 'Let me have your bank details when you've opened an account and I'll arrange to have money paid in every month.'

'I've got them here. Have you got a pen?'

'Gosh. That didn't take long.'

She doesn't respond to that, merely dictating the numbers he needs to know.

'I'll make the first transfer today,' he says. 'And I'd like to come and see you.'

'Come to England, you mean?'

'Yes. Of course. Come there.'

'Not here as in here, Ted. We'll meet somewhere.'

'Oh. Okay. Will you bring Tammy?'
'I don't think that's a good idea, Ted.'

He flies to England. They pick restaurants out of the *Good Food Guide* and eat there. They walk in Richmond Park. They visit Westonbirt Arboretum, Brighton, Burford and Chipping Norton. Just the two of them. Ted asks Michelle to bring Tammy but she never does.

Each time they meet they agree to forget about the past and focus on having a good time, two friends together, but before the visit is over she's unpicking their relationship again, pointing out where he went wrong, explaining why she left and the many aspects of his failure as a human being. When they walk on Beachy Head he senses such hostility that he makes sure she's always between him and the edge, afraid she suggested this place in order to have the chance to push him off.

He loves her still, he'd do anything to be back to what they were, he'd move to England today and buy a house for them anywhere she wants, a house where the three of them can live and from which Tammy can go to an English school. But she is implacable. It's a word he comes back to time and again. No other seems remotely to fit. Implacable. Not to be placated or appeased. Irreconcilable.

"I will never have you back". She repeats it, at every meeting and in every conversation. "I will never have you back". He hasn't dared ask her to have him back, but the compulsion to reject him can't seem to leave her. It begins to madden him more than anything else between them. In the end, he says, 'Look. I want to make a deal.'

'What?'

'I will promise that I will never, ever, ask you to have me back. Not now, not in twenty years time, not ever. And in return you will promise that you will never, ever again, tell me that you won't.'

She stares at him. 'Have I been saying that a lot?'

'In just about every sentence you utter.'

'I'm sorry. I hadn't realised.'

'Is it a deal?'

'Okay. All right. It's a deal.'

He's in England for six weeks and he doesn't see Tammy once. 'She's my child, Ted. She isn't yours. She thinks she is, and you seem to think she is, but she isn't. She's mine. She has to get used to not having you in her life.'

'Does she ask about me?'

Michelle's eyes mist. 'I think it's better if I don't talk about Tammy to you.'

He flies back to Fuerteventura. The villa feels empty. For a while, he can't stay in it. He spends time on the boat. He goes to bars and restaurants. He visits friends. He picks up women. Intelligent women, interested in sex and fun to be with; but all suffer from one drawback they will never be able to overcome.

They aren't Michelle.

He stops dating. Not overnight and not by conscious choice. He simply loses interest. He wakes up one day and realises he hasn't been with a woman for more than a year and he doesn't care. There is no sense of loss in his mind. He isn't celibate by choice; he's celibate because he can't be bothered to be anything else.

Once, loving someone had meant answering their calls. That changes. He'd said to Sarah, 'You want the advantages of being in a relationship without any of the drawbacks.' He says it again to Michelle when they've been apart a year and she telephones to ask him for an extra ten thousand pounds to clear her credit cards.

He says yes but suggests she should get a job. She says she will. He says relying on him isn't healthy for her, and funding that reliance isn't healthy for him. She says she agrees. Agreement is plentiful. They have no trouble reaching agreement. They agree that she will start looking for work. They agree that his money will stop when she finds it.

For another eighteen months, she'll say she's looking and he'll say he knows she'll find something. She's clever, she's personable, she has a lot to offer. What becomes clear, though, is that she isn't looking and won't start looking as long as she's getting money from him. He calls her on it.

'This is about making me pay. Isn't it? For the end of our relationship?'

'Is there any reason you shouldn't?'

'But you ended it.'

'You wanted me to. It was what you wanted.'

'Michelle, that's bullshit.'

'I'm not arguing with you.'

'I did not want our relationship to end.'

'Sure you didn't.'

'I've been supporting you for two and a half years. For most of that, you've been promising to look for work. And you haven't been. Have you?'

'Why should I?'

'Why say you are if you're not?'

'I'm in this position because of you. I gave up opportunities to build a career because of you.'

'What opportunities? What career?'

'I thought you loved me.'

'I did. I do.'

'If you loved me, you'd go on supporting me until I can make enough to look after me and Tammy.'

'And how will you do that if you won't look for a job?'

'I'll start.'

'I suggest you do. Because the money tap just ran dry.' He hangs up.

There's the occasional anguished telephone call and he usually responds with cash, but he feels better about himself now that he is no longer regularly financing a woman who wants his money but doesn't want to be with him. Then she writes, out of the blue, suggesting they can be occasional companions, occasional lovers. She rings him. He says he isn't interested in being her occasional lover. She says okay. Afterwards he marvels at what he's just done. He, Ted Bailey, offered the chance to sleep with the most rewarding bed partner he's ever known, said "No". What he'd really meant was "Not on those terms", but still.

Then contact ceases. He's at peace with that. He knows it's over anyway, so why draw it out?

He takes a holiday in England, visits his parents and then drives wherever the fancy takes him. One place it takes him is Bournemouth. Actually, that isn't just his fancy; there's a marine electronics company there that makes a special radar device that Ted wants and you can't yet buy in the Canaries. He's walking along, looking for somewhere that might serve acceptable coffee and realising he's in the wrong place entirely, when he's hailed from the other side of the street.

He waits as she crosses, using the time to recall her name. An old friend of Michelle who visited them in Corralejo for a couple of weeks with her husband and their children. She shows him the way to the nearest coffee shop.

They exchange greetings and news. He can see she's agog to tell him something and he lets it come. After the small talk, the news of children, the inquiries after his and his parent's health, and is that divine little bodega still on the corner? He knows, of course, that Michelle has a new man? That she and Tammy have moved in with him? He didn't know? Oh. She's sorry if she's...he's sure he doesn't mind? Positive? Oh, that's good. She really wouldn't have wanted to upset him. She's glad he feels that way and, yes, she certainly will pass on his very best wishes next time she sees Michelle. Who, by the way, is blissfully happy with Ted's successor.

Not that she sees her very often these days. Then she says, 'She should have told you really. After all, you paid for it.'

'What?'

'She asked you for money for household repairs. You gave her five thousand pounds.'

'How did you know that?'

'She told me. She told everyone. She thought it was hilarious. Young Tammy was disgusted. There weren't any repairs. Your money paid for a wedding in the Seychelles. Air tickets, hotel, ceremony. She laughed about it. But please don't ever tell her I told you.'

He flies home two days later. He wants to believe that he isn't hurting. It isn't true. It's almost true, but not quite. There's a tiny scrap of pain there. Of regret. All this time he's accepted that their relationship was over. Sure. But there was always the chance. He couldn't ask her to have him back. That was their agreement, the deal they had made. But she could ask him.

He knows how he'd have reacted. He should do; he's played it out in his mind often enough. He'd say, "Well, I'm really going to have to think about that very hard, Michelle." And then, almost without a break, "Okay, I've thought about it and how soon can you move in?" And she'd punch him on the chest, a bit playfully and a bit for real, and say, "I'll *smack* you!"

And she'd move in right away, she and Tammy. And he'd do anything she wanted. Move to England? Sure. Buy a house? Anywhere. She can choose. Fifty-fifty, so it's his cash but she's on the title with all the security that brings? Wouldn't have it any other way.

It could have happened. It was never really going to, he knew that, but it could have. It was always a possibility. Remote, almost non-existent, nothing but a dream really, but there.

And now it isn't.

He's good at dreams. He's just beginning to realise how good.

He feels like a break. Just back from England and already he needs a holiday. He sails the boat to Puerto del Carmen. He checks into a hotel. He plans to devote the week to walking, eating and swimming.

The second day, he's on a sun lounger by the pool. A girl is looking at him. She was looking at him yesterday, too. Should he recognise her? Is she someone he knows? The daughter of a friend? There's something familiar about her, but not familiar enough for him to place.

It's early, in the season and in the day, and most of the loungers are empty. The girl comes hesitantly towards him. She sits on the little table between his lounger and the next, which is unoccupied. She smiles.

Ted says, 'Do we know each other?'

'Would you mind pretending we do? Or the hotel might ask me to leave.'

'You're not staying here?'

'I pretend I am. I've been sleeping on the beach.'

'You're English. Obviously.'

'Obviously. I'm also skint. Obviously.'

'I'm sorry. Do you need something? Want to take a shower in my room? Get your laundry done?'

She coughs. She's having difficulty getting this out. 'How much would you pay to have sex with me?' It comes out in a rush.

'What?'

'Please don't make me say it again.'

'Bloody hell.'

'I'm sorry. If you're disgusted, I'm sorry. But I need the money. Desperately. I can't stay on the beach. I've had two close calls already.'

All his bells are ringing. A little while ago...what does he mean by that? Before he heard that Michelle had a new man. That's what he means. Before he heard that Michelle had a new man, he'd have responded to this plea the way he always did to a woman in need. He'd have found out how much she needed and given it to her. Before he heard that Michelle had a new man.

'Look, love,' he says. 'I haven't been with a woman for ages. Years. I can't remember when. I can't even remember when I last had an erection. I don't know if I can still get it up.'

The girl looks disappointed. 'But you would if you could?'

He smiles. 'Undoubtedly.'

'I can get you some Viagra.'

'Don't you need a prescription?'

'Not if you know where to go. I'd need a hundred euros.'

She's giving him a way out. He hands her a hundred euros, she pretends she's going for the pills, he never sees her again. A win-win. A result for both of them. He smiles. Reaches for his wallet. Takes out two fifties and gives them to her. Then he adds a third. 'In case they're dearer than you think.'

He watches her heading for the beach. Nice arse. The nicest he's ever seen on a confidence trickster. Pity, really. She had lovely skin. Smooth and taut the way only a young woman's can be. A little recreational rudeness might have been nice. But there you are. He knows he'll never see her again, which means he's free to dream.

Does he dream too much? Maybe. But he doesn't hurt people any more, Lenny's death was the end of all of that, and he knows which way of being he prefers.

Idly, he wonders what Michelle's sex life is like with her new chap. He'd like to be able to hope it would be disastrous, but somehow he can't bring himself to do that. He wishes her well. God knows, he wasn't the easiest person to live with. She was right. He was a selfish bastard. Still is, probably. Maybe she's enjoying the payoff now. He hopes so. Even if he does hate the very thought of the man she's enjoying it with.

Just let the guy be good to Tammy. And to Michelle, of course.

He smokes a Gitane. Then he dozes.

He's woken by a hand gently rocking his shoulder. It's the girl. The girl he never expected to see again. She hands him some euros and a small polythene pouch containing blue pills. 'There's your change,' she says. 'I got them for eighty.'

'Keep it,' he says, astounded. 'I mean the money.'

'Thank you. Listen we didn't actually agree the...what you'd pay.'

'How much do you need?'

She gulps. 'Three hundred would be good. I know that's a lot, but...'

'I'll give you five.'

'Five hundred?'

He nods. 'There's an ATM in the lobby.'

'I don't know what to say. You're a hero. A doll. Look, I don't want to rush you but I think those things need time to work, you know?'

'I'll have to get some water.'

'We could go over to the bar? You could get me an ice cream, maybe? And a coffee?'

'When did you last eat?'

'A while ago.'

'When?'

'Yesterday.'

'For goodness sake. They're still serving breakfast. Let's go.'

She goes back three times to the buffet. Ted pours himself a glass of grapefruit juice to wash the pills down.

He's heard stuff about Viagra, idle talk in the locker room, and he knows this isn't how it's supposed to work. You don't walk around with a stiffie all the time. You respond to the usual things and if there's nothing to respond to you stay limp. Idly he wonders what substitute she was sold. How dangerous it might be. And whether she knows. He's astounded to realise how little he cares. Aloud, he says. 'I never had a hard-on like this. Not even with Annabel.'

'You're having it with Annabel now.'

'What?'

'That's my name. Annabel. My Mum calls me Bella. Why are you staring at me like that? Doll? Are you all right?'

Is there...? Maybe about the eyes...? Of course not. That's ridiculous. Even so. The way she looks at him. As though she knows him already. As though there's a private smile there, a secret she isn't going to share. Ted shakes himself. It must be the heat. He's just woken up and he feels woozy. 'I'm all right. I knew a Bella once.'

'Yes. I gathered that. Look, I need a shower. Would you think me awful if I asked you to have one, too?'

They shower together. She's beautiful. She smiles sweetly at him as he soaps her all over, gives at least the impression of enjoying it when he pays particular attention to her breasts, the place between her legs, the furrow between her buttocks. She must find his sagging body and the hair growing out of his nose repellent, but she doesn't let it show. That there may be fifty years between them you would not know from her demeanour.

When they come out of the bathroom, Ted gives her five hundred euros. She puts the notes in the pocket of the jeans she's dropped carelessly on the floor. She kisses his cheek. 'You're a doll,' she whispers.

He tells her he has a hankering for doggy style and she arranges herself accordingly. Her bottom, smooth skinned and now sweet-smelling, is raised invitingly. He kneels behind her, his hands on her hips. She reaches back between her open thighs and guides him into her, looking over her shoulder as she does. She smiles encouragingly at him. With something between a sigh and a sob, he leans forward and kisses her gently on the back of the neck.

'You're a doll,' she says again.

The pain starts low in his chest and spreads, upwards and outwards. It won't let go. He knows what's happening. He's read about it often enough. He's supposed to put an aspirin under his tongue and let it dissolve. He has a packet of aspirin bought for just this purpose and never opened.

It's on the boat.

What will happen to this poor kid if he dies on top of her? He has to get off her. Out of her. He has to let her up.

He can't.

He collapses slowly. Bella is pressed, squealing and twisting, to the bed. He struggles to withdraw. He fights to twist himself off to the side, give her space to crawl free.

He can't.

Chapter 23

The others have left, wondering why they were invited when it's clear the decision had already been made.

Peter has asked Alex to stay behind, and Alex is in no such doubt. 'That wasn't about Ted, was it? It wasn't him you were looking at at all. It was us.'

Peter smiles, if one of Them can ever be said actually to smile. 'The others will have to stay a little longer,' he says. 'But you, Alex. You're ready to go to the Next Stage. Well done.'

The Next Stage. She should be excited. In fact she is nervous. What is the next stage? She's heard it talked about since she got here but no one knows what happens there any more than anyone when she was alive knew what happened Here. 'How do I get There?'

'The same way you got Here. You will simply pass. In fact, I'll take you.'

'Is it different from Here?'

'As a loaf of bread is from a grain of barley. Have you never wondered whether getting Here was worth it? Never found it a bit boring? Would you want to spend eternity not doing what you haven't been doing Here? I don't think so. The Next Stage is also the Final Stage, Alex. It's where you get your reward.'

'A reward! What is it?'

'It's whatever you want it to be. As long as it doesn't hurt other people, and you wouldn't be going if you could still want to hurt other people.' He grins a most unsaintly grin. 'Grilled fish is a central part of mine.'

'You can eat There?'

'You have all the appetites There, Alex. And the means to satisfy them.'

It's a question that has baffled her since she got Here. 'Why me?'

'There are many paths. You reached it because of who and what you have been. And we have decided to return Ted Bailey to life, at least for now. He will have a second chance because of how he changed, who he became and what he did. Human compassion and remorse are valued Here more than shows of devotion.'

'Ellie Mason swung it for him? And the children in the fire?'

'You know, humans are shackled by so many false ideas about God, and that is one. And it is so unnecessary. If you can believe that Man was created in God's image, why is it so hard to look at the way people are and realise that God must be that way, too?

'Life is not fair, yet people believe that God is. God has favourites. The Moslems know this. God loves every human being as a mother or a father would, because that is what God is—their mother, their father, their creator. Do parents love all their children equally? There is another love, a warmer, closer love, the love that in Arabic is known as *Hub,* and God gives this warmer love or withholds it. Yes, Alex, withholds it. People have died who men would have deemed exemplary, but God did not care for them and they are not Here.'

'But why did He not like them?'

'And why do you persist in calling God "He" when I avoid it? No, I will tell you. You do it because yours is still the same patriarchal world that you pity mine for being. You have not found that Here and you should stop.'

'But surely…God wants everyone to be good, so that they can join Him. I'm sorry, I mean Her. I mean…what do I mean?'

'What nonsense! In the first place, God does not want to be surrounded by people, any more than I do or you would. However loved they may be. You know what grandparents learn?'

'I'd have liked the chance to find out.'

'They learn that it is wonderful when their grandchildren come to visit, and just as wonderful when they go. You can love people without wanting them under your feet all the time. And good people can be so boring. God likes to be entertained.'

'Isn't that a little capricious?'

'And people are not? Have you listened to a word I've been saying? From time to time, someone slips into Here who perhaps should not; and numberless are those who have followed every commandment, put others first, prayed daily and loved their neighbour as themselves, and yet at the last were turned away because they were just too boring to be around all day. You may never sit on another panel like this, but in case you do I'll offer you a word of advice. Probably the most valuable advice anyone coming Here can have. Do not, whatever else you do, let someone in Here who God will find boring. And don't be boring yourself. You bore God at your peril.

'But, in any case, it wasn't just Ellie Mason or those children. People save other people all the time and they don't necessarily get any reward for it. There was a house of refuge for women whose men did them harm. The landlord wanted to evict them. An anonymous donor bought the house and gave it to them. There are scholarships at the Royal Grammar School for the talented children of women living alone who could not afford the fees. To list everything bought for hospitals in poor places would be tedious. I say nothing of cricket equipment given to schools in those same areas. Money for holidays for children who would not otherwise have them. The running costs of a hospice. Get rid of this idea that human logic can explain God's grace. It can not.'

'But Ted will survive?'

'He will. For how long, I cannot say. Let us see how he fares when he knows he is to be a father.'

'When he *what?*'

'The girl. The new Annabel, who just may be the old Annabel, but don't ask me because I won't answer. She cannot know it yet, but she is with child. Bailey impregnated her in the moment of his heart attack. And now it is time. Will you give me your hand?'

'A child. His own child. After all this time. That child will be so lucky in its father.'

'We shall see. Your hand?'

'Peter. Does anyone ever choose to go back instead of on?'

'Back?'

'Back There.'

He sighs. 'Oh, God. I should never say that but, oh, God. Why would you want to do that?'

'Does anyone ever do it? Can it be done?'

'No. It can not be done. Your life as Alex Hughes is over.'

'I understand that. I was thinking, as I believe you know, of entering into an unborn child and living that life.'

'Alex, for pity's sake. We should never have sent you Back. Leave it. You will be yourself again soon.'

'Can it be done?'

'It is done all the time. But not from Here. All the Calvinists do it. You cannot come through the darkness if you believe you are predestined to do so. Calvin himself came through the darkness sixty years after the death of the man the world knew by that name. John Knox endured many lives and in the end became Gordon Brown. Though Knox was never really a Calvinist, of course. Even so, consider his fate. From a man unafraid of anything the world might say or do to one who married for no reason but to stop people asking a question he feared would cost him the prize he sought. A prize, like all earthly prizes, that when he had it he wished he had it not.

'He wrote a book about courage but was afraid to look into his own self. And now his final chance is almost certainly gone. He is not likely even to be permitted another life after this one. Which will, at least, save some poor infant mouth-twitching misery and allow a newly minted soul its tilt at Life.

'That is what you must bear in mind, Alex. People imagine some sort of inevitable, inexorable climb towards the Light but that is not what happens. If you went back from Here you would lose everything you have won. You would forget all you have learned. Your memories of this place would fade within your first year and your chances of Life would be no better than those of everyone around you. It is not worth it, Alex.'

'But it can be done.'

'Think of those first months of consciousness. You retain the memory of what happened Here, but you cannot communicate. And the memory fades.'

'Then it can be done. Or you could not know that.'

'By the time you can communicate, it is gone. From time to time you will remember that there was something, but what it was you know not. Only one man in the history of the world was ever allowed to keep it, and his reward was to die on the cross. He felt such compassion for those he had left behind that he went back to help them, and they killed him for it. Another man preached violent revolution, hatred instead of love, and they called him Bar Abbas, the Son of God, and they released him from prison and the man who in his pity and love had come to save them they killed. People think the Jews are a pliable race who can be pushed around, and we are not. How could we be, and still have been chosen by the God I'm trying to help you to see? But I tell you, God turned away that day and never fully turned back. The loss, Alex. The loss! And you may never get back Here. You who have earned Life may never enjoy it.' He smiles. 'Not just the grilled fish, Alex. Not just the pleasures of the body. But to know God. And to understand Why.'

'But it can be done.'

'Why would you run such a terrible risk?'

'Can it be done?'

'Why? Why did God ever give free will to such a vexatious creature as Man?'

'Will you help me?'

'Alex. In my day and in my country we dealt with women as women's nature required they be dealt with. We told them what to do and they did it.'

'But you will help me.'

Ted is back in the angle of wall and ceiling, watching himself. Watching the poor girl flattened beneath him. Tear tracks have dried on her face. There is a yellow stain on the sheets where she has pissed herself. Oh, the poor child.

But, oh my God, the pain is easing and the darkness retreating. The distance between Ted and his lifeless body is reducing. Re-entering it is like clambering into a dinghy. It comes alive, rocks, then steadies. He raises himself onto his elbows and kisses the girl tenderly on the back of the neck.

If something else had not already done it, her scream would wake the dead. He leaps backwards in shock, coming out of her with a pop like a champagne cork.

She turns and hurls herself at him, pounding his chest and shoulders with both fists. He lets it happen. At last she falls sobbing upon him. 'I thought you were dead. I thought you were dead.'

He kisses her gently on the forehead. 'I am so sorry.'

'What happened?'

'I've no idea.'

'Have you been taking something?'

'Nothing.' He rolls her gently to one side and stands up. Even after death, it's always him who takes charge. 'I think we both need another shower. Then maybe we should get out of here. The bed's a bit of a mess. I'll leave a couple of hundred for the chambermaid.'

She cries quietly.

'Bella?'

'I thought I'd won a few days, at least. A little space. Some peace from the men on the beach. They wouldn't leave me alone. The times I've had to pick up everything in the middle of the night and run… I thought you'd let me stay in your room till you left.'

'You can come with me if you like.'

She sniffs. 'Give me a hanky, will you? Thanks. Go with you where?'

'My boat's in the harbour. I've got a villa on Fuerteventura. You're welcome to stay as long as you like. No strings. There's a very nice guest room. I won't expect anything from you.'

She won't look at him. 'Why should you do that?'

'Because of what I've put you through? Because I like you? Because you're another human being and you're in need? Because you remind me of another Annabel? Maybe I'm just the old fool there's no fool like.'

She gently holds his arms as she raises her face to kiss him. 'You're a doll.'

'I meant what I said about no strings.'

'I know you did.'

'I just have to find a woman called Maggie Leghorn and then we'll be on our way. She should be around somewhere. I want to give her a cheque.'

As they go to the door he hears the sound of faint sobbing. He looks round. There on the floor, his back against the wall and his legs thrust out anyhow, his chin resting on his chest, Ras Tafar is weeping tears of disappointment. He looks up for a moment and sees Ted's eyes on him. He lifts one limp hand and waves Ted away. In the corridor, a man in a green suit that is too small for him is walking away. When he sees Ted, he raises a finger to his forehead in salute. Ted says, 'Who are you? *What* are you?'

The look the man gives him is almost touching in its affectionate warmth. 'If you pass this way again, who and what I am will become clear.'

'And if I don't?'

'Then you have no need to know the answer.' And he vanishes from Ted's sight.

It is evening when they leave harbour and the warm darkness of an African night engulfs them.

'Look!' Ted says, holding the wheel steady as they come out into the open Atlantic.

'At what?'

'Usually when you see a shooting star it's going across the sky. From one side to the other, and unimaginable distances away. But look at that one. It's coming straight at us.'

'What do you suppose it is?'

'I've no idea.'

The star speeds towards them, ice blue and glowing and tiny. It skips above the dark ocean, sometimes skimming the waves and sometimes climbing almost straight upwards as though in breathless, playful joy. As it approaches the boat it shakes itself, spins dizzyingly and dips below the bow. It disappears from sight.

Annabel gives a sudden shudder. Ted looks at her, eyebrow raised. She says, 'Just for a moment I had the strangest feeling. As though something had touched me. As though... '

'Are you all right?'

She trembles. The glowing ice blue of the shooting star flashes for a moment in her eyes. 'It's nothing. It has passed.' She smiles, touches his arm. 'Did I tell you you're a doll?'